FINDING Ronan's HEART

NEW YORK TIMES AND USA TODAY BESTSELLING AUTHOR

MELANIE MORELAND

CORP

BOOK 2

D1089562

Dear Reader,

Thank you for selecting the Vested Interest: ABC Corp series to read. Be sure to sign up for my newsletter for up to date information on new releases, exclusive content and sales.

Before you sign up, add melanie@melaniemoreland.com to your contacts to make sure the email comes right to your inbox!
Always fun - never spam!

My books are available in both paperback and audiobook! I also have signed paperbacks available at my website.

The Perfect Recipe For **LOVE**
xoxo,
Melanie

Age of Ava (Vested Interest: ABC Corp #4)

Insta-Spark Collection

It Started with a Kiss

Christmas Sugar

An Instant Connection

An Unexpected Gift

Mission Cove

The Summer of Us Book 1

Standalones

Into the Storm

Beneath the Scars

Over the Fence

My Image of You (Random House/Loveswept)

Changing Roles

Happily Ever After Collection

Revved to the Maxx

Heart Strings

The Boss

Finding Ronan's Heart by Melanie Moreland
Copyright © 2020 Moreland Books Inc.
Copyright #1181587
ISBN Ebook 978-1-988610-50-4
Paperback 978-1-988610-49-8
Audio 978-1-988610-53-5
All rights reserved

MORELAND

BOOKS INC.

Edited by
Lisa Hollett—Silently Correcting Your Grammar
Cover design by Karen Hulseman, Feed Your Dreams Designs
Photo Adobe Stock

publication/use of these trademarks is not authorized, associated with, or sponsored by the trademark owners.

Quote Permission from Her Virtuous Viscount by Scarlett Scott @2020

DID YOU KNOW?

Even an author can learn a thing or two.

It is Lego™. Not Legos or Legoes. Just simply Lego™.

Here is the official company explanation:

https://twitter.com/LEGO_Group/status/
842115345280294912?s=20

And for a giggle, another explanation:

https://twitter.com/LEGO_Group/status/
1359856214591627269?s=20

DEDICATION

Beth,
Thank you for all your support, help, honesty, and
care.
Keep your chin up and fight the fight, my friend.
You are loved.

Scarlett,
Thank you for the loan of your words, your
generosity, and your ongoing kindness.

Matthew
My beginning and my end.
Plus all the wonderful moments in-between.
They are yours, as am I.
Always.

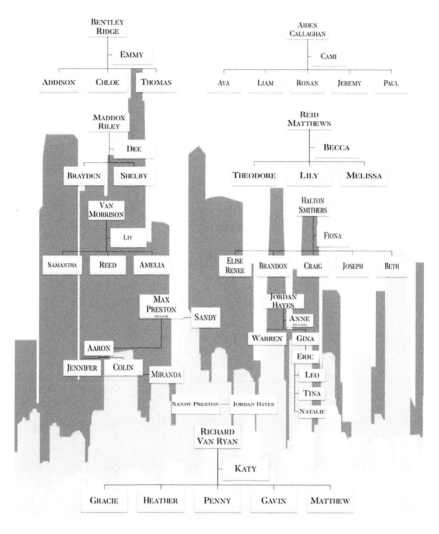

FAMILY TREE

The Contract **VESTED INTEREST**

NEW YORK TIMES AND USA TODAY BESTSELLING AUTHOR

MELANIE MORELAND

CHAPTER ONE
RONAN

I stared at the screen, tilting my head and squinting.

"No, something is off."

Paul looked over my shoulder, his large frame casting a shadow across the screen. "Too much?" he asked.

"Or not enough," I replied.

I erased the double columns, replacing them with heavier, single structures. I added detail to the bottom, then shaded them black on the top.

"Perfect." Jeremy clapped his hand on my shoulder. "That makes it unique."

I pulled off my glasses and rubbed my eyes. I really needed to get them checked.

"I'll send it to Addi and see what she thinks."

Jeremy flung himself into the chair beside me. "She'll love it. We'll start on the room layouts tomorrow. She only wants twenty-four, right?"

I reached for the thermos of water I carried everywhere. I liked it cold. Ice-cold, so the large double-walled flask was filled several times a day, and I added lots of ice each time.

"Yeah. All luxurious, self-contained. Separate bedrooms, kitchen area, sitting room, and spectacular baths."

Paul chuckled as he poured a coffee and sat down. "This is going to be amazing."

"It took us long enough to acquire the old Port Albany hotel. Addi wants it to handshake with the winery. Stay at the resort, visit the winery. Host an event at the winery, book your guests at the hotel. She plans on shuttles, cross-promotion, all of it."

"Heather already has ideas for the interior. The whole beachy vibe thing. She's been sketching for days."

I grinned. Heather VanRyan was one of our "cousins." We had a massive extended family, and many of us worked here at ABC Corp—a division of BAM that specialized in business and land development outside the Toronto area—or the GTA, as it was known. Our fathers pretty much had that city sewn shut. As the next generation, we brought a new energy to the mix. We bought the land, created the businesses, and ran them. The talent in our family was rich and varied, and we worked well together, having grown up surrounded by one another. We'd never felt any pressure from our fathers to be part of their world. Thomas, Bentley's son, was a marine biologist and had zero interest in the corporate world—except the money his father donated to the causes dear to his son's heart. Shelby, Maddox's daughter, was an artist and preferred her

2

canvases to that of a boardroom. Each cousin found their own path, and those that led to ABC were welcomed. We supported one another with the love and respect our parents had taught us.

Melissa Hanson, one of the office assistants, knocked on the door, holding a bag. "I got your lunch."

Paul grinned. "Awesome. I'm starved."

Jeremy reached for the bag, but I frowned. "I never gave you my order."

She laughed. "As if I need it. Turkey on white, lots of lettuce and mustard. All the same for the threesome. You guys are so easy."

"Actually, I prefer extra tomatoes and mayo. No mustard or lettuce. And sourdough."

She looked startled. "Pardon me? You always get the same."

"Because no one ever asks," I muttered under my breath. "It's fine," I said loud enough for her to hear. I'd eat the damn thing, because I always did. "It's all good."

"And I got some chips," she added and left.

I didn't ask what kind. There wasn't a hope in hell they would be sour cream and onion.

Sure enough, Paul pulled out three bags of salt and vinegar chips.

I took them without complaint. It wasn't worth the hassle over a sandwich and chips.

We worked most of the afternoon together, perfecting the design and the specs for the building.

It was early evening when I slapped the laptop shut. "We should celebrate tonight. Tacos?" I asked hopefully.

Paul and Jeremy exchanged a glance, and I frowned.

"What?"

"Um, we have a date."

I lifted my eyebrows in surprise. "Again?" It had happened several times lately when they had turned me down. Used to being part of a threesome that hung together constantly, I was missing my brothers.

I was the eldest triplet. Born four minutes before Paul and six before Jeremy, I loved flaunting my older status. We weren't identical triplets, although we were similar. We were all tall and broad like our father, Aiden. We had green eyes that came from our mother, Cami. Our personalities were more like our dad's—loud, boisterous, and happy. Paul and Jeremy were most alike—I was slightly taller, a little broader, and as my brothers liked to tell me, the worrier. I kept it hidden quite well, but I did tend to watch over my brothers, as if those four- and six-minute differences in our ages made me the responsible one. I was quieter than they were, not that many people noticed. They saw the group, not the individual, most of the time. People often exclaimed how much we looked alike, but if you took a moment, you would realize how different we actually were.

I narrowed my eyes. "You both have a date, or are you seeing the same girl?"

They laughed. "No. We're each seeing a different girl."

"Oh. Friends?"

Paul looked uncomfortable. "Sisters, actually." He exchanged a glance with Jeremy. "Twins."

"You're seeing *twins*?" I repeated. "Why didn't you tell me?" I asked, feeling oddly hurt. "Where did you meet them?"

Jeremy leaned forward. "At Oscar's Tavern—a few weeks ago. That night we went to the bar after the gym and you went home."

I nodded in remembrance. I wasn't as big on the bar scene as my brothers were. Overall, I tended to be more serious and lived a quieter life. I headed home and did a little more work, while they headed to the bar for some beer and wings. We each had a condo in Toronto in the same building. I also had a house in Port Albany, where I spent a lot of time. That was another difference between us—they liked Port Albany to visit but preferred the bustle of the city. I enjoyed the peace of living by the water and, more often than not, went to Port Albany on the weekends and some weeknights. We'd grown up there, and to this day, I felt more at home in the quieter area than the craziness of Toronto. Paul and Jeremy were the opposite—another difference between us most people didn't see.

"We didn't tell you…" Paul paused and looked at Jeremy. "We didn't say anything because we didn't want you upset, Ronan. We didn't want you to think we were abandoning you."

I had to laugh. I had noticed they weren't around as much, even when I was in the condo. "You're not abandoning me. I'm happy you're seeing someone. Or two someones. I can't believe you met twins. I mean, what are the odds?"

"I know. And the girls are great."

"Do you double-date all the time?"

"No. Some nights. Other times, we go our separate ways. We want the girls to meet you."

"I'd like that." I hesitated. "Do your girls have names, or do you just call them 'the girls'?"

Paul laughed. "Kim and Diane."

Jeremy smiled. "They're awesome. Kim, my girl, is a teacher. Paul's girl, Diane, is a nurse. They have a friend we thought might suit if you…" He let his words hang in the air.

I shook my head. "Not interested, but thanks."

"Not everyone is like Loni," Paul offered, his voice low.

I held up my hand to stop that conversation. "I know. I'm just not interested."

"Okay. Wanna come meet them with us? We're going for pizza and a movie."

I held back my grimace. That sounded like a planned date and me being a third wheel. No thanks.

"No. You go ahead. Maybe we can meet up this weekend?"

"Great. We'll check with them and talk tomorrow."

We high-fived and they left, already discussing their plans and forgetting about leaving me there.

I shook my head at that strange thought. It wasn't as if we were glued at the hip. Our parents had always encouraged some separation, even growing up. The truth was, that plan often failed. We were in the same classes at school when we were younger, and the teachers always kept us together for projects and groups. Even older, when choosing our own classes, we ended up together since we all were headed in the same direction, career-wise. Our lives were always interwoven, although we had our own friends and all of us had dated different girls at one time or another. We were incredibly close. Somehow, we always traveled toward the same goal, always a part of one another's lives. This was the first time Paul and Jeremy were doing something together I wasn't part of that seemed long term—not a simple "we've decided to go away for the weekend without you," sort of thing.

It felt strange.

I shook my head. I was a grown-ass man, and I was perfectly fine being on my own. I took my laptop to my office, grabbed my gym bag, and shut the door. I wasn't surprised to find I was the last one in the office as I headed down the hall and took the steps. That happened a lot these days. Addi and Brayden had been married almost two years but still acted like newly-weds. Gracie's daughter, Kylie, was almost one, and she liked to be home as early as possible. Reed and Heather were in Port Albany today, overseeing the last of the new building setup. After many months of delays, we had finally broken ground on a building that would hold ABC Corp, and we would be moving within the next few weeks.

I planned on moving to Port Albany permanently. So had Paul and Jeremy. It had been their plan as well since we'd be working there every day—it only made sense. My steps faltered when I thought about that idea. Now that they had met these girls, did that change their plans on moving? I had never lived anywhere but with or close to my brothers. Hell, even our condos were next to one another on the same floor of the building. I always knew that one day that would change. We would marry and settle down. But somehow, I had thought we'd be in the same zip code.

Suddenly, I didn't want to use the gym in the building. I didn't want to be alone. Changing my direction, I headed out the front door and to the gym a few blocks over. It was a nice spring evening, perfect for a walk. A good workout was what I needed to clear my head.

Two hours later, I wiped my forehead as I slowed down the treadmill. I had done a lot of weights, some cardio, and taken a yoga class. I loved anything that helped calm my mind and keep me strong. It had been what I needed. I talked to some of the trainers and other people working out, enjoying the hum of the machines and music around me. I liked this place and would miss it once I moved, but I hoped to convince the owner to add one out in Port Albany. His philosophy of small and personal worked. His staff was stellar and his equipment top-notch. We had a great home gym in the BAM compound, as we called the cluster of houses where we lived, but at times, such as tonight, I liked being with other people.

I grabbed a quick shower, towel dried my hair, and headed outside, inhaling the bracing cool night air. It was only just past nine, but I decided the craving for tacos had passed. I inhaled again, the scent of coffee and something savory and delicious hitting my nose. A small coffee shop-type throwback restaurant had opened up recently across the street. The sign was lit up and people were inside, but it wasn't packed.

Deciding a burger and coffee would hit the spot, I headed across the street, the scent of the grilling meat too much to resist.

I stepped in, the aroma intensifying. I headed to a corner booth, taking off my coat and sliding onto the vinyl-covered bench. Glancing around, I had to smile. It was decorated to look old. Formica countertops with round stools lined the wall by the kitchen. An open pass-through let you see the busy cooks at work. The floor was distressed to appear dated. The walls were covered in bright posters, and there was even a jukebox. I liked it.

I plucked a menu from the holder and studied it, suddenly starving.

The sound of a throat clearing and a soft voice interrupted my study of the menu.

"Welcome to Nifty Fifty. Are you ready to order, or do you need a minute?"

I shut the menu, already responding. "Nope. I'm good. I'll have—"

I looked up and froze.

Dark-brown eyes, soft and gentle as a fawn's, stared at me. A face I could only describe as adorable was surrounded by hair the color of sand in sunlight. Golds, blonds, and browns were woven into wild, chin-length corkscrew curls that moved as she tilted her head, waiting for me to continue. She had rounded cheeks, a full mouth, and a nose with a perfect line of freckles across the bridge that stood out on her pale skin.

She frowned at my silence. "Did you want to hear the specials?"

I cleared my throat. "No. Double cheeseburger with grilled onions and the works—except lettuce."

Those expressive eyes widened, and she nodded, the corkscrew curls on her head bouncing.

"I know, right? Hot lettuce is wrong. It's for salads. Not a garnish."

I grinned. "Exactly. I'll have one of those too. Ranch on the side. Onion rings and fries. And a vanilla shake. Ice water." I pointed to the display of cakes under domes that lined the counter. "Probably a slice of the hummingbird cake after with coffee. Please," I added.

She glanced over her shoulder. "Is someone joining you?" she asked, a grin playing on her full lips. Her eyes twinkled in amusement.

"Nope." I slapped my chest. "Growing boy. I need to keep up my strength."

She blinked, and I was sure she muttered, "God give *me* strength," before she turned and hurried away.

I was mesmerized by her full ass. Curvy. The perfect handful. I guessed her to be not much over the five-foot mark. Maybe by a couple of inches. She was cute. Sexy. I liked the freckles.

I shook my head to clear it. Where the hell were these thoughts coming from? I wasn't looking for a relationship.

Still, my gaze followed her around as she worked. Smiling, laughing with customers. Filling coffee cups, clearing and wiping tables. She walked my way, a large salad and ice water balanced on the tray along with the milkshake. The metal container glistened in the light, and I could hardly wait to taste the cold, creamy concoction. She set everything down in front of me, including a slice of cake, wrapped on the plate.

"There you go, big guy. Burger will be up soon. I snagged you one of the last pieces of cake, and I added a little extra frosting. I figured you for an icing lover."

I grinned. I was, indeed, an icing lover. Especially cream cheese icing.

"Thanks, ah…" I trailed off, unable to see a name tag.

She smiled, her dark eyes warm.

"Elizabeth. But my friends call me Beth." Her cheeks colored adorably, and she cleared her throat. "My name is Beth."

Her oversharing made me grin. "Nice to meet you, Beth. I'm Ronan." I held out my hand, and she shook it, her small palm settling on mine as if made to go there. Her fingers were petite, just like the rest of her, and I squeezed them before releasing her hand.

I indicated the cake. "And thanks."

Two darker circles of color pooled under her skin, and she blinked.

"No problem."

She hurried away, my gaze once again drawn to her before I reached for the salad, wondering why my night suddenly seemed a little brighter.

It had to be the cake.

Right?

CHAPTER TWO

RONAN

I polished off everything Beth had brought to me, exhaling in contentment as I pushed away the empty plates. I had enjoyed the meal a lot, and part of me wondered if it was only the food, or if the occasional visit from the pretty waitress had anything to do with it.

I had watched her the entire time I had been eating, purposely doing it slowly to draw out my stay. She was like a humming-bird, constantly busy, never staying in one place too long. She was friendly with the customers, often talking with one hand on her hip as she filled cups or responded to a question. I had gotten up at one point to grab a bottle of ketchup from the table beside me just as she came around the corner, almost colliding with me. For a moment, we were close. Close enough I could see the flecks of gold and green in her dark eyes. She had put a hand out to steady herself, and I caught her elbow to do the same. Our eyes locked, hers flaring with surprise. I judged her to be a foot shorter than I was, and the odd thought that I would have to kiss her sitting down in order to prevent a sore neck flitted through my mind as we locked gazes.

Or even better, pull her onto my lap. My fingers tightened on her arm at the thought.

She cleared her throat. "Is everything okay, ah, Ronan? You need something?"

Reluctantly, I released her elbow, but not before I let my fingers drift over the softness of her skin. "Nope." I held up the ketchup bottle. "Needed a refill."

"Oh. Anything else?"

"Some more water would be great when you can."

She nodded and hurried away, once more giving me a glimpse of her sweet ass. I'd never thought of myself as an ass man before, but I had a feeling that had just changed.

She approached the table, lifting one eyebrow as she gathered the empty plates. "Would you like me to get you a box for the cake?"

I shook my head, grinning widely. "More coffee, please."

"I guess you burn off a lot of calories over there." She indicated the gym across the street.

"Yeah, I do. And I like to eat."

She pursed her lips, a smile playing on her full mouth. It drew attention to a small beauty mark to the right of her lips. One dimple appeared in the same cheek, giving her an impish look.

"Really," she drawled. "I hadn't noticed."

She made me laugh as she moved away, returning with the coffeepot and filling up my cup.

I thanked her and reached for the cake, humming around the first mouthful. The pineapple and banana flavors hit my taste buds, and the cream cheese frosting was rich and decadent.

"Damn, that's good," I groaned, licking my lips, glancing up and meeting her dark gaze. She was watching me, her lips parted, eyes wide, the coffeepot hanging from her fingers.

Something passed between us. Something that wrapped around us, alive and vibrant. Throbbing heat filled my veins as our eyes locked. Green meeting brown. Intense longing I had never experienced pounded in my chest. My hands itched to reach out and pull her to me. Taste her full mouth. Run my hands along those inviting curves and cup her full ass. Slowly, I settled my fork on my plate as my body shifted to bring itself closer.

And a customer called out, "Hey, is that coffee just for him, or can we get some too?"

The moment shattered, and I was shocked to find I was halfway out of my booth. Beth was gripping the corner of the table as if to stop herself from coming closer. Both of our chests were moving rapidly as if we'd just run ten miles.

She blinked and hurried away. I sat back down, shocked.

What the hell just happened?

I ate my cake slowly, watching her more intently than I had been. The diner slowed, the hour getting late. The other waitress who had been here disappeared into the kitchen. Beth moved around, filling napkin dispensers, wiping down tables, getting the place ready for the morning.

A group of younger guys came in, sitting down and ordering food. They were loud and had obviously been drinking, with one of them standing out as the leader of the pack. He leaned back in his chair, watching Beth, making inappropriate remarks to his friends, and calling her over far too often for my liking. More than once, she evaded his wandering hands, still being polite, even as I saw the flash of anger cross her face. I pushed away my coffee cup, shaking my head as she came over and offered a refill.

She slid the bill my way as I looked over at the loud table. "Assholes," I muttered.

She shrugged. "I ignore them. They'll eat, act like jerks thinking it makes them cool, then they'll leave." She sighed.

"Hopefully they'll leave a decent tip too," I added.

She shook her head. "Not usually." She walked away, and I glanced at the bill, deciding to make sure, tip-wise, her night was a good one, at least.

I drained my water and stood, walking down the hall and using the restroom to wash my hands that were sticky. On my way back down the hall, I heard it.

"Let me go."

I increased my pace and rounded the corner. Beth was at the table of troublemakers, her face like thunder. The leader of the pack had his hand around her wrist, pulling her toward him.

"Come on, sweetheart. Sit that sweet ass on my lap, and we can talk about the tip. Yours or mine, whichever you prefer."

I was across the diner in a heartbeat, yanking his arm away and tugging Beth out of the way.

I loomed over him, furious. "You wanna show a little respect, asshole?"

He looked up at me, fright replacing the cockiness that had been there a moment ago. I was taller and outweighed him by a good fifty pounds of muscle. I could wipe the floor with him on my worst day—and with the anger he had just roused? I could take on all three of them right now and walk away whistling a merry tune while they struggled to get the license plate of the semi that hit them.

"Just having a little fun."

"Take your fun elsewhere." I leaned closer. "Pay your bill, tip the lady, and fuck off. Or deal with me. Your choice."

He muttered something, and I tightened my grip on him. "What did you say?"

He yanked his arm away. "I said we're leaving."

I stood, crossing my arms, knowing how large that made me look. "Good choice."

I returned to my booth, grabbed my gym bag and the bill, and waited. The asshole and his sidekicks headed to the register, and Beth processed their tabs. When the guy who'd grabbed her was in front of her, I approached, watchful. He leaned close to Beth, saying something that angered her. He had the audacity to try to touch her again, but before I could get there,

16

she grabbed his hand, bent his finger back, and smiled sweetly as he whined like the little dog he was.

"I think my friend asked you to leave. Now, I'm telling you. Get out, and don't come back."

I halted my progress, surprised and impressed at the move, and slightly turned on by her actions.

"I oughta report you to the manager," the asshole groused.

"Feel free," I said, heading their way. "I'm a witness, and I'll tell them you crossed the line."

A cook stuck his head out of the pass-through. "So will I. You heard the lady—get out and don't come back."

Beth pushed the asshole away, eyeing him balefully.

He glared but walked out, not dropping anything in her tip jar. He narrowed his eyes at me as if daring me to do something about that. His friends had dropped in some bills, at least. She deserved them.

I set down my bag and handed her my bill. She watched until they had left, then sighed and rolled her eyes. "Exactly what I didn't need tonight. Mike isn't going to be happy when I tell him."

"I'll vouch for you."

She smiled. "Thanks."

I handed her some twenties and took the change, slipping it in her jar. She shook her head.

"No need for that."

"Great service deserves a good tip."

She handed me a small container. "So does being a hero."

I flipped open the lid, grinning at the slice of cake inside. I wasn't going to refuse that. "Thanks."

She laid her hand on my arm. "Thank you," she responded. "It's been a long time since someone came to my rescue."

I looked down at her fingers resting against my skin. Small, pale, and delicate. One finger had a slender braided silver ring on it. The nails were short, buffed, and neat. Her hand looked tiny on my arm, and before I could think about it, I covered it with mine, squeezing her fingers.

"At your service, my lady," I quipped. "Knight in shining armor is my side hustle."

She laughed, stepping back and withdrawing her hand. "Trainer by day, damsel rescuer by night—is that how it is? Good plan."

I laughed. "With the move you just pulled, you didn't really need me. Impressive."

She shrugged. "A girl needs to protect herself." She sighed. "Okay, I have to finish up and head home. Thanks again, Ronan. I hope to see you again."

She moved away before I could say anything else. I paused, but I took my cue, picking up my bag and the container of cake. I quickly dropped a couple of extra twenties into her jar, then headed outside. She deserved them after dealing with that jerk. I glanced at the gym across the street then behind me at the diner. She thought I worked at the gym. Twice, she had mentioned it, and I never dissuaded her.

I headed back to the office, throwing my bag in the back of my car and driving toward the condo. I wondered why I hadn't told her. The first time, it didn't really matter—she was my waitress and it didn't seem worthwhile to correct her. The second time, though, I should have told her I just worked out there on occasion, not let her assume I actually worked at the gym. I was an honest guy, so I wasn't sure why I hadn't fixed her wrong assumption.

Except, it had been nice to be just Ronan for a bit. Just a guy having a burger after work. Not one of the triplets. Not the son of the rich business tycoon Aiden Callaghan. Or the wealthy man I was in my own right. Beth had zero clue who I was, and it seemed as if she didn't care.

After what had happened to me the year before, I liked that.

And the bottom line was, aside from the occasional night I went to the gym, I probably wouldn't see her. I had no idea of her schedule, hadn't inquired, or even asked her for her number. Maybe she didn't work every night. Maybe I had imagined that connection I felt toward her. Maybe I had been the only one to feel it. For all I knew, she had a boyfriend. She hadn't offered her number either, so perhaps the odd sensations had been only on my end.

I parked in the garage and headed up to my empty condo, wondering why those thoughts made me feel strangely sad.

CHAPTER THREE

BETH

Ronan disappeared around the corner. I absently wiped the tabletop, watching his long strides as he moved away, a strange ache in my chest when I could no longer see him.

He'd caught my attention the moment he entered the diner. I was sure he caused that reaction most places he went since he definitely stood out in the crowd. He was tall and broad. Massive. His shoulders were wide, his arms thick, sinewy and strong. I was fascinated by the way his forearms rippled with muscles as he moved them. He used his hands a lot when talking, drawing my eyes to the sexy gestures.

When I approached his table, I wasn't sure what to expect. I had seen him come from the gym, and I assumed he was one of the many trainers who worked there. He certainly looked like one. Quite often, the staff at the gym ordered a salad or the protein plate to go. They rarely engaged much if they ate in. One had pushed me constantly about becoming a member, only stopping when I informed him there was no way I could afford their fees. He had paid his bill and left after that, and I hadn't seen him again.

Ronan's voice surprised me. It was surprisingly low, rich, and deep. He spoke softly, although his words were clear and easy to hear. But when he laughed, the sound boomed. I had a feeling he laughed a lot at times from the crinkles around his beautiful green eyes. Bright and warm, they were set off by long lashes under thick eyebrows that suited his masculine face. His nose was long and straight, his wavy hair a deep brown that brushed the back of his shirt. Scruff showed off his expansive jaw. His smile was wide and friendly.

I also noticed a trace of sadness in his eyes, even when he smiled. But he was polite and charming. His order surprised me. I liked how he responded to my teasing. The massive amount of food he inhaled wasn't what I expected, but then again, I had a feeling nothing Ronan did was the norm.

He ate slowly, cleaning off every plate I had brought him. I'd made sure to add lots of extras to the salad and that his burger was hot and had extra pickles when he mentioned he loved them. I cut his piece of hummingbird cake larger than normal, hoping he would enjoy it.

The way he polished off the cake, there was no doubt he did.

I couldn't begin to describe the way it felt when he appeared beside me, telling off the asshole and making sure I was okay. I was used to taking care of myself. I had to. I knew enough moves, I could have brought the idiot to his knees in a few seconds, but having Ronan stand up for me left a warmth in my chest. The way he'd tucked me behind him, ready to defend, made me feel special and...*protected*. Safe.

I wasn't used to feeling either of those.

I sighed as I wiped down the table and replaced the condiment holder.

The feeling had faded when he left. He never asked for my number. I was sure he was going to, and for the first time in years, I hoped to be asked. Every time I had looked his way, our eyes had connected. He seemed to find excuses to call me to his table. He asked questions so that I lingered. More than once, I thought I had felt something pass between us.

But he left. I had obviously mistaken the signs—he was just a nice guy who had flirting down to a science. With those killer eyes and muscles that went on for miles, it would make more sense.

I doubted a short, curvy, overworked waitress was his style. I imagined he dated tall, voluptuous blondes who looked perfect, even while working out. Maybe he'd been watching me so closely, mentally tabulating the ways he could improve my figure.

I flipped the lock closed and pulled down the blinds, grateful this part of the night was over. I rolled my tired shoulders. I had one more job to do, and then I could head home.

I headed to the kitchen, anxious to be done.

It was past one when I let myself into the house, my breathing easier once I shut the door behind me. It was a short walk from the bus to the little house, but at this time of night, I always felt relieved when I stepped in the relative safety of the door.

I hung up my coat, slipping off my sneakers and rubbing my feet, wondering if I could stay awake long enough to soak them for a bit.

I rounded the corner, surprised to find Paige awake, flipping through a magazine.

"Everything okay?" I asked anxiously.

She waved her hand. "Yes. Everything is fine. Couldn't sleep, is all." She lifted her arms over her head, stretching. "How was work?"

I flung myself on the sofa. "Fine, aside from a jerk-off with wandering hands."

"Ugh. Did you use your moves?"

I chuckled. "The second time, yes. The first time, a customer stepped in and told him off."

"That was nice, but apparently he didn't listen."

I yawned. "Nope—his ego was too big to hear a word. So, when he tried again, I bent his fingers back."

She grinned. "Did he squeal?"

"Like a little girl." I laughed. "With ribbons in her hair."

She high-fived me. "That's what I'm talking about."

I indicated the hall. "They okay?"

"Yes," she assured me. "They played some video game for a while, and Lucy fell asleep. Evan did some homework and went to bed by ten." Her voice was tender. "He is so patient with her, showing her the controls—I think he let her win just to make her happy."

23

"He's a good kid. They both are."

She leaned over and squeezed my hand. "We're lucky to have you."

I squeezed her palm back. "We're lucky to have you."

"You need to get some sleep. You have an early class tomorrow."

"I know." I stood. "I'll check on Evan and head to bed. I'll peek in on Lucy too."

"Thanks."

I headed down the hall, stopping at Lucy's room. She was asleep, surrounded by pillows and stuffed animals. Her long dark hair was tied up in a ponytail, and she was adorable, clutching her favorite bear. The blankets, as usual, were flung off, and I tucked them back around her, making sure she was warm, even though I knew she'd fling them off again soon enough.

In Evan's room, I watched him sleep for a few moments, his deep, even breathing helping me to relax. As usual, his room was neat and orderly—exactly the way he liked it. One of his crutches had fallen over, and I placed it upright next to the other one, my smile fading as I did.

I wished he didn't need them. I wished I could go back to two years ago and change what happened. But that was impossible.

Instead, I bent and tenderly brushed away the hair that fell over his forehead. "Sleep well, kiddo. I love you."

Then I headed downstairs to bed, somehow feeling the weight of my responsibilities even stronger than usual.

That night, I dreamed of warm green eyes and dimples. Strong arms and a smile so wide it made my heart soar.

But when I woke up, I was alone—and somehow, I felt the pain of that more than I had ever experienced before now.

———

RONAN

I punched at the bag, ducking and weaving to avoid bounce back, hitting it hard. Sweat poured down my back, and my shoulders began to ache from the strain.

"What has the bag done to you lately, son?" my dad drawled as he walked into the gym we had set up in the building.

I stepped back, stilling the motion of the bag, and grinned. "It was looking at me funny."

He chuckled, rolling his shoulders. "Wanna spar with your old man, instead?"

I tapped my gloves together. "Bring it on."

His laughter filled the room as he picked up a set of gloves, using his teeth to pull on the second one. He wore a pair of workout pants and a tight shirt, showing off his still-impressive physique. He had always been into fitness and had spent hours with us as kids sharing his passion. He was patient and knowledgeable and made sure we knew how to look after ourselves. He taught us all self-defense, including my sister, Ava, who now held a black belt in karate. No one messed with my elder sister—and she wasn't above using one of her stellar moves on us if we pissed her off.

For the next twenty minutes, the room was filled with nothing but trash talk, the squeak of our footwear on the mats, and grunts as we advanced and retreated, jabbing punches and uppercuts, and generally enjoying ourselves. I loved sparring with him, learning as he quietly corrected my form, laughing as he pretended to be insulted when I would "land" a punch, chuckling at his insults.

We tapped gloves, tore them off, and both drank deeply from cups we filled at the water cooler. We sank to the floor, our backs resting against the cool cement walls.

"Working out your frustration?" he asked.

"Just letting off some steam." I patted my face with the towel.

"Wanna talk about it?"

I tilted my head to the side, meeting his gaze. "Talk about what?" I asked, wondering who had asked him to come see me.

"Whatever is bothering you."

"I don't recall saying anything was."

"Your mother noticed you were quiet at dinner on the weekend. Your brothers are worried about you."

"No need for them to be worried," I stated mildly. "I'm fine."

"They think you're upset over their new girlfriends."

I swallowed a long drink of water. "They're wrong. I went to dinner with them last night. I liked both Diane and Kim. They seem very happy."

"And you're on your own."

26

"Dad, it's not the first or the last time. We all have our own lives. You and Mom made sure of that. I'm a little preoccupied with all the problems the ABC build is having. Finishing all the details for the hotel. Going back and forth between here and Port Albany."

"How do you feel about your brothers thinking about not moving?"

"I wasn't surprised when they told me about meeting the girls. It makes sense they want to stay closer for the moment. And they've never wanted to live in Port Albany the way I have."

"What about you?"

"I still plan on moving out that way permanently—especially once the building is done and we start concentrating on the whole southwest area of the province."

"No one holding you here?" he asked.

I sighed. "No, Dad. You know there isn't. And there won't be," I added, even as a set of dark eyes and wild curls flitted through my mind. I hadn't been back to the diner since last week. I had been tempted but resisted.

"She was an anomaly, Ronan." He paused, frustrated. "I wish you'd tell us what happened. Maybe it would help."

"Doesn't matter. It's in the past, and I'm over it. I don't plan on letting it happen again." I shoved off the wall and extended my hand to my dad. He grabbed it and pulled himself up, laughing as his knee cracked.

"Jeez, I'm getting old."

I clapped him on the shoulder. "Never. Just a little stiff."

"That's what your mother said last night."

"Oh God, no. Don't even start that," I groaned. "No sex stuff about you and Mom."

He waggled his eyebrows. "She still can't get enough of me."

"Whatever."

He suddenly became serious. "Ronan, I know you feel lost in the shuffle sometimes. Part of a group. But I also know you're different. You hide it, but your mother and I know."

"You're probably the only ones who do," I couldn't help but say.

"You're the protector, the worrier. Your brothers know it too. They love you, and whether you like it or not, the three of you share an incredibly strong bond. You have from the moment you were born. We couldn't separate you for the longest time. Growing up, you all stayed together. You finished one another's sentences. You felt one another's pain. But you felt theirs even more. Even apart, you were together. You can't ignore that connection."

"I'm not trying to. But our lives will veer away from one another, Dad. They have to. It won't sever the connection, but we each have to find our own happiness. Our own path. Not every part of our lives can involve the others." I lifted my shoulders. "And we all have to cope with that in a different way. They each found a girl they're interested in. The fact that they're twins is just a fluke. But their lives remain on the same track, and right now, mine is on a different path. We'll come back together. We always will. But I need to step back a little and let them do this without me."

He shook his head. "I'm still worried. You're spending a lot of time alone."

I barked out a laugh. "I'm with them every day. Addi is there. Gracie. Ava. Reed and Heather. Theo now, too. I'm surrounded all day. We had dinner on the weekend, and I saw them last night. I'm hardly alone."

He met my gaze with a serious one. "You can be alone in a room full of people, Ronan. I know that all too well."

"Dad, honest, I'm fine. I'm thrilled for Paul and Jeremy, and I liked the girls. I know they're planning on bringing them out to meet you and Mom soon too."

"Will you be there when they do?"

"Yes," I assured him. "I will."

"You need to find your happiness too, Ronan."

"I know that. But you can't expect my schedule to be the same as theirs. We're not *that* similar."

He rubbed his chin. "That's it, isn't it? The three of you have always been so synced. Now, life is changing for you in a big way. They're going in one direction, you're in another."

"We're still close. Them falling in love isn't going to change that. My time will come," I added, trying to sound positive for my dad.

"Yes, it will," he agreed. "You'll find your heart. I found your mother, and she changed my life."

I couldn't help the grin that crossed my face. "Mom says she found you, and you fought her tooth and nail."

He laughed. "She's right. I was stupid. But once I got my head out of my ass, I held on tight. You'll find a girl you feel that way about. I promise."

"We'll see what happens."

He studied me, obviously deciding he'd lectured me enough. "Okay, I'll drop it for now. But your mother is going to check on you a lot. Be warned."

"Does that mean she'll send food?"

He frowned. "I suppose."

I hooked an arm around his neck, dragging him in for a hug. "Thanks, old man. I know you hate sharing."

He wrapped his arms around me, holding me tight. For a moment, I let myself draw from his strength. Dad had always been demonstrative with us. With our mom. With the entire extended family. He gave great hugs, and sometimes I thought it was because he needed to feel them as much as he needed to give them. I hugged him back tight.

"Thanks, Dad."

He stepped back. "Anytime. I'm always here, Ronan."

I smiled and squeezed his shoulder. "I know."

He picked up his bag and left, waving at me. I watched him go with a sigh. I hadn't exactly lied when I told him I was fine, but the truth was, I was feeling off-kilter. I slid down the wall, sipping at my water.

He was right. I was missing my brothers. Even when our lives took us in different directions, we were somehow connected.

There was an unbreakable bond between us being triplets. Even when we'd been with our own groups of friends, girl-friends, and internships, somehow we were still together. We knew one another better than anyone. We were so close, we sensed how the others were feeling at times. It was a bond we couldn't explain and we didn't try because, for us, it was simply part of being a triplet. We'd all gone to university together, and although we'd done our internships at different compa-nies, we had still been connected on a daily basis. We even shared a condo until we decided it was time to live on our own once we graduated. But now, for the first time, our paths felt as if they were traveling in separate lanes rather than criss-crossing over one another. It was an odd sensation.

I thought of growing up. Even our careers were similar. We shared a deep love for architecture, although in different ways. I preferred commercial architecture, Paul concentrated on sustainable/green architecture, and Jeremy was the interior space expert. Together, we were one hell of a team. In fact, the entire Callaghan clan, aside from my mom, was involved in the BAM/ABC empire in some way.

Our elder brother, Liam, loved the outdoors. He had been into plants and gardens for as long as I could remember. My earliest memory of him was being with him outside as he dug and weeded a vegetable garden, fussing with his plants, showing me how to water them properly. He became a horti-culturist and operated his own company. He did a lot of work for BAM and ABC as well as many other companies, and his services were in high demand all the time.

Our sister, Ava, worked at ABC, functioning as the liaison for all the projects we took on. I didn't know another person as organized or meticulous with paperwork and keeping all the pieces of the puzzles together and running smoothly. Our adopted grandfather, Jordan Hayes, had held that position at BAM and insisted Ava learned everything she knew from him and had surpassed him ten times over. We were lucky to have her.

But the truth was, the three of us were the closest. Even when I had been seeing Loni, we remained so. After our nasty breakup, I had fallen into the habit of being alone. Licking my wounds in private. And even after I moved past the trauma, I had never felt quite the same. She had left a scar on me that hadn't healed properly. My brothers had been their usual understanding selves, never pushing me, but they had also moved forward with their own lives. And this time, it felt as if the separation was the start of something bigger. Something lonelier for me.

Last night, I had dinner with them and their twin girlfriends. Kim and Diane were like us in that they were similar in looks, but not identical. Kim's hair was a light brown, while Diane's was a deep mahogany. Both had blue eyes. They were tall, slender, and pretty. Intelligent and well-spoken. Easygoing. They suited my brothers well. Diane was quieter, which suited Paul's outgoing personality. Kim radiated exuberance and chatted constantly, Jeremy encouraging her with his wit and his ability to talk on a vast array of subjects. It was easy to see the four of them were comfortable with one another.

"What grade do you teach?" I asked Kim.

She smiled as she replied. "Grade one."

"I bet that keeps you busy."

"All the time. I love kids, and I enjoy being with them. They're open and honest, you know? Their reactions are real." She paused with a laugh. "Sometimes too real, but it keeps the days interesting."

Remembering what a handful we were in school, I could only imagine.

"Any twins or triplets in your class?"

"Not this year. I had a set of twins two years ago. They were identical. Inseparable. Luckily, their mother dressed them differently, or I would have been lost."

"We used to switch outfits." Paul chuckled. "We'd be one another some days just for fun."

"I'm sure the girls did that a few times," Kim agreed. "But you're not identical?"

"We looked pretty similar when we were younger," I explained. "Then I got better-looking than these two clowns." I winked.

"Bigger, you mean," Jeremy scoffed. "We all know I'm the best-looking one. The looks improved as we came out. Longer baking time."

It was my turn to laugh. "Yeah, those six minutes made a big difference."

He nodded. "I knew you would agree."

We all laughed. Kim hugged his arm and whispered something to him, which made him grin and turn his head, kissing her hard.

I felt that odd pang in my chest again watching them.

Kim looked flushed as she met my eyes. "Jeremy says you're the driving force of the design team."

I shrugged. "We all bring something to the table."

"Paul says the same thing," Diane offered quietly. "He says your talent astounds him."

I looked down, fiddling with my fork. It was rare I heard what my brothers thought about me from someone else. We supported one another and fed off the artistic vibe when working, but they rarely offered simple praise.

I picked up my drink, striving to keep the mood upbeat. "I am pretty awesome."

That led to more teasing. The meals were served, and the conversation was light. They had a lot of "couple banter" between them, and at times, I felt very much the odd man out, watching their closeness from the outside. I wasn't part of the inside jokes or the memory of that great sushi place they'd been to the week before. I couldn't laugh as loud over the story of how Paul had tripped over his untied shoelace in the theater, the popcorn he was carrying being flung over everyone in the vicinity. I laughed at the image it brought to mind, but not the shared recollection.

Diane talked about her job at the hospital a lot, sharing amusing stories.

"I'm a pediatric nurse," she explained.

"You love kids too, I assume."

"Yes. But I am a horrible teacher. I can cajole, give shots, calm a child down, get them to let me look in their throat or something, but teach them anything? No."

"I'm sure you're better than you think you are."

Kim leaned forward, grinning. "Trust me, she isn't."

Everyone laughed. Paul leaned back, playing with Diane's fingers. "She can't explain things to adults either."

34

Diane chuckled. "Good thing I have you to do that now."

He kissed her. "Yep."

They weren't as demonstrative as Jeremy and Kim, but each couple was very close. I found the fact that both girls loved children interesting. Jeremy and Paul had always expressed their desire for having a big family like ours. They had picked the right girls, it would seem. Unlike my choice.

I enjoyed meeting Kim and Diane but left after dinner when plans for continuing the evening were far more suited to couples rather than a plus-one. I invented an excuse and left.

With a groan, I let my head fall back against the wall. I had spent the rest of the night alone in my condo. I highly doubted my brothers returned to their places, or if they had, they weren't alone.

I looked at my watch. It was only just after eight. I was hungry, but the idea of going back to the condo and ordering in didn't appeal to me.

I stared at my feet, knowing exactly what did appeal. Some good music playing on the jukebox, something delicious and filling, and the dark, smiling eyes of a certain waitress. She had been on my mind a lot. I replayed our conversations in my head, remembering the pleasing cadence of her voice. The gentle disposition she had shown me. The strength she displayed when that asshole crossed the line. She was full of surprises, and I liked that. Probably more than I wanted to admit.

I ran my hand over my hair with a grimace. I had no idea if she even worked tonight. Just because she had been there last

Thursday didn't mean she would be there today. Yet the yearning lingered.

I pushed myself up off the floor.

There was only one way to find out.

CHAPTER FOUR

BETH

I came from the kitchen with a full tray, concentrating on the heavy order I was carrying and nothing else. I delivered the full plates, checked on refills, then turned to scan the diner. I had heard the bell ring, so I knew there were more customers to look after. It had been a busy night, and I hoped it would slow down soon so I could start clearing sections for the morning.

I had to stop for a moment and collect my thoughts when I spied the new customer.

Ronan was sitting in the same booth as last week, studying the menu. He was dressed in a tight-fitting Henley, the material stretched over his barrel chest and large arms. His biceps flexed as he turned the pages of the menu, his brow furrowed and his full lips pursed. He squinted in concentration, then huffed and reached into his jacket pocket for a pair of glasses, slipping them on his nose.

I had no idea how a simple pair of glasses made him look even sexier than he had only a moment ago, but they did. I noted there was no gym bag tonight, and I wondered if he had left it at work or was only on a break.

He looked up as I approached, our eyes locking. His brows lifted as he studied me, a smile playing on his lips. He pulled off the glasses, holding them in his large hands.

"Hi," he said as I got to his table. "I didn't know if you'd be here."

I held up my hands. "Here I am."

He leaned back in the booth, laying his arm along the top of the bench. "There you are," he replied, his voice pitched low. It made me shiver, and for a moment, we stared. I had to clear my throat before I could speak.

"Do you know what you want?"

He rubbed his bottom lip, looking thoughtful. "Not sure if what I want is on the menu, but I was wondering if the clubhouse is pressed turkey or the real stuff?"

"They roast the turkey daily."

"Then a clubhouse. And a salad."

I paused, my pen hovering over the pad, waiting, but he didn't say anything else. "On a hunger strike today, Ronan?"

He laughed, the sound booming in the restaurant. "Soup any good?"

"It's vegetable today, and yes. Delicious."

"I'll have that too. The sandwich comes with fries?"

"Yes."

"Great. Add a shake, water, and coffee. And save me a piece of cake."

"Hummingbird or carrot?"

He frowned, rubbing his chin with the arm of his glasses. "Maybe one of each?"

"Okay."

"And one other thing."

"Sure?" I asked, waiting for his order.

"Maybe you could join me for coffee when the place slows down."

"Oh, ah…"

He reached out, waiting until I placed my hand in his. He wrapped his fingers around my palm firmly, although his touch was gentle. "Is that against the rules? Having coffee with a customer?"

"No."

"Great." He beamed.

"I don't know when it will slow down."

"I'm not in any hurry."

"Okay, then." I waited then tugged. "But I need my hand back to do my work."

"If I have to." He relinquished his hold, but not before dropping a fast kiss to my wrist. My heart rate sped up at the touch of his mouth on my skin. I suddenly wondered how his lips would feel on the rest of my body. My mouth. I felt my cheeks heat, and I turned and hurried away.

"Extra pickles," he called out. "Please."

"Got it," I responded over my shoulder.

Amazingly, it no longer mattered if I got the tables cleaned early.

I was having coffee with Ronan.

I refilled Ronan's coffee, poured myself a cup, and sat across from him. Luckily, the last few customers had seated themselves in Jane's area, so she was looking after them. She had looked shocked when I told her I was taking a break. I never took breaks. But when she saw the direction I was heading, I got a subtle thumbs-up from her and a grin. I hoped my cheeks weren't red when I sat down.

Ronan finished off his dinner, wiping his mouth and pushing away his plate. "That was good."

"You eat a lot."

He chuckled. "So I've been told."

"You must have been hard to keep filled up as a teenager." Evan was only twelve, and it felt as if he was constantly eating.

He poured the last of his shake into the glass and sipped it. "Yeah. I think my mom went grocery shopping at least twice a week. Four boys."

I lifted my eyebrows. "*Four* of you?"

"And a sister. Ava never ate as much as we did, though."

"Big family."

He nodded, not offering any other information.

"Are you close?" I asked.

He hesitated, but again, nodded. "Too close at times. What about you?"

I looked down at the table, took a sip of my coffee to stall, then drew in a deep breath. "There's just my brother and me. My parents died a few years ago."

He reached across the table and took my hand, the warmth of his encompassing mine. "I'm sorry," he said sincerely. "That must have been rough."

I swallowed the thick feeling in my throat I always got when thinking about my parents. "Yeah, it was. Still is."

"I can't even imagine."

I looked up and met his gaze. It was warm and caring. Concerned. Honest.

"I look after my brother now."

"Big responsibility."

"He's my family," I responded.

"Of course."

I glanced down to where our hands were entwined on the table. His large thumb traced gentle circles on my skin in comfort. His caress was light, his skin warm, and his touch welcome. I looked up and met his eyes.

"I wasn't sure you were coming back," I blurted.

"I wasn't sure either," he admitted. Then he inhaled, his eyes never leaving mine as he studied me. His chin dipped slightly as if he had made a decision.

"But I forgot something."

I frowned in confusion. "I don't think anything was turned in."

He chuckled. "No, I forgot something more personal."

"Oh?" I asked, suddenly feeling breathless.

"I forgot to ask you out."

I blinked, hoping I had heard him right.

"Ask me out?"

"On a date." He lifted his shoulders. "Would you let me take you to dinner, Beth?"

Happiness surged through me, and for a moment, I basked in that feeling before reality kicked in. I frowned as I looked down at our hands, surprised to see they were still clasped together.

Ronan stiffened at my hesitancy. "Maybe I've overstepped." He began to pull back his hand. "You probably have a boyfriend."

I grasped at his fingers. "No. No, I don't."

"You don't want to go out with me?"

"It's not that I don't want to…" I trailed off, unsure how to explain.

"Are you hiding from the law?" he asked, leaning forward and talking low.

A smile tugged on my lips. "No."

"A serial killer?"

"Nope."

His eyes widened. "Would you prefer it if I were a woman?"

I burst out laughing. "No."

"I'm so hideous that you won't be seen with me?"

I tilted my head. "No. It's just——"

"Just what?"

"My life, Ronan. It's crazy. I work here four days a week. I go to school. I study. I look after my brother."

"What about time for yourself?"

I laughed. "That's rare. My shifts are Wednesday to Friday night. Every Saturday. Sunday is errands, schoolwork, and whatever else I have to catch up on. Monday is usually study group. I'm always running late. Always behind. Always playing catch-up. I would love to go out with you, but it's not fair. You aren't the sort of guy someone slots in when they have time."

"I'm not?" he asked, lifting one eyebrow.

"No."

"Maybe I'm okay being slotted in."

"You deserve more than that."

He looked surprised by my words, and he smiled.

"You didn't say anything on your schedule about Tuesdays."

I blinked. "What?"

"It sounds like Tuesday is an open day. Aside from school, your brother, and everything else."

"Usually, I study or relax if I can."

He leaned forward, taking my other hand between his and holding them both tightly. "Maybe you could relax with me for dinner?"

"I'm not a fancy girl, Ronan. I don't have a lot of dressy clothes in my closet."

"I love tacos," he announced.

"Um, who doesn't?" I responded, wondering what tacos had to do with my lack of wardrobe.

"Tuesday is taco night. Tacos don't require fancy clothing. So, you see, the planets have aligned, and now you must come with me and have tacos." He nodded decisively. "On Tuesday."

He looked proud of himself. Boyish. Happy.

And the thought of having tacos with him made me feel the same way.

Happy. And after all, it was just tacos. What could happen over tacos?

"Tuesday, it is."

He smiled. Widely. Showing me his even, white teeth. Crinkling the skin around his eyes that danced in elation.

"Tuesday."

Ronan finished his coffee and approached the cash register. He held out his bill with some twenties and shook his head at the change.

"You gave me too much last week," I argued. "I know it was you who put the extra into the jar."

"I have no idea what you're talking about."

"It's not necessary."

"I disagree. I said it before—good service, good tip. My aunt was a waitress. She said there isn't a more unappreciated job." He reached over the counter and tucked the money into the jar.

I rolled my eyes but didn't fight him. His tip last week had given Evan a new set of Lego. Evan loved Lego sets and building things.

"You know what else is necessary?" he asked.

"What?"

He held out his phone. "Your number and address where I can pick you up on Tuesday."

I took the phone, noticing the sleek new version of the iPhone that had only come out a few months ago. Mine was an older, used phone, many generations behind his. I added my phone number and address and sent myself a message so I had his number, then handed it back.

"Six okay on Tuesday?"

"Six is fine."

"Great."

I came around the counter and handed him a small box. His face lit up. "Another piece of cake?"

"Yes. The last of the hummingbird."

"This is awesome." He leaned down, his hand light on my shoulder. He pressed his mouth to my cheek, his lips lingering, his warm breath drifting across my ear.

"I can hardly wait until Tuesday," he murmured.

He pulled back with a smile, and I watched him leave, his stride fast. He disappeared around the corner.

It wasn't until I caught sight of myself in the glass window that I realized I was holding my cheek, the one he had kissed, in my hand. It was as if I were holding his caress to my skin, branding myself with it.

I shook my head as I turned to start clearing tables.

How silly.

Sunday morning, I was up early as usual. My body was so used to my schedule, I never slept in anymore. When I was younger, it was my favorite thing to do on the weekend, but no longer. I needed every hour of the day I could find to keep up. I sat at the small kitchen table, sipping a cup of coffee, going through the budget. I had been able to work all my hours and my tips were decent, so we were in okay shape as long as there were no major surprises. Using my laptop, I checked my bank account, sent a transfer to Paige for my share of the rent and utilities and signed out.

I looked around the homey kitchen, pulling a leg up to my chest. I was grateful we had a place to live, that Evan had company while I was at work or school, and we were doing all right. It wasn't the way I had planned my life to be, but the reality of the actual world and the one I had pictured were vastly different. Still, Evan and I were together. That counted for something.

Paige appeared, running a hand through her dark hair and yawning. "Morning."

"Morning. Coffee is in the pot."

"Thank God," she muttered, pouring a mug and taking a sip before sitting down. She indicated the laptop. "What are you working on?"

"Just checking the budget. I sent you rent and utilities."

"Thanks."

"I have a favor to ask."

"Sure. What do you need?"

"Um, I have a date. On Tuesday. Would you be okay with that? Watching Evan again?"

Paige's eyebrows shot up. "First off, Evan is never a problem. And second—a date?"

"Yeah, remember the guy—the customer—who tried to help me with that asshole? He was in the diner again last night, and he asked me out for tacos."

She chuckled. "Tacos? Is that what we call it now?"

I laughed. "Apparently tacos are one of his favorite foods. I told him how busy I was, but he insisted on Taco Tuesday and asked me out. I said yes."

"You must like him a lot. You haven't said yes in years."

I thought about Ronan's warm eyes. His size and strength. His gentle voice and loud laughter. How safe he'd made me feel when he stepped up to protect me.

"He seems like a nice guy. Decent."

"What does he do?"

"I think he's a trainer at the gym across the street."

"A muscle guy? That is not usually your style at all. He must be special."

"I'm not sure I have a type." I chuckled. "But Ronan seems really nice. Honest and genuine." I laughed again. "And his appetite is like nothing I have ever seen."

"Is he picking you up here?"

"Yeah, as long as that's okay."

She grinned. "Sure, I'd love to meet him. He knows about Evan?"

"He knows I have a brother I take care of. That's all he needs to know. I'm not letting him get involved with us or you until I'm sure he'll be around long enough."

She gripped my hand. "Carson was a jerk."

She was right. I had met Carson at school. He'd seemed great. We dated for a while, and I thought we were getting serious. Until the accident and my responsibilities grew. I remembered the way he looked at me the day we broke up. Cold, removed, and uncaring.

"This wasn't in my plans, Beth. I didn't count on a kid who needs help and a girlfriend who isn't around much. It's not really worth it. We weren't forever anyway." He lifted a shoulder. "You understand."

"Understand what?"

He laughed, the sound unpleasant. "You were a great distraction for now. But not the girl I'd bring home to my parents. Not the one I'll spend my life with. I need...a little more than you can offer. Someone worthwhile."

And he had walked away as if I meant nothing. As if we'd meant nothing.

Even now, I felt a flash of pain as I recalled his dismissive voice and attitude. His painful words. It didn't matter I had just lost my parents. That my brother was injured and needed help. The fact that my whole word had just been turned upside down meant nothing to him aside from an inconvenience. Add in the fact that he showed me his true colors that day, proving he wasn't the person I thought him to be. And he had been wrong. He was the one not worthwhile. Still, it hurt, and it took me a while to recover.

He was the last man I had dated. He'd shattered my trust and self-confidence completely.

Paige frowned. "It was him, not you. You know that, right?"

"Yes." I sighed. "Ronan is different. Or at least, he seems different."

"Ronan. Unusual name. I like it."

"I like *him*," I confessed.

"I look forward to meeting him."

I heard the patter of tiny feet, and we both grinned as Lucy shuffled into the kitchen. Her hair was a dark cloud around her face, and her pajamas were covered in daises. She loved flowers of any kind, but daisies were her favorite. And kittens. Puppies. Anything soft. Anything sweet. She was a real girlie little girl. She was affectionate, bright, and adorable. She looked like Paige with her dark hair, small stature, and sunny disposition. She had wide, hazel eyes, the irises a rich mixture of green and brown. She inherited those from her father, with one big difference. Lucy's shone with warmth and happiness. She was impossible not to love, unless you were Paige's ex.

The fact that she was born with only one fully developed arm had proven to be too much for the man Paige described as exacting, cold, and indifferent. *"He hid it well,"* she stated sadly. *"I fell for the outward charm and didn't see what lurked underneath."*

Unable to accept his daughter could be less than perfect, he had walked away the day she was born, abandoning them. He divorced Paige, signed away any parental rights, and she never saw him again. His lawyer was nasty and underhanded, and Paige had neither the money nor desire to fight him.

"Once he was gone, I realized how horrible he was. How badly he treated me," she confessed. *"I never want Lucy to be treated that way. We're both better off without him."*

I had met her one day in a support group, and we bonded. I was dealing with the aftermath of the accident that claimed my parents and left my brother injured, and she was struggling with a toddler with special needs, on her own with no family. Both of us recognized a kindred soul, and we became close. When we needed a place to live, we pooled our resources and rented a small house together. Paige worked from home as an insurance adjuster, so she was there with Lucy and Evan during the day when I was at school or work. The days I was home, I took over to give her a break. We relied on each other, and we were our own little family.

Lucy scrambled onto her mom's lap, holding a stuffed animal tight under her arm. She amazed me the way she coped with only one working hand. Paige explained because she'd never known any different, Lucy adapted easier than someone who lost it later in life. I knew Evan was struggling with his disability, although I hoped in time it became easier. I hoped one day a treatment could be found that would work on improving his life.

Lucy held up her stuffed animal. "We hungry!"

I grinned at her, still shocked anyone couldn't love that little face. She was pure sunshine.

"What are you hungry for?" I asked, already knowing the answer.

"Pandcakes!"

I laughed. We had "pandcakes" every Sunday. They were a favorite for all of us.

The sound of metal crutches met my ears, and Evan appeared in the doorway. He regarded us with a grin. "Did I hear the word pandcakes?"

I stood. "You did. Come join us, and I'll start them."

"Bacon?" he asked hopefully.

Luckily, tips had been good again. "Yep."

"Awesome." He sat down beside Lucy. "Hey, Lucy-loo. What's shaking?"

She giggled, and my heart melted watching them. They were like brother and sister. He taught her video games, ever patient with her disability, and she was getting better all the time. He read to her, watched TV shows he had no interest in because she loved them. He watched over her. She looked at him as if he hung the moon, not caring that he walked with crutches or that outside the house he was so shy he could barely speak. She waited by the window every day for the school bus to drop him off, not caring it took him a long time to get down the steps or hobble up the sidewalk. Here, he was her Evan, and she adored him.

And I adored all of them.

An odd thought jiggled in my head as I gathered the makings of our Sunday morning feast.

How would Ronan react to them?

CHAPTER FIVE
RONAN

Tuesday took forever to arrive.

Twice, I drove past the diner on Saturday, but I didn't stop. I saw Beth through the windows. The first time, the place was busy, and I saw three other servers, all rushed off their feet. The second time, it was slower, but there were only two of them then, and I knew she wouldn't have time to talk to me. Feeling like a stalker, I drove out to Port Albany. I walked around my finished house, knowing I needed to buy some more furniture and make the decision to move permanently. The kitchen was well equipped, but the only things I had in the house were a bed and a large chair in the living room. It sat in front of the huge bay window overlooking the water. I loved to sit and watch the changing skies, the way the waves hit the shore, and how the color of the water altered with the light. Clouds fascinated me, and I often watched them moving across the sky, sometimes puffs of white, other times dark and stormy. Watching the weather change over the water was something I never got bored of, no matter the season. I liked being here. The offices of ABC would open here soon, and I really didn't want to make the commute daily.

Except suddenly, I wasn't as anxious to move. Dark eyes and wild curls the color of sunlit sand came to mind, and I had to shake my head at the ridiculousness of those thoughts.

I didn't even know her.

"That's what Tuesday is for," the voice in my head whispered.

I heard the light tap on the front door, and my mom walked in, holding a plate.

"I saw your car. I thought you might be hungry," she said with a smile.

My mother, Cami Callaghan, was an elegant, talented woman. Always dressed to impress, yet somehow never over the top, she was astounding. Having given birth to five kids in three years, she was simply extraordinary the way she handled all of us and our father. He was a handful just on his own.

He adored my mother, and she was equally as passionate about him. They were great parents, loving and demonstrative. He nurtured our bodies and taught us to respect them. She nurtured our souls, encouraging us to love art, music, and learning. Growing up, we took as many trips to the museums and concerts as we did trips to the gym and wrestling matches. Neither of my parents had experienced good childhoods, so they made sure we did. Between them and the extended family they created with BAM, growing up here had been nothing short of magical.

I hoped one day to give that to my own kids.

"Aren't I always?" I replied, bending to kiss her cheek. Her green eyes were tender as she cupped my face, her dark hair shot with silver and highlighted with purple—something she still did "for fun"—hanging to her shoulders. She was beautiful, and I loved my mother.

But I had a feeling there was a hidden agenda behind the plate of fried chicken she had brought with her.

"Aunt Dee been cooking?"

She laughed. The one thing my mother didn't do overly well was cook. Her meals were simple, but my aunt Dee, her sister, was great in the kitchen, and they often cooked together.

"Yes. She, Emmy, and I made a whole pile of fried chicken today. Brunch tomorrow, you know."

I reached for a piece. "I'll be there."

"So, you're staying overnight?"

I nodded around a mouthful of the crispy treat. "Thought I'd unpack the TV I bought and set it up. Maybe wire up the sound system." I paused. "Damn, this is good."

She laughed. "I know. We taste-tested it earlier."

I chewed and swallowed. "I think there's a new piece of equipment Dad mentioned at the Hub I might try."

"Your brothers in town tonight?" she asked.

I smiled at her obvious attempt to be innocuous.

"Yes, Mom, they are. And yes, I know they are bringing Kim and Diane out to meet you tomorrow." I set down the chicken, wiping my fingers. "And yes, I'm fine with it. I met them. I liked them."

"It's just…" She trailed off, and I patted her hand.

I hated seeing the worried look on her face. The way the frown pulled her mouth down.

"Mom, it's okay." I hastened to assure her. "Things are changing. You didn't really think we'd all fall in love at the same time and set up house together or anything, did you? You knew we'd all find different paths eventually."

"I know." She sighed, looking at me as if I were crazy. "*Of course* I know that. But they've both done it at the same time, meaning you're alone. That must leave you with some residual negative feelings."

Part of me wanted to tell her, yes, it did. But I knew it would only upset her more. So, I opted for what people expected of me. I joked around.

"Mom, have you been watching a lot of *Dr. Phil* lately or something? *Residual negative feelings?* What are you reading these days?" I lifted my hands. "The boys are seeing a couple of great girls. I'm with them every day at work and still some evenings," I fibbed a little. "I'm fine, they're fine. Everyone is fine. Stop worrying."

She stood, crossing her arms and tapping her foot. Instantly, I knew she wasn't buying it. Not for a second. The toe-tapping was a dead giveaway when she was upset.

"It's my prerogative to worry. I'm your mother. And if you think I can't see through you, Ronan Adam Callaghan, you are sadly mistaken. I know you're hurting. I know you're lonely. Of the three of you, you have always felt things more intensely. Worried more. I'm not sure if it comes with being the firstborn of triplets or if it is simply part of your DNA, but you are different from Paul and Jeremy." She patted her chest. "Inside. You are different."

I blinked at her lecture.

"I'm fine," I repeated, thinking if I said it enough, it would be true. That I wouldn't feel slighted or ignored. Lost. I had no reason to feel that way. What I said was true. I liked the girls, and Paul and Jeremy seemed happy. We were still connected and saw one another every day.

I ignored the little voice that reminded me they saw each other way more often, but I was no longer included in those moments.

Mom slapped her hand on the table. "If everything were fine, you would not be sitting alone in an empty house on a Saturday night, eating fried chicken and setting up a TV."

"I'm not alone. You're here."

She stalked to the door and spun on her heel. "When you are ready to be open with me, you know where I am. Until then, enjoy your chicken." She paused. "And it's not *Dr. Phil*. It's a new book I got at the library on channeling your inner therapist. Obviously, I struck a chord, and you're using sarcasm to push me away."

She flounced out, the door slamming behind her. I blinked at her anger. Then the door opened and she raced in, flinging her arms around me.

"I love you, Ronan. Come over later and have dessert."

Then she was gone.

I tried not to laugh. Mom never could stay mad at any of us. Especially Dad. He did the stupidest stuff, and she forgave him. Like the time he snuck into Ava's graduation dance to check on her, and he got caught when he stumbled and fell through the curtains covering the gymnasium walls and landed on the dance floor, in a pile of rented fabric. He embarrassed Ava in front of her whole class, and when he tried to make a joke, she kicked his feet out from under him again, leaving him lying in the fabric once more. Mom had to go pick him up at the school and she was furious, but by the next morning, she was more amused than angry. Ava, on the other hand, didn't talk to him for a week. It was epic. Bentley and Maddox still teased him about it.

I didn't want her to worry about me. I didn't want anyone to worry about me. It was my job to worry about my brothers. The tug of loneliness, the feeling of being cut off from them, would fade. I was certain about it.

I wondered why I hadn't mentioned my date with Beth. I munched on another piece of chicken as I mulled it over, realizing, for the first time, I was doing something completely on my own. I had a date with a girl who knew nothing about my family, and about whom they knew nothing. Beth was just for me, and I didn't have to share. She was all mine.

I kinda liked that feeling.

———

Tuesday night, I pulled up in front of a small, neat bungalow. The lawn was freshly cut, and some flowers were planted in the front, giving it a cheerful look. It was an older house, but well kept up. I smoothed a hand over my head, feeling decidedly nervous. It was just tacos, I reminded myself. Tacos with a pretty girl. Only the two of us.

Sunday had been loud and crazy. Brunch became drinks and games at the Hub. Some of the family that was around came to meet Kim and Diane. They clustered around, laughing and talking. The girls seemed fine with it all, not the least bit worried about the crush of strangers or how they fit in. Paul and Jeremy never strayed far from their sides. There were moments I felt invisible and alone, which was weird when I was in a roomful of people I loved and who loved me. But usually when the family was together, we three boys were a unit. We sat together, ate together, teased the group from our spot. We entertained and made everyone laugh. It was always the same.

Except, today, it was the *four* of them, and I sat to the side, talking to Jaxson or Dad most of the time, trying not to feel left out—and failing. Still, I smiled and covered up my unease.

I wandered down to the beach, needing to escape for a while. Gracie had followed not long after, linking her free arm with mine. We were quiet for a minute before she spoke.

"You okay?" she asked.

"I'm good."

"Too much back there?"

I sighed and was honest. "At times. It's a freaking circus."

She laughed quietly and squeezed my arm. "I know. I feel the same some-times. Paul and Jeremy seem happy."

"Yep."

Gracie was never one to mince words. "Are you feeling left out?"

"I'm not sure how I'm feeling. I'm happy for them, though."

"You'll find the right girl. And you'll want her to be part of the circus."

"Maybe."

"You will," she insisted. *"You need to find your person. The one who loves Ronan. It makes a world of difference."*

"Like Jaxson is for you?"

Her smile was wide and happy. "Yes. I belong to him, and he is mine. When we're with the family, it's fun and great, but our life is together and separate in many ways. Right now, the family is the focus for you. Being part of it. You need to find your life outside it and build a world that includes it, but that isn't the entire focus." She huffed. "You share your life with the family, but your world is the person you love. If that makes any sense."

"It does."

"Good. You'll find her, Ronan. I know it. And she'll be awesome."

I was tempted to tell her about my date with Beth, but I refrained. I still didn't want to share her with anyone. I had no idea if anything would come of it. If there would be a second date. If it would lead to anything.

I sighed and climbed out of the car. There was only one way to find out.

I rang the doorbell and stood back. Beth opened the door, and my breath caught in my throat. Her hair was shiny, the curls wild around her face. She was wearing a pretty green blouse and a skirt that flowed around her knees. She smiled and accepted the small bunch of flowers I had picked up. I didn't know her favorite kind, so I let the lady at the shop make a bouquet.

"These are lovely!" Beth exclaimed and leaned up to kiss my cheek.

I grinned. "So are you."

Her cheeks darkened, and she indicated for me to come in. I met three sets of eyes as I entered the living room.

A pretty woman with dark hair and blue eyes stood.

"This is Paige, my roommate," Beth introduced us.

I shook Paige's hand. "Nice to meet you."

She put her hand on the little girl's shoulder. "This is my daughter, Lucy."

I crouched down, trying not to look so tall. "Hi, Lucy. I'm Ronan."

Hesitant hazel eyes met my green. "You're big."

"I am."

"Are you scary?"

I laughed. "I try not to be."

She held out her left hand, and I was surprised to see the artificial limb on her right. I switched hands and shook hers gently, then stood and faced the young boy who was staring at me.

Beth smiled. "This is my brother, Evan. Evan, this is Ronan."

He looked at me, his curiosity evident. He studied me for a moment. I took in the metal crutches he leaned on. The way he favored his right side. The obvious lean. He'd been injured badly at some point and never recovered.

"Hey, Evan. Good to meet you."

He was silent, then pursed his lips. "Are you a body builder?"

"Nah. I just like to work out."

Beth cleared her throat. "He works at a gym."

I opened my mouth to correct her, but Evan spoke.

"Cool. So, you know how to work all the machines and everything?"

I let it go, deciding I would address my job with Beth later. "Yeah, I do."

"Wicked. My school has some, but I don't use them."

I stepped closer. "Why?"

He indicated his leg. "I don't know how, and the other kids…" He stopped talking and shrugged.

Instantly I understood. "Maybe I can help you there."

His eyes widened. "Really?"

"If it's okay with your sister." I met her gaze, which seemed overly bright right now.

"I'm going to go put these in water. Evan, we'll talk about it later." She turned and hurried away, and Evan's shoulders slumped.

"That probably means no."

I met Paige's eyes, suspecting why Beth was hesitant. I smiled and patted Evan's shoulder. "I can be persuasive."

A tugging on my pants made me look down. I met the wide gaze of Lucy. She was adorable as she grinned at me, a couple of her teeth missing. "Me too?"

Chuckling, I bent and scooped her up into my arms. "I think you're too little, Lucy. But I could use you instead of pumping iron." I pretended to do arm curls with her, careful to hold her tight so she didn't fall. She shrieked in laughter, the sound making me grin. Evan chuckled, and Paige smiled as I teased Lucy.

"You're the perfect size for this. No more growing, or you'll get too big."

"Good luck," Paige laughed. "She grows every day."

I sighed dramatically and put Lucy down. "Shame."

"Maybe you grow too," Lucy said.

It was my turn to laugh, and I ruffled her hair. "Maybe."

In the car, Beth smiled. "You were very good with them."

"I like kids."

"I think they liked you."

"Lucy..." I let my voice trail off.

She sighed, knowing what I was asking. "She was born with one arm not formed. We hope once she's older she can get one of those prosthetics that work with your brain. She has an artificial one now that has to be changed as she grows, but it's more for looks than anything. She doesn't really like it, and she does very well without it."

"She is adorable. Her father not around?"

"He walked out when he found out she had a *defect*."

The way she snarled the word, I knew it wasn't the way she saw Lucy.

"Asshole, I assume?"

"That's being polite."

We pulled up to the restaurant, and Beth looked around the parking lot. "Looks busy."

"They know me here. I have a table reserved," I assured her. "And they'll have extra tacos ready with no lettuce for me."

She laughed. "Oh boy. This I gotta see."

Over margaritas, I discovered Beth was exactly what I thought her to be. Witty, smart, and fun. Her laughter was low and sultry. She was well-read and knowledgeable.

"You mentioned school. University, I assume."

She nodded.

"You must have just finished exams?"

"Yes, thank goodness. My last one was two days ago. Now, I'm starting some intersession courses next week."

"No summer school?"

"No. I work during the summer."

I had a feeling I knew why, so I didn't push the subject. "What are you taking?" I asked as I lifted a heavy nacho, already anticipating the bite of the jalapenos and the crunch of the chip and peppers on my tongue.

"Science. I'm specializing in meteorology."

I chewed and swallowed. "Are you shitting me? Like clouds and storms?"

She smiled and nodded around her mouthful, pausing to sip her drink before answering. "Yes. Clouds and storms."

"How freaking cool is that?" I breathed out. "I love watching clouds." I leaned forward. "So, you know the names of all of them?"

She looked startled. "Yes."

"Hit me with a few."

"Um, well, there is cumulus. The stereotypical puffy cloud you probably drew a lot of when you were a kid, they are dense, individual clouds that are bright white on top and gray under-neath. They typically appear earlier in the day when it's sunny."

I nodded. "I know that one. What is a storm one called?"

"Well, cumulonimbus are the classic 'thunderstorm clouds.' Seeing them is a sign that a storm is likely on its way. Or there are nimbostratus. Those clouds form a thick, dark layer across the sky, often blotting out the sun. Like cumulonimbus, they're associated with rain, but you can't pick out individual nimbo-stratus clouds."

I leaned back and looked at her.

"Gotta be honest. I am totally turned on right now."

Her sudden loud peal of laughter made me grin. If I thought her low chuckles were sexy, this had ten times the effect. Her curls bobbed, her mouth turned up in a sexy smirk, and the color on her cheeks was a light pink. Her dark eyes danced in mirth.

"No one has ever said that to me before. Not about clouds."

"It's not just the clouds. It's you talking about them. How many years do you have left in your degree?"

A flash of pain crossed her face. "I had to stop going to school, so I'm behind. I have another year left, then I want to get my masters, so that is another two."

"And you're twenty, ah…?" I paused, waiting for her to fill in the number.

"Twenty-five."

She was younger than me but very mature for her age. I had a feeling it was due to her responsibilities and her personality. She had an old soul, much like a lot of the women in my family—wiser than their years.

"What do you want to do with your degree? Not a weather girl on TV, I'm assuming."

"I want to work behind the scenes. Research. I want to study weather trends and their effects on plants, animals, humans, and the world's oceans. Research can also study historical atmospheric data to find clues that help the scientific community understand how weather events shape the earth's ecosystems. I want to be part of that."

I sat back, admiring her. "I just came in my pants," I deadpanned. "Beautiful and smart? Poke me with a fork, because I am done."

That got me another burst of laughter. A little more color in her pretty cheeks. I wondered if her skin would be warm if I kissed her right now. It took all I had in me not to lean across the table and find out.

"I have to finish school first and find a job."

I had a feeling she could do anything she put her mind to.

"You will," I assured her. "I have no doubt."

"You hardly know me. How can you be so sure?"

"I'm a great judge of character."

She shook her head, but I saw her smile.

And I liked it.

———

Beth regarded the large platter of tacos in front of us.

"I wasn't sure what you liked, so I got an assortment," I offered. "You told me you weren't a vegetarian, but I wasn't sure if you liked beef. So, there's pork, chicken, and shrimp too."

"Not even you can possibly eat this many tacos," she said, lifting her gaze to mine. "Can you?"

"Not an issue."

"Wow," she breathed out.

"I gotta keep up my strength. Make sure I'm ready to battle anything out there to keep you safe."

She lifted one eyebrow. It was sexy. "Is a ninja attack imminent?"

"You never know." I lifted a taco. "Better safe than sorry. You're my responsibility until I kiss you goodnight and make sure you're safely inside."

"Who says you're getting a good-night kiss?"

I grinned. "Hopeful."

She took a taco, shaking her head. But she was still smiling. She bit and chewed, then moaned low in her throat. "Oh my God, these are so good. I hope you got enough."

I threw back my head in laughter, grateful for her humor. The sound of her low moan had made my cock twitch. We both wanted to hear it again. Hopefully while my mouth was on hers.

We were quiet for a few moments, concentrating on the food. I filled her glass from the jug, and she regarded me wryly.

"Trying to get me drunk, Ronan?"

I laughed. "No. They make these special for me. Less than half the alcohol. Then I can drink two of them and be fine to drive. Two at full blast, I would be wasted."

She pursed her lips. "You come here a lot, I assume."

"Yep. Have for years. It's long been a family favorite. My dad used to bring my mom here."

"I see. I guess you work it off with all the exercise you get being a trainer."

I cleared my throat, not able to look her in her eye as I kept lying. "I'm not a trainer at that gym. I just go there because I like it. It's small and well equipped. Great classes."

She didn't seem to notice my unease. "Oh, you train elsewhere but use those facilities?"

I hesitated, not wanting to tell her yet. I squirmed in the booth a little, feeling guilt trickle down my spine. I was enjoying being Ronan. Just a guy. No huge family, no triplets, no expectations. "Something like that. I have another job elsewhere. I help out on occasion if John needs it. Otherwise, I'm just another customer."

She frowned, but she seemed to understand. "Ah."

I changed the subject, grateful she didn't push. "I know a place. It's great to watch clouds. See the water and have a picnic. Maybe on a Sunday?"

"I usually spend Sundays with Evan. I hardly get to see him during the week."

I quickly went over the area I was thinking about in my mind. It was on the very edge of the BAM property, behind the woods, and no one ever went there but me. "He could come along. The path is pretty level."

"He'd like that."

"What about his sister? Would she like that?"

She picked up another taco. "Yes."

"Great. We'll figure out a day when we know there will be some clouds around. You can show me."

"All right."

I ate another taco. "Was it an accident?" I asked. "The reason for the crutches?"

She swallowed, setting down the taco she was eating. She took a sip of her drink, not meeting my eyes. "Yes."

"I don't want to pry or upset you."

She lifted her gaze to mine, and the pain in her eyes was prevalent.

Without thinking, I reached for her hand and squeezed it. "I'm sorry. You don't have to say anything."

She shook her head. "No, it's fine. There was an accident. A drunk driver. He plowed into a crowd. He killed my parents and left Evan badly injured. They weren't sure he would walk again."

"But he did."

"Yes. He needs the crutches, though."

"Does he have trouble at school getting around?"

She sighed and wiped her fingers. "He does okay. It's a pretty small school. I think he gets picked on a lot, though. He refuses to tell me, and I know he ignores a lot of it, but…"

"You hate it."

"Yes."

"He seems like a great kid. He's a lot younger than you."

She smiled. "He's twelve. He was a whoops baby. My parents had tried for years after me and gave up. I was in my teens when they had him. I adored him from the moment he was born."

"So, you're very close."

She met my gaze. "Yes. He is a huge part of my life."

I knew what she was saying. Evan came first. She had responsibilities. Lots of them, I was discovering. It didn't faze me, though, or make me want to get to know her any less. If anything, I only admired her more. Wanted to spend more time with her.

"So, you said you were close to your family?" she asked.

"Yes. We're pretty tight," I admitted.

She smiled, picking up her taco again. I decided to keep the rest of the night light. I had a feeling she didn't get enough light.

"Enough about families," I announced. "Tell me about Beth."

"What do you want to know?"

"Everything. Your favorite color, food, movie, book, season. Anything you are willing to tell me, I want to hear."

"You're a great date, Ronan."

"Just getting started, Beth. Trust me."

After churros, we took a short drive and ended up at the waterfront. We strolled around, got ice cream, and walked along the water's edge. It was getting later, the sun disappearing fast and not many people around. It wasn't even close to being as nice as Port Albany, but for Toronto, it was okay. She sighed as she looked over the water.

"You like that?" I asked. "Water, I mean?"

"Yes. I love to swim."

I thought of the Hub. The pool. The lake. The exercise room I could help out Evan in. It was on the tip of my tongue to tell her. But then the whole family thing, the triplet angle, all of it would come up. I decided to stay silent until I was sure there was something ahead of us besides tonight.

When I was ready to share.

"There's a pool in my condo building," I offered.

"Maybe," she replied. "I might take you up on that."

I nodded, looking out over the water. The desire to kiss her was predominant. She stood close to me, her head barely grazing my shoulder. I could feel her warmth. Smell the scent of her light perfume. Flowery, pretty. Unique—like her. She finished her ice cream, wiping her lips, the action bringing my gaze to her mouth. Her lips were full. Pink. Would they be as soft as they looked? Would she taste of the cherry ice cream, the cinnamon of the churros? Both?

I wanted to know more than I had wanted anything in a long time. She turned her head, her eyes meeting mine. Slowly, everything around us faded. All I could see was her. Wild hair, dark eyes that beckoned. A full mouth I wanted to claim. Her lush curves that invited my hands to sculpt over them, pull her to me.

She blinked, her long lashes fluttering. "What are you think-ing?" she whispered.

The atmosphere was heavy. Serious. Too serious.

I gazed into her dark eyes. "I was wondering if I should switch my home and auto insurance to Geico," I deadpanned.

For a moment, there was no reaction. Then she laughed. The loud peals I found so enticing. And suddenly, she was in my arms and our mouths fused together, her amusement shared only between us. I kissed her deeply, her lips parting for me right away. I tasted the ice cream. The cinnamon. Her. She delved her hands into my hair, pulling me closer. We both groaned. I bent, lifting her into my arms so I could kiss her longer. Harder. She was perfect in my embrace. Soft. Warm. Melting into me as if she belonged there. Nothing existed outside this moment. I slanted my head, kissing her deeper, taking everything she gave me and wanting more. Every nerve in my body lit up as if on fire. My heart pounded a fast rhythm in my chest, her name echoing with every beat. She whimpered as I dragged my lips across her cheek to her ear.

"Beth," I moaned. "You are so sweet."

"More," she replied. "Kiss me more."

I was happy to comply, capturing her mouth with mine.

I knew right then there was no going back. I was all in. No matter her limited time, no matter her responsibilities, I wanted to be a part of them. Part of her life.

I kissed her until she was breathless. Until I was dizzy with desire and want. Until I knew I had to stop or I would drag her back to my car and have her in the back seat. Or the hood. I wasn't picky. Neither was my cock. Hard as a rock, aching and pressed between us, he would take her any way he could.

And it was too soon for that. She deserved better.

I lowered her to her feet, cupping her face as I kissed her one last time. I drew back, already missing the feel of her mouth underneath mine.

I pressed light kisses to her cheeks, eyes, then the end of her nose. She opened her eyes, the dark eclipsed by her pupils, her expression one of soft protest. "You stopped."

I wrapped her in my arms. "I had to, or I wouldn't be responsible for what would happen next."

"Oh." She nestled closer. "I might not object."

I shut my eyes. "Don't tempt me, Beth. You deserve better. A fast fuck in the car isn't my style, and I highly doubt it's yours either." Opening my eyes, I tilted up her chin and met her gaze. "I'm not in a hurry. We'll get to know each other, and I promise you—" I lowered my head and kissed her again "—it'll be worth the wait for us both."

She sighed. "You're right. Damn it, Ronan, you messed with my head."

I stepped back, keeping one arm wrapped around her. "Come on, I'll take you home. If I keep you out too late, Evan might smack me with one of his crutches."

She chortled. "He might."

In the car, I turned on the heater since it was getting cooler and glanced over at her. "I had a really good time tonight."

"Me too."

"Could I take you out for coffee after work on Thursday?"

"Oh, that's cake night."

"Cake night?"

"The night I bake the cakes at the diner."

"You bake those cakes?"

"Yes. I get a cut on every slice they sell."

I promptly decided I would call and order some cakes in the morning. The office would love it.

"I could help."

She frowned. "Not much fun for you."

"If you're there, I'm good."

"Really?" she asked, sounding unconvinced.

"Really."

"Okay, then. I'd love the company."

"Great."

She shook her head. "I don't think I'm prepared for you, Ronan."

I grinned.

She hadn't seen anything yet.

CHAPTER SIX

BETH

I knew he was in the diner before I saw him. Ever since Ronan had taken me home on Tuesday, he had been on my mind. He had kissed me again before I got out of his car. Then caught me on the steps for another kiss. His mouth was addictive, and his caresses left me longing for more. More of him. I had never felt that way about a man before now. Especially one I didn't really know. Given how Carson had treated me, I should be more cautious, but Ronan seemed open and honest. He was caring and asked a lot of questions about Evan and Lucy. He wasn't intimidated or daunted by their disabilities. He didn't seem overly interested in their physical conditions, but rather the person. It was nice to talk about them, share stories about their lives.

I did, however, notice his lack of sharing about his own life. I assumed there was a story there and he would tell me when he was ready.

I turned from the table I was serving to meet Ronan's bright-green gaze. He watched me intently, smiling as I drew close.

"Welcome to Nifty Fifty."

He leaned back in the booth I had come to think of as his, with a grin.

"Do you need a menu?" I asked, trying not to get lost in his warm eyes.

"Are you on it? Because I'll take the order to go," he replied, leaning forward and tugging my hand from my chest. He lifted it to his mouth and kissed the inside of my wrist. "With whipped cream on the side."

"What are you going to do with the whipped cream?" I asked breathlessly.

He chuckled. "Oh baby, if you only knew what I was thinking."

I felt the flush of color on my cheeks. The rush of heat through my body. Regretfully, I pulled back my hand.

"Hello, Ronan."

He leaned forward expectantly. I realized he was waiting for me to close the distance and kiss him. I quickly glanced around then pressed my mouth to his cheek. He caught me before I could pull back and kissed my mouth, flicking his tongue over my lips, then sitting back looking pleased.

"Hello, Beth."

I rolled my eyes. "Did you have dinner, or are you eating?"

"Eating."

"What would you like?"

"It's late, so I'll go light. I'll do the house chopped salad. Extra chicken. And the soup. A couple of rolls." He paused, looking over my shoulder. "Is that a new kind of cake over there?"

I chuckled. "Spice cake with raisins. It's been a big hit."

"A slice of that."

"Holding back, I see."

He grinned. "I had a late lunch."

"Hmm."

"You'll sit with me for coffee?"

"Yes."

"And we'll be alone later?"

"I have to make cakes, Ronan."

"I'll help. But if we're alone, I can say hello properly. Maybe throw in a goodnight, a how are you, good job—whatever else I can think of."

The heat pooled in my stomach, slithering up my spine. I met his gaze, watched as his tongue ran along his bottom lip.

"I'll get your order," I mumbled, forcing myself to leave before I launched myself at him.

What was that man doing to me?

———

I grabbed a cup of coffee and sat with Ronan briefly. I wanted to get everything done and start making the cakes as soon as possible, but I couldn't resist having a few extra moments with him.

I slid into the booth, eyeing the empty plates. "Everything was okay?"

His reply was enthusiastic. "Awesome. That spice raisin cake? Wicked good."

"It's an old recipe from my grandma."

"I loved it." He took a sip of coffee. "Quieter in here this week."

"Not much happening downtown tonight. Less foot traffic."

"No assholes to contend with," he mused.

"Not tonight," I replied with a grimace.

"You had another one?"

I sighed. "You get them all the time in this business, Ronan."

"Punks."

"Last night was the type I hate the most. Your age, dressed in a suit that would pay my rent for a year, double-parking his expensive car outside. Demanding, rude. He went off because I didn't have any whole wheat buns for his veggie burger. It was ten o'clock, and we had run out. I offered the gluten-free or the regular one, but it wasn't good enough. He ranted at me for five minutes and, of course, got personal." I shook my head. "I dislike that type the most. The wannabe businessman who's had Daddy hand him everything and acts as if he is better than anyone. Filled with a sense of entitlement. Who thinks people like me are beneath him. Who pretends to be something he is not."

A strange look passed over Ronan's face.

"So, you hate businessmen?"

"No, that would be the same as saying all younger guys are jerks. They aren't. I dislike the unjustness sometimes. The haves versus the have-nots. Those who have to work hard, and those who get everything handed to them on a plate." I shrugged. "Ignore me. He was terrible, though."

"What did he say?"

"It doesn't matter."

"It matters to me."

I sighed. "It's fine, Ronan. He yelled, he didn't get what he wanted, and he stormed out, but not before making sure I knew he was much better than I was. Informed me it was hardly a surprise I was the one in the apron. That he mattered, whereas a waitress like me did not."

"Not all young businessmen are like that."

I smiled. "I know. Like I said—he was just a jerk. You must have to deal with the same problem at the gym sometimes. People." I shook my head. "Anyway, he left, and I ate a perfectly acceptable veggie burger on a white bun since he refused to pay for it and I refused to let him have it for free."

Ronan laughed, but he still looked troubled. "Good."

I stood. "I'm going to finish up."

I felt his stare the whole time as I kept busy in the diner. It surprised me how much the rude customer seemed to bother him. I dealt with cranky and mean patrons all the time.

Anyone who worked in the public sector did. I would have to get him to tell me some stories about people at the gym. I was sure he had some amusing ones.

I wanted to have as much ready for when we closed as possible. Jane was working and set up her tables for the morning, and since it was quieter, she helped me prep my area as well. I liked working with her. She was friendly and a hard worker, always willing to help out. She didn't question Ronan's extended stay but instead nudged me with her elbow before leaving for the night.

"Damn, that is one fine mountain man you have there."

I had to laugh. Ronan was large. Tall. Broad. I wasn't a small girl—my curves were too plentiful for that—but beside him, I felt tiny. The other night, he had lifted me as if I weighed nothing and held me close, as if the effort were easy. I had loved it.

I had also loved the feel of his mouth moving with mine. The man knew how to kiss. Possessive and deep. Passionate and fierce. There had been no doubt of his desire. I had felt him hard and pressing between us. My response to him was nothing short of explosive. It had taken all I had in me not to kiss him the way he wanted when he arrived. But I would have ended up on his lap and putting on a display for the restaurant. Somehow, I knew that without a doubt, so I had held back.

But soon, we'd be alone. The kitchen staff always cleared out as soon as possible on Thursdays so I could bake the cakes.

I checked that everything was ready in the kitchen and headed into the diner, stopping when I realized that Ronan was wiping down the last few tables. The muscles in his arms bunched as he polished the tabletop, and his jeans stretched tight over his ass as he leaned over, making short work of the job. He stood and nodded, pleased with his efforts.

I flicked off the lights, and he followed me to the kitchen. I pointed out a chair in the corner.

"You can sit there and talk to me while I bake."

He frowned. "I can help. I used to help Emmy all the time in the kitchen. She baked scones for a coffee shop when she was younger, and she always loved to bake at home. She let me help."

"Emmy?"

"My aunt. She was a waitress. She put herself through school. Like you." He stepped closer. "Let me help."

I handed him an apron, unable to resist his earnest voice and pleading eyes.

I had a feeling he was going to prove to be that way a lot.

"Okay, let's do this."

Forty-five minutes later, I slid the first of the cake pans into the oven and shut the door.

"You do this every week?"

"Yes. Eight cakes now. When we opened, it was three. And now on Saturdays, I often have extra orders. But it's great. I make a little more money. I bake them and take them out to cool. I make the icing while they are baking, and in the morning, they'll ice them and store them."

"No one else can do it?"

I waggled my eyebrows. "If I gave them the recipes, maybe. But I refused—the recipes were my mom's and her mom's. This pads my income a little. My classes are later on Friday mornings, so I can work late Thursday baking, get Evan ready for school Friday morning, and relax a little before class. The extra ones I make I do between rushes on Friday night and Saturday." She smiled. "The owners are very accommodating."

"Because it's damn good cake."

Ronan rinsed the last of the bowls as I wiped down the counter. I had already whipped up the massive tub of icing, and I pulled off the beaters, offering him one. He took it, licking away the frosting. "Damn, I love cream cheese," he muttered.

I tried not to stare. To fight down the wish that I was the beater he was using his tongue on. I failed at both, and he caught me looking, a teasing smirk pulling at his lips.

"See something you like?"

I swallowed, gasping in surprise as he moved fast, lifting me to the counter and standing between my legs. "Well?" he asked, plucking the other beater from my hand.

"Yes."

He licked the beater, slowly twirling it on his tongue.

"That was mine," I whined, not really caring. Watching him lick it was far more satisfying.

"Come get some, then," he murmured in a low voice. He pressed closer, covering my mouth with his. I groaned as he swirled his tongue along mine, tasting the sweet icing and Ronan. The combination was highly addictive. So was the feeling of being wrapped up in his arms. I felt his strength, carefully held in check. His muscles that rippled under my hands as I stroked his back. The silkiness of his hair as I ran my fingers through it.

His erection, that, like the rest of him, was massive and hard.

I whimpered.

He kissed me deeper, pulling my ass to the edge of the counter and grinding himself against me. I wrapped my legs around his waist and rubbed myself on him. He groaned low and deep in his throat in satisfaction. I heard the sound of the beater he'd held in his hand hitting the floor as he gathered me closer. Our kisses turned frantic. Wetter. Deeper. Wilder. Our teeth clashed. Tongues dueled. Our noises grew louder, our movements frantic.

Then the timer went off on the oven, the loud beep pulling us apart.

We stared at each other, our breathing fast. His hand was under my shirt, his skin warm against my back. I had his Henley gripped in my hand, the material twisted between my fingers. The timer sounded again, and Ronan looked toward the oven.

"We heard you." He grinned in amusement. "I think your oven is a little judgmental."

I started to laugh, and he wrapped his arms around me, kissed my head, then lifted me to the floor. "Check your cakes."

I opened the oven door and, satisfied, slid the pans onto the cooling table. The air was instantly filled with the scent of sweet and spice. I slid in the next batch, shut the door, and set the timer.

"So, we have another hour?" he asked.

"You should go. I know you have to work. What time do you have to be at the gym?"

"I'm good."

I began running a knife around the edges of the pans to loosen the cakes. "Really, Ronan, it's fine."

He picked up a knife and imitated me. "No, I like being here with you."

I liked hearing him say that.

"Tell me a funny story about some asshole at the gym. I bet you get people all the time."

"Oh, not really. I guess I've been lucky," he mumbled.

There was something in his tone, and I glanced up. There were slashes of crimson across the tops of his cheeks, and it occurred to me that perhaps he didn't like to talk about the gym, so I let it drop.

Ronan watched as I flipped the cakes onto the racks to finish cooling. I explained I would put parchment paper between the layers and wrap them tight. "They'll get frosted in the morning, rewrapped, and put in the fridge to be stored."

"Do they ever run out?"

"Yes. I think I'll have to start doing this twice a week. Making double batches."

"Do you have time?"

I shrugged. "I'll make time."

All too soon, the next batch was ready. I had to admit, having Ronan there was a treat. While I was wrapping the cakes, he scrubbed the pans. He helped me carry the cakes to the shelves. He lifted the heavy container of icing into the refrigerator. He let me talk, asking a ton of questions about clouds and storms and the classes I took. He said very little, but I gleaned he loved to work out, swim, hike, and above all, eat. He lived alone, saw his family when he could, and listened to music a lot. He also confessed to loving theater shows.

"My mom and aunts took us when we were younger. My brothers weren't so big on them, but I loved them. When I was older, I went with my mom and my sister."

"Musicals too?"

He grinned as he leaned forward and kissed the end of my nose. "Those were my favorites. I bet I could sing any song you threw at me."

And for twenty minutes, he did. He had a loud singing voice, way off-key, but his enthusiasm was catchy and he made me laugh with his overdramatic gestures. His *Man of La Mancha* was especially zealous. I clapped at the end.

"Maybe I could take you to one," he suggested as I began to wrap the last of the cakes after his performance ended.

"I'd like that," I said.

"Me too."

I wiped off the counter. "Done."

"Okay. I'll walk you to your car."

I shook my head. "I don't have a car."

"How do you get home?"

"The subway is at the corner."

"It's past one in the morning."

"They run until two."

He frowned. "That's not what I meant. It's late. You're alone."

"I don't drive, Ronan. I don't own a car."

"What about a cab? An Uber?"

"If the weather is bad, then I take one. But otherwise, I take the subway, or the bus if it's later."

His lips thinned in displeasure. "So, you take the subway every night?"

"Yes. Every morning too. Quite often in the afternoon as well," I teased, wanting him to stop looking so upset.

"Not tonight." He held out his hand. "I'm driving you home."

"That's not necessary."

He grabbed my hand and pulled me close. He looked down at me, his eyebrows drawn tight. I could see the small flecks of brown and gold around his pupils. "Yes, it is. Get your purse."

Then he kissed me, and the argument I was about to start somehow was erased from my head. The words were gone, and all that I cared about was his mouth on mine. Even when he pulled away, I couldn't speak.

"Get your coat."

And I did.

Ronan pulled up in front of the house, cutting the engine. He had been his usual gentlemanly self, opening my door, helping with the seat belt, and making sure I was warm enough, but he had been quiet.

I turned to him, laying my hand on his arm. "Thanks for the ride, Ronan. Unnecessary, but I appreciate it. I appreciate everything you did tonight. You made the work fun."

A reluctant smile crossed his lips. "It was fun. I enjoyed myself."

I laughed. "You are too sweet." I leaned over and kissed his cheek. "Good night."

I was partway to the front door when he caught up with me, holding my elbow and spinning me around. His eyes glittered in the low light. "I don't like thinking of you riding the subway late at night."

I didn't know what to say. It wasn't as if I had much choice. Cabs, even Ubers, would add up fast and negate the cake income.

"It's part of my life, Ronan. At least for now."

"It's not safe."

"There are two bars between the diner and the corner. They're open late, so there are people around. The subway stop is less than a block from here, and often others get off when I do. I walk on the road and make sure I am aware of my surroundings. I've taken self-defense courses. I can take care of myself."

He crowded me. "What if I told you I wanted to take care of you?"

I blinked up at him. "I would say no."

"Why?"

"I can't get used to having someone around who might walk."

"Not going to happen."

Then his lips were on mine. Hot, hard, seeking. He tugged me to his chest, devouring me with his mouth. I whimpered, wrapping my arms around his neck. He lifted me, letting my feet dangle in midair as he kissed me. Endless moments passed until he broke away, leaning his forehead to mine. Our eyes locked, intense green meeting confused brown.

He set me on my feet.

"I am not walking away."

"My life isn't mine to give you right now."

"I'll fit in wherever you have space."

"Ronan—"

He cut me off with another kiss. "I have never felt this attraction to another woman before, Beth. You're all I can think of. Don't ask me to walk away. Don't end us before we begin. Especially not because of time. We can figure it out. Please."

I sighed, unable to resist. Not wanting to.

"Come for breakfast Sunday," I whispered. "But Ronan, my brother is part of the package—you need to understand—"

He interrupted me. "Yes."

"I don't know—"

His mouth pressed to mine. "Yes."

I sighed. "Okay. Sunday. Ten."

He kissed me again. "Yes."

CHAPTER SEVEN
BETH

Sunday morning, I was up even earlier than usual. Knowing Ronan would be here with us today made me excited. And nervous. I wasn't sure which sensation was the most prominent. The diner had been busy on Friday and Saturday, plus there was a last-minute order for three extra cakes that had come in early on Friday from a company downtown, so I'd gone in early Saturday to bake some extras to cover the ones purchased and delivered on Friday. I didn't mind because the extra income was a bonus. My boss was thrilled because the company paid extra for last-minute plus delivery. He gave me a bonus for it, which meant my bank account breathed a little easier.

I made up the pancake batter, doubling the usual amount since Ronan would be there. I grated potatoes to make hash browns and started the bacon. Evan would be thrilled. In his opinion, bacon was a food group unto itself and should be served with every meal.

Paige smirked as she watched me putter around. She sipped her coffee. "This guy has you spinning in circles. Although," she drawled, "seeing those muscles, I understand why."

"Stop it. There's more to Ronan than muscles."

She leaned her chin on her hand. "I bet there is. Is he packing?"

I gaped at her, and she shrugged. "Come on," she teased. "I have to live vicariously through you."

"How would I know?" I asked.

"From the look of your swollen mouth and mussy hair the other night, I would say you do."

My cheeks flushed. I had been rather disheveled on Thursday when I stumbled in the front door. Paige had been awake, and the grin on her face had made me blush, mutter about being exhausted, and head downstairs as fast as I could.

I shook my head. "You're awful." Then I waggled my eyebrows. "And he is."

"I knew it."

Evan walked in, rubbing his eyes. "Bacon?" he asked hopefully.

"Yep." I wiped the back of my neck. "Ronan is going to have breakfast with us."

He frowned. "The big guy who was here?"

"Yes."

"Cool. I liked him." He sat down beside Paige, who ruffled his hair. He swiped at her hand, pretending to be annoyed, but he grinned as he did it. "So, is he your boyfriend?"

"Um, we're friends?" I said, making it sound more like a question.

He crossed his arms on the table. "I'm old enough to know what a boyfriend is, Beth. As long as he doesn't tell me what to do, I'm cool."

"I don't think he'd do that."

"Okay."

I turned back to the stove, trying not to smile.

Boyfriend. I whispered the word under my breath, wondering how Ronan would feel about being called that. We'd only had one date, so it was too soon to put a label on us. I needed to know more about him. He was such an open person until I asked him questions about himself or his family. Maybe there was bad blood or a break between them. I would give him time to trust me—I was sure he would tell me once we got to know each other a little more.

An hour later, I was ready. The food was mostly done except for the eggs. Everyone liked them differently, and I always made them last. Scrambled for Evan and Lucy. Fried for Paige. Poached for me. I wondered how Ronan would like them.

The doorbell sounded, and I sucked in a deep breath as I walked down the hall. I guessed I was about to find out.

I opened the door, Ronan's broad shoulders filling the doorway. His smile was wide as he cast his gaze over me. He stepped closer and lowered his head.

"Morning, little bird."

I laughed quietly. "Little bird?"

"You remind me of a hummingbird—always on the go." His kiss was warm on my cheek. "Hello."

I turned my head and pressed my lips to his quickly. "Hello." I stepped back before I could do something silly like fling my arms around his neck and kiss him the way I longed to do. "Come in."

He walked in, filling the small hallway. He handed me a bunch of flowers. "To say thanks for breakfast."

His gesture made me smile. Especially considering his hands were still full with other offerings. I watched as he greeted everyone. He handed Paige a bouquet, crouched down to offer Lucy a bunch of daisies, then grinned at Evan. "Figured you for more of a chocolate kind of guy," he said and handed him some Kinder eggs. Evan loved those. I had mentioned that the other night, plus the fact that Lucy loved daisies. It touched me that he remembered.

Evan grinned in delight. "Awesome. Thank you!"

Ronan bent again and handed Lucy an egg as well. He looked at Paige. "Hope that's all right."

She smiled. "It's fine. Thank you, Ronan. Sit and we'll put these in water and get coffee."

"Do I smell cinnamon buns?" Ronan asked, sniffing the air. "I love cinnamon buns."

"Beth makes the best," Evan told him. "Lots of cinnamon and icing."

Ronan met my gaze, running his tongue along his bottom lip. "Icing. My favorite."

I knew what he was thinking. Remembering, the same way I was, about our kiss in the kitchen. How we'd both tasted of the icing. I felt the color flood my cheeks, and I turned and hurried to the kitchen. Paige followed me, reaching past my shoulder to get a vase.

"Nab him," she muttered. "If you don't, I swear I will. Flowers? Gifts for the kids? The way he looks at you? Damn it, girl. Does he have a brother?"

I had to laugh at her enthusiasm. She was even more hesitant than I was about men. Ronan had charmed her as well.

"Yes. I have no idea if they are younger, older, married…" I trailed off.

She hip checked me. "Find out, you selfish bitch. Stop hogging him."

We both laughed, and it felt good. She grabbed the coffeepot and filled the mugs waiting on the tray. "You take this into the living room, and I'll handle the flowers."

I smiled and accepted the tray. "Okay."

I walked into the living room, my smile getting wider. Ronan was on the floor, leaning against the sofa. Lucy was on one large leg, chatting at him, and he was listening intently. Evan was perched on the sofa beside him, also adding to the conversation. Ronan looked relaxed, not at all put out about being with the kids or annoyed at being used for a cushion. In fact, his wide hand was resting against Lucy's back, making sure she was stable. I felt a lump in my throat as I watched them. I had never seen either of the kids respond to someone the way they were responding to Ronan. He seemed to have that effect on people. He certainly did with me.

He glanced up with a grin on his face. But he didn't interrupt Lucy. I handed him a cup of coffee after adding cream the way I had seen him do. He watched me, accepting the cup with a wink, but never wavered his attention from Lucy. I sat down, observing him. He asked her questions, listening as she responded.

"I have sixteen stuffed animals," she told him.

"Sixteen?" he repeated. "That's a lot. Do you have a favorite?"

She scrunched up her face. "Mr. Teddy. He's a teddy bear," she added in case he was unsure. "I had him since I was a baby. He didn't care if I only had one arm."

Ronan nodded. "Good man."

"I love him even if he only has one paw."

"What happened?" he asked, as if it was the most important piece of information he was going to get today.

"A dog bit it off at the park. He tried to take my bear, and I pulled. All he got was the leg. Momma stitched him up so he was good."

"So, you match."

She nodded. "Yes. Do you have any stuffies?"

He leaned down, his voice low. "I have one. I keep him in my room. My dad gave it to me when I was little, and I have kept it all these years. He sits on my dresser."

"Does he have a name?"

"Skittles."

She rubbed her nose. "I like that."

"Me too." Then he turned to Evan. "Your sister tells me you love Lego. I did too." He grinned. "Still do."

That started another excited conversation. And the whole time, he held on to Lucy, making sure she didn't fall.

Paige perched on the arm of my chair. "Damn it," she whispered. "He is the whole package, isn't he? Look at him with them."

"I know," I said quietly. "I know."

RONAN

The kids were awesome. Well behaved, chatty, and funny. Lucy was adorable, and I had a feeling she would capture my parents' hearts fast. Evan was smart and quick. His love of Lego was obvious and he wanted to show me his collection, but Beth stood.

"After breakfast, Evan. It's almost ready. Ronan, how do you like your eggs?"

I looked at her, unsure. "Whatever is easiest."

She grinned. "I do them all. Lucy and Evan like scrambled. I prefer poached, and Paige likes fried. So, whichever is your favorite, I can do."

I had to take a second to think. No one ever asked me. I had always eaten scrambled because that was what Jeremy and

Paul liked. I didn't mind them, but I really preferred poached. I always ordered them if I was out for breakfast, but no one ever seemed to notice, and I always had scrambled with the guys.

"Poached?" I asked.

Beth grinned. "Runny yolks?"

"Please."

"Okay. On it."

Lucy slid off my lap. "I help," she informed me. "I mix the eggs."

"Good job," I replied.

She toddled off, making me smile. She was very cute. Determined, too. I made a mental note to find out more about prosthetic limbs.

Evan adjusted himself, a small grimace crossing his face. I turned in his direction so he wouldn't have to bend to see me.

"Beth says you work in a gym?" he asked, looking hopeful.

I blew out a long breath. "I don't work there."

"Oh," he said, looking disappointed. "I thought maybe you could show me a few exercises to help my leg."

I scratched my head. "I'm not a trainer, but I know a lot. My dad taught me, and I took some courses. Maybe I could suggest some things."

His face brightened. "That would be awesome!"

I chuckled. "I like working out. I go to the gym a lot."

"If you don't work at a gym, what do you do?" Paige asked behind me.

"I, ah, build things," I said, feeling uncomfortable as I lied once again. I shifted on the floor, picking up my coffee and draining the liquid.

"Oh, construction," Evan enthused. "Cool. You know how to fix stuff too?"

"I'm pretty good with my hands."

"My desk is wobbly."

"Evan," Beth chastised as she walked into the room. "Ronan is a guest. He's not here to work."

I shook my head as I stood. "Happy to look at it."

"Maybe after breakfast."

"Sure."

"It's almost ready. Come sit down."

I followed her to the kitchen, sitting at the table. I looked around the room. Like the rest of the house, it was small but tidy. Drawings were stuck to the fridge. Jackets hung by the back door. The linoleum was worn, but clean. It was homey and inviting.

Evan sat beside me, and I watched him maneuver into the chair, another small grimace crossing his face. I added another item to look into. I would talk to my dad. He would probably have some advice. Of course, he would have a lot of questions as well, but I would figure that part out.

I inhaled, the scent of breakfast making my mouth water. Salty bacon, sweet cinnamon, and rich coffee filled my head.

"Smells awesome," I said as Beth and Paige began filling the table with dishes of food. Beth grinned as she set plates of scrambled eggs in front of the kids, then handed me mine. Four perfect poached eggs sat in the center, steaming and looking delicious. She sat next to me, her plate holding only two eggs. Paige sat across from me and handed me the plate of bacon.

"I've heard stories of your appetite, Ronan. Don't disappoint me today."

I had to laugh. "I'll do my best."

I sat back, replete and happy. I couldn't remember the last time I had enjoyed a meal so much. It wasn't only the food, but the company. I loved hearing the kids talk, answering their questions, watching Beth interact with them. It was obvious that this house was full of love and that what my dad always said was true. Family was more than blood. These two women had created their own family, and it was as close as my large one. It felt odd at first when questions were directed only to me. It always seemed that Paul, Jeremy, and I were talked to as if we were one unit. And accordingly, we seemed to act that way. More so when we were younger, but it still lingered. We always sat together, finished one another's sentences, knew one another's thoughts. Much like the scrambled eggs, we each had our own likes, but often deferred them when we were together. I ate scrambled eggs, white toast, and never asked for poached or thick sourdough bread.

Today, I had both and I loved them. I even had peanut butter on my "pandcakes," showing the trick to Evan and

Lucy, who declared it their new favorite. Paul and Jeremy both disliked peanut butter, so my mom never thought to put it out unless I asked. Which I rarely did. I just ate it when I was on my own.

"That was amazing," I complimented Beth. "Those cinnamon buns were incredible. Do you make those at the diner too?"

She laughed. "No. They take too much effort." She beamed as she picked up her coffee. "I had to make three extra cakes on Saturday. A company ordered one of each cake for pickup on Friday, so I had to replace them. It was a great bonus. Mike told them there was a fee for a last-minute order, as well as a delivery fee, and they agreed."

I bit back my grin. I had offered to pay that fee, hoping Beth would get a bigger cut. I put one of each cake in the lunchroom, and they had disappeared fast and everyone raved about them.

"That's great," was all I said. "I hope the order is worth your effort."

"It is. Mike said they already placed an order for next week too."

"That's awesome."

Lucy spoke up. "Momma, can we go to the park?"

Paige frowned. "I have to go do a few errands. Maybe we can go later."

"Beth, you take me?" Lucy asked.

"Um…"

I clapped my hands. "Why don't you both go? Go do your errands, go to the park. I'll stay here with Evan. We'll clean up the kitchen, and I'll look at his desk."

"You don't have to do that," Beth said quietly.

I squeezed her hand under the table. "That's the rule at my parents' place. If the women cook, men clean up. Evan and I can handle it, right?"

He nodded. "I can dry."

"Perfect. You ladies go and do your errands. Have fun in the park. It'll give us guys a chance to get to know each other."

Beth worried her lip, and I leaned close. "He'll be fine with me, Beth. Promise."

"I know that."

"Then go and enjoy a little girl time." I had a feeling she didn't get to do that very often.

She surprised me with a swift kiss to my cheek. "Thank you."

I winked, lowering my voice even more. "You can thank me more later."

I chuckled as she flushed then stood.

"Okay, girls, let's head out before he changes his mind."

They left, their voices fading away. I stood, picking up dishes.

"Not a lot of food to put away," I commented.

Evan laughed. "You eat a lot," he said with the honesty of a child.

"Yep, I do."

"What kinds of things do you build?" he asked as we started dishes.

"Buildings, mostly."

"Here in Toronto?"

"No, out of town," I replied.

"Are you my sister's boyfriend?" he asked abruptly, changing the subject before I had to.

"Ah, I think that's up to your sister."

"Do you want to be?"

"I like your sister. I'd like to take her out again."

"So, that's a boyfriend, right?"

"I guess so."

He nodded, drying a pan I handed him. There was a dish-washer—old, but serviceable, so we had loaded it with the plates and cutlery, leaving only the pans to hand-wash. "There's a girl at school I like," he said quietly. "She doesn't make fun of my leg or how shy I am."

I leaned against the counter. "Are you shy because of your leg?"

He sighed, the sound long and low. It said everything he didn't speak out loud. "That's part of it. I'm skinny and I wear glasses. I walk funny. I get picked on a lot."

"Are you bullied?" I asked.

"Sometimes. There is one group of boys that likes to push me around."

"Have you told Beth?"

He pushed up his glasses and regarded me sadly. It was the gaze of someone much older than twelve. "It wouldn't do any good. She's tried. The guidance counselor has tried. But they're smart. They don't hurt me. They just say stuff. Hide my crutches. Push me around a little when no one is watching." He shrugged. "I know it's because I'm scrawny. I can't fight back. I don't wear cool clothes, have new sneakers or a cell phone." He paused. "Or parents." He met my eyes again, the sorrow in them spilling out. "It makes Beth sad, so I don't say anything. I know she misses them too. And the other stuff —Beth can't afford it, and I don't want her to know. It would upset her. You can't tell her."

Something in my chest clenched. This kid needed some help. He needed a friend. Someone to talk to other than his sister. Maybe, just maybe, what he needed was me.

And that was another new thing for me. To be needed just for being Ronan.

I finished the last pan and let him dry it.

"Show me what you can do with that leg, Evan."

"Why?" he asked.

"Because I may have a few things I can show you. Let's see if we can help strengthen it."

His expression was excited. "Really?"

I nodded. "Really."

CHAPTER EIGHT

BETH

I should have been nervous leaving my brother alone in the house with someone I barely knew, but I wasn't. I trusted Ronan. Paige commented on the fact that, strangely enough, she did as well. He seemed genuine. And I had seen the way Evan's eyes lit up at being called one of the men. He wanted to help out more. He always did. Ronan had made him feel normal with a few simple words. Unknowingly, he had notched up my affection for him without even trying. Just by being himself.

I had heard him tell Evan he didn't work at a gym but built things. I wondered if he was ashamed of being in construction. He talked about his family but never offered much personal detail. Perhaps they didn't approve of his job. There was no shame in being in construction. It was good, honest work. Hard, as well. I sighed as I thought about it. I somehow had to let him know I was fine with it without just blurting it out. I didn't want to scare him away. I had to admit, I liked him far too much.

We reached a bench in the park, and Paige sat down, placing the rolling basket beside her. We'd done some shopping, and it was now Lucy's time for the park. She headed directly to the swings, kicking off and pumping her legs hard. We knew not to offer to help her. She was independent and fierce. Aside from the monkey bars, she played on everything, finding her own way to do so with her one arm. She was an amazing little girl.

"So, Ronan," Paige murmured. "He is something."

"Yeah," I agreed. "He is."

"Is he hiding something?"

I looked at her. "What do you mean?"

"He dresses well. Drives a nice car. He talks as if he's well educated. He belongs to a pricey gym..." She paused. "Can you do that on a construction worker's salary?"

I pursed my lips. "I have no idea." I hadn't really paid attention to his car or his clothes. "Can't construction workers talk well? Or have nice clothes?"

She laughed. "I suppose so. I confess, I don't know any. Maybe he's a foreman or something. He certainly seems smart."

"I think maybe his family doesn't approve of his job. He gets uncomfortable whenever I bring them up."

She nodded. "Could be. Maybe he grew up with money, and they don't approve of his choice." She sent me a side glance. "Of course, one way to find out is to ask him."

"We've only had one date. I'm sure we'll talk about family stuff. He doesn't know about me either."

"True. Interesting, though. He's got me curious."

"I thought you only wanted to know if he had a brother."

"Well, there is that too." She nudged me. "Two questions you need to ask."

I laughed, even while a niggle of doubt worried my brain. What if I didn't like the answers to my questions?

I sighed and shook my head, concentrating on watching Lucy. I would figure out Ronan soon enough.

We walked back into the house, hearing the echo of shared laughter. I paused for a moment, enjoying the sound. Evan was always too serious for his age. Hearing him laugh was wonderful. I headed to his room, Lucy racing ahead of me. I paused in the door, taking in the sight. Evan and Ronan were at his table he kept in the corner, building Lego together. Ronan looked huge in Evan's room, perched on a chair that was too small for him, no doubt uncomfortable, but not at all worried about it. He looked like a kid, reaching for a Lego brick , talking about his favorite set he liked to build when he was Evan's age.

"My brothers and I would spread out all the pieces on the floor and have contests of who could build something the fastest. My dad always stepped on a piece and yelled at us. My mom would laugh every time. Then my dad would get in on the action, and we would have a competition," he told Evan, who was watching him. "I always liked to build stuff, even when I was a kid." Without breaking his concentration, Ronan lifted Lucy onto his lap. He dropped a kiss to her head as if it were the most natural thing to do. "Hey, Lucy-loo. How was the park?"

She giggled. "Evan calls me that."

"I know," he said. "He told me. I like it. Is it okay if I call you that too?"

She nodded. "Can I help?"

He handed her a partially built item. "Put this piece here," he said patiently. He met my gaze across the room, his gaze warm and welcoming. "Hi."

"Hi yourself. Having fun?"

"A blast," he replied.

Evan grinned at me. "Ronan is so cool."

Ronan held up his hand and got a high five. "Darn right, I am."

I laughed, watching as Lucy lifted her arm, wanting one. Her hand looked tiny against his large one. He flipped her hand over and tapped it. "Baby five, Lucy-loo. A tiny one, just for you."

She giggled. "That rhymed."

He nodded. "Yep."

She leaned up and kissed his cheek, and he beamed down at her. Behind me, I heard Paige's fast intake of air. We had never seen Lucy kiss anyone but us. I turned and met Paige's gaze. Her eyes were damp, and she squeezed my hand. Her voice was a whisper in my ear.

"Construction worker or whatever, I'm telling you, he's a keeper."

I wanted to laugh. Except a little piece of my heart was already agreeing with her.

I needed to rein that part in.

Lucy fell asleep on Ronan's shoulder, and he stood, carrying her to her room. He laid her gently on the bed and watched as I tucked her in.

He followed me to the kitchen. I could hear Paige on the phone in her room, and Evan was busy still working on whatever design was taking shape on the table.

"The desk just needed some tightening. I found a screwdriver and some glue. It's fine," Ronan informed me. "Need anything else done?"

"No. Thank you, though."

He scratched his head. "So, I saw Evan's room. Lucy's. Paige's is obviously the other bedroom. Where do you sleep?"

I indicated that he should follow me, and we went downstairs. There was a little laundry area, a bathroom with a small shower, and an unused family room that we'd turned into a bedroom for me. It was modestly furnished with a double bed, dresser, and nightstand. A chair I had recovered was in the corner with a small bookcase beside it, holding my favorite books. An old table held a lamp and a bag of wine gums—my secret stash I kept for the rare times I could curl up and read.

The desk held my laptop and books. A fluffy rug kept my feet warm against the cold concrete floor.

"No door?" he asked, running his hand along the doorframe.

"No."

"The framing is in place for one," he observed.

"I think there used to be one there. The landlord said we could add one." I shrugged. "It's not a high priority, budget-wise."

"You should have a door. I could get a crew in to take care of that for you."

"I have lots of privacy."

"No, it's a fire code thing. You should have a door."

"Oh."

"I'll arrange it."

"So, you're a construction worker?"

He ran a hand over the back of his neck, looking flustered. "I work in that field, yes. More of a boss than a hands-on crew member, but I know how."

So, Paige had guessed right when she said foreman. I wasn't surprised. Ronan seemed like a natural leader. I was, however, a little shocked how uncomfortable he was on the subject of his job. There was obviously a story, but I didn't want to push.

"I don't want to bother you for a door, Ronan."

"Not a bother. I'll measure it before I go and arrange it. We have tons of doors from jobs kicking around. It'll only take a couple of hours."

I worried my lip. "A fire code thing?"

"Yes. Every bedroom has to have a door." He ran a hand through his hair. "This isn't exactly a legal bedroom, but it still needs it."

"It was the only option. Evan can't come down easily with his crutches. Paige wanted to be close to Lucy. It was either make my room down here or share a room with Paige."

"Oh. This is better then, I think."

"Me too. I kinda like it down here. It's private and quiet."

"Do you get much chance to enjoy that quiet?"

"I study down here when I can. The reading thing doesn't happen as often as I want, but once I'm done with school, I hope it will."

He nodded. "You have a lot on your plate."

"Many people do. I'm not alone in that situation. Paige and I help each other out."

"I can see that."

He looked at me, his green eyes intense. I felt the hairs on the back of my neck rise. Goose bumps broke out on my arms, and I shivered.

"I'll get you that door."

"Okay."

"I'm glad you don't share a room with Paige," he murmured, reaching out and tucking a stray curl behind my ear. His gentle touch made another shiver run down my spine.

"Why?"

"Because I couldn't do this."

He swept me into his arms, pulling me tight to his chest. His mouth settled on mine, firm and demanding. I opened for him, and his tongue glided along mine, exploring and hot. He tasted of cinnamon and coffee. Ronan. Addictive.

I wound my arms around his neck as he yanked me closer. Our mouths fused, the kiss becoming deeper, harder. I whimpered. Ronan groaned, the sound low and sexy. He slid his hand up my shirt, spreading his big palm across my back, holding me tight. I gripped his shoulders as he lifted me, sitting down on the edge of my bed, my legs straddling his thick thighs. I felt him hard and pressing between us. He slid his hand to the nape of my neck, holding me close. I played with his hair, the strands soft and silky under my fingers. I was lost to him. To everything that was Ronan. His strength. His taste. The way he held me close as if he didn't want to let me go. The intensity of his kisses, the scent of his skin. It was a combination of ocean and citrus—I had never smelled anything like it before now. It was uniquely Ronan and highly addictive.

So was his mouth.

He dragged his lips to my ear. "Jesus, I want you, Beth. I want to roll you over on this bed and have you."

I tightened my hold on his neck. I wanted that too.

He stilled and sighed, wrapping me in a tight embrace. "We need to stop."

I nodded, my head resting on his shoulder. He was right. We couldn't do this with my brother upstairs, Paige and Lucy potentially walking down the steps any given moment.

"Can I take you out on Tuesday?"

I pulled back. "Paige has an evening meeting," I said regretfully.

"How about I bring dinner and come here?" he asked hopefully. "I can install the door too."

"Not much fun for you."

"No, it is. I like the kids. I get to see you. It's all good. Maybe once Paige comes home, we could go for a drive. Have dessert somewhere."

I lifted one eyebrow. "Dessert?"

He laughed. "Dessert," he said firmly. He kissed me again, a light tease of his mouth. "It can be whatever you want."

"Okay."

His smile was wide. "Awesome."

———

RONAN

Monday morning, I was in a good mood as I made my way to ABC Corp. It was early as I headed to my office. I paused in the hall, my attention drawn to the sight of Addison standing in front of the window by her desk. Her husband, Brayden, was behind her, his arms wrapped around her waist. Their displays of PDA were nothing new or unusual, but this was something different. I studied them, unnoticed, the two of them too wrapped up in each other to see me there. Brayden's hand was spread wide on Addi's stomach, protectively. She was leaning back against him as if absorbing his strength. She held a piece of paper in her hands, and they were both staring at it. Instantly, I realized what I was witnessing. Addi and Brayden had a secret of their own. From the looks on their faces, a joyful one. I was thrilled for them but wondered how long it would be until they shared. Part of me wanted to rap on the doorframe and let them know I was there, but the newer, more aware part of me knew they needed this moment, and they would share when they were ready. I smiled as I quietly kept going. It explained a lot. Brayden's constant smile, Addi's devouring of the cake I had brought in last week, then the way she had wept because she thought she was being greedy wanting more of it. Brayden had laughed, taken her to her office, then returned and cut another slab of cake.

"Get more next time, Ronan. We're gonna need it."

It all made sense now, including her unusual emotional display. The fact that I wasn't the only one with a secret somehow made me feel better.

Later that afternoon, I walked into the boardroom, whistling under my breath. Gracie was at the table, studying the screen on her laptop. I stopped and pressed a kiss to her head. "Hey, Gracie-girl."

I sat at the end of the table, not because it was the position of being the head, but because of the room it afforded me. My shoulders were wide, and I hated being crowded. I reached over and snagged a Danish, smiling at Grace, who was observing me carefully.

"How's my Goddaughter?"

She smiled. "Fine. Growing too fast. Jaxson laments it daily."

I chuckled. Jaxson doted on his wife and daughter. He was head over heels in love with them both, and he was a very hands-on daddy. Gracie was my favorite "cousin" in our large extended family, and I had grown close to her husband. They had married under odd circumstances, but he was a good guy, and I was glad they had worked it out. Gracie had never looked happier, and I enjoyed being part of their life.

She tilted her head. "You weren't at brunch yesterday."

That had been the only bad part of yesterday. I had completely forgotten about brunch in Port Albany. My mom had texted me asking where I was, and I had apologized but said I couldn't make it. I had felt her displeasure in her brief reply. *"Your brothers will be disappointed."*

I would have to make it up to them.

"I had plans."

"Jeremy and Paul brought their girls to meet everyone."

"I've met them. I've had dinner with them, and I was there last weekend for brunch at Mom and Dad's. You saw me there."

"It seemed odd you not being there yesterday, though. It was sort of more official."

"We're not joined at the hip," I snapped, sounding angrier than I expected to. "I can do things on my own without them."

Grace looked surprised. "Of course you're not joined at the hip. I was only saying you were missed."

I ran a hand over my face. "Sorry, Gracie."

"Are you okay?"

"I'm fine."

She frowned, tapping a pen on the desk as she studied me. That was not good. Her tapping meant she was thinking. All the women in my family seemed to tap when they were thinking. It was never a positive sign.

"You haven't been yourself lately. You've been quieter. I haven't seen you much."

"Like I said, I've been busy."

"Are you seeing someone?"

I hesitated, which was a big mistake. Gracie jumped right on that.

"You are," she breathed out. "You're seeing someone."

I hunched forward. "Keep that to yourself."

She frowned. "Why?"

I traced the design in the wooden boardroom table with my finger. "I'm not ready to share, Gracie. Her, me, us. We're too new. It's too complicated."

"Complicated?" She snorted lightly. "I excel at complicated, Ronan. Jaxson and I were the epitome of complicated."

I met her eyes. "I like this girl. She likes me. *Me.* Not my family. Not my money. In fact, she knows nothing about them."

She frowned. "How does that work, exactly?"

I shrugged. "I just don't discuss them. To her, I'm Ronan. Singular. I'm letting her get to know me before I tell her about the whole triplet bundle thing. The family."

We both heard footsteps approaching, and I shook my head, silently ending the conversation. She leaned toward me.

"They are a part of you, Ronan. Trust me, keeping secrets is not the way to build a relationship. I went through that. You don't have to keep us secret, keep who you are secret in order to have her to yourself. Let her know all of you. Trust me on that."

She sat back with a frown. "Don't break her trust before you can build it. It won't work."

Addi and Brayden came into the room, smiling. My sister Ava was behind them, laughing at something one of them had said. I heard Reed's loud voice in the hall. My brothers would appear soon. I shook my head to clear Gracie's words. I had to concentrate on work. She didn't know anything about Beth and me. I wanted Beth to get to know me more. Just me. It was the first time in my life I'd had that happen.

I wasn't giving it up just yet.

"What are you doing?" my mother asked, coming into the storage room at the Hub that night. I had driven to Port Albany, enjoyed the last of the evening, then come to find my old Lego sets. I was sure my mother had kept it.

I straightened, moving another box. "Looking for something."

"Well, that's apparent. What exactly are you looking for? I know where most things are."

"My old Lego stuff. I know we had bins of it."

"It's on the other side. This is all Christmas and holiday décor."

"Oh." I pushed all the boxes back into place and followed her to the other side of the large storage area. Each family had a section to use—most were full, but all of them neat and tidy. My mom indicated some boxes.

"Move those, and they should be at the back."

I did as she instructed and found the bins. Each one was labeled with our names. I found mine and dragged it out, replacing the others back into the order she had them in.

I opened the lid, grinning. There were some box sets plus a ton of extra pieces. Evan would love them. I looked up to find my mom staring at me.

"What?"

"What made you want your old Lego kits? I was saving them for your kids. They're always popular."

"Um, a friend's son. He's really into them. I thought I'd show him mine."

"Do I know this friend?"

"No."

She tapped her foot, saying nothing. I stifled a sigh. More tapping.

"Look, Mom. It's just a friend I met at the gym. We've been hanging out."

The tapping kept going. I snapped the lid closed. "Can I take this?"

"They're yours."

I lifted the box. "Great. I'll bring them back."

"Once *your friend's* son is done with them," she stated.

"Yes."

I headed toward the stairs, her voice stopping me before I could climb up.

"How important is this *friend*, Ronan?"

"All friends are important," I shot back. I had no idea why I was so determined not to tell anyone about Beth. I told myself it was because of how new we were. I had no idea where this was going. I ignored the voice that laughed at those thoughts. That said I was keeping this to myself for other, more selfish reasons.

"So is family," my mom called. "You missed an important day for your brothers. They wanted you there."

I faltered in my steps and turned to look at her. She gazed up at me, worry making her frown.

"And I'll make it up to them, Mom." I scrubbed my face. "I met Kim and Diane. I like them. I was there last Sunday. There isn't an issue, so please don't try to make one."

"Then where were you?"

"I had to do something else. Something important to *me*."

She sighed.

"How many times do they have to be 'introduced' anyway?" I mumbled, using my fingers as quotation marks. "It felt a little over the top, to be honest."

"Ronan," she rebuked me, aghast. "What is going on with you?"

"Nothing," I insisted.

She stepped closer, her voice worried. "Are you all right?"

My mom was the epitome of love to me. She was forgiving and caring. Always there for us. For me.

"I'm fine, Mom. I just—I need some space, okay?"

"Space for what?"

"For me."

That made her hesitate. I could tell she wanted to push more, but she let it go. At least for now.

"I love my family," I assured her. "That will never change." I smiled. "I love you most of all, Mom."

Her expression was still concerned, but she returned my smile. "We're here, Ronan. We're always here."

I turned away, heading upstairs and putting the boxes in the trunk.

That was part of the problem. They were *always* there.

CHAPTER NINE
BETH

I was surprised when I got home Tuesday to find a strange truck in the driveway. There was no name on it, no sign as to whom it belonged, but from inside the house, I heard the sound of power tools. A saw was set up in the driveway, the sawdust piles indicating work was being done. I went in and found Paige in the dining room at the small desk she used for work. She was typing but looked up with a smile.

"Hi."

"Hey. What's going on?"

She grinned. "Your man is downstairs installing a door." She waggled her eyebrows. "He's hot when he's in construction mode."

I rolled my eyes. "He's not my man."

"Really," she replied sardonically. "I think he'd say otherwise. His helper is pretty hot too. Older, though, and married. Shame."

"I wasn't expecting him to do this."

"I know. He called this morning, and I talked to the landlord to make sure it was okay. Ralph was fine with it, and I let Ronan know. They showed up a while ago."

I set down the bags I was carrying and headed downstairs. Ronan was holding a door as another man fitted the hinges. They had used the wide space to add a set of double doors, and I had to admit, they looked great. Ronan saw me and grinned.

"Beth." His stare was warm and frank. "How was your day?"

"Good."

The other man stood, and I blinked. He was as big as Ronan, his muscles rippling as he swung the door to test it. "Hello." He dipped his chin and held out his hand. "I'm Van."

"Hello, Van." His handshake was firm and strong, yet gentle. His voice was low-pitched and pleasant. He was older, as Paige stated, but attractive. "Thank you for doing this."

He clapped Ronan on the shoulder. "Any friend of Ronan's is a friend of mine. Happy to help." He checked out the level of the doors and nodded. "Okay, I'll measure the trim. You add in the hardware," he said to Ronan. "Then we're done aside from a lick of paint."

Ronan ran his hand over the door. "I had them primed and the first coat put on already. Same with the trim. I'll add a second coat once we're done."

"Great." Van took some measurements and headed back upstairs.

I looked at Ronan. "I didn't expect this."

"I know. But I figured we had them in the shop, and I'd put them in today. Van's schedule was light, and he offered to help."

"You work with him?"

"He runs his own division. He's, ah, he's my uncle."

Another tidbit of information about his family. They dripped out like syrup on a cold day, slow but satisfying.

"Oh, that's very kind of him. You work together with your family."

He nodded, a frown on his face. "Some more than others," he stated, then changed the subject. "What time does Evan get home?"

"About four." I glanced at my phone. "So, about half an hour."

"Great. I got a surprise for him."

I shook my head. "You can't do this, Ronan."

He stepped closer. "Do what?"

I waved my hand. "Come in here with doors and gifts and your smiles."

"Why not?"

"I can't reciprocate. I don't know how to repay—"

He cut me off. "No repayment is needed. All I want is to spend some time with you. And what I have for him isn't a gift. It's a loan."

"Can I pay for the doors?"

He slid his hand under my chin, lifting my head. He met my gaze, his bright-green eyes burning into mine. He stroked along my jaw—featherlight strokes of his fingers that I felt right down to the soles of my feet.

"Yes," he murmured. "You can."

"How—"

His mouth silenced me. His lips were firm and warm. He snaked his arm around my waist and pulled me close. His tongue splayed across my lips, and I opened for him with a low moan. He kissed me deeply, holding me tight to his chest. Everything left my mind but his touch. The feel of his mouth on me, his tongue sliding along mine, possessive and gentle at the same time. I never wanted him to stop.

Until a throat clearing made me stiffen, and Ronan drew back. He lifted his eyebrows as if to say "Busted," then kissed the end of my nose.

Van walked past us, chuckling. "As you were."

Ronan grinned, reaching for me, but I pulled back, slapping at his hands. He only laughed.

"Paid," was all he said.

I headed up the stairs, unsure how to respond. If he accepted kisses for doors, his bonus was going to be dinner. And I had a feeling he was going to love it.

Van and Ronan came upstairs, and I watched from the kitchen window as they loaded stuff into the truck and swept the driveway clean of sawdust. As they stood talking, Evan's bus pulled up and he got off, making his way toward them. I expected him to say hello and come inside, given his shyness with new people. But I was shocked to see him greet Ronan enthusiastically and shake Van's proffered hand. Van bent down on one knee, talking to Evan. Ronan copied him, and the three of them seemed deep in a serious discussion. Paige came up beside me.

"He's talking to them. Both of them," I breathed. "Like he knows them." I met her gaze. "Like he is comfortable."

She smiled. "Ronan has that way with him. I guess Van does too. He seemed really nice."

"He's an uncle."

She elbowed me. "Were my instructions not a single brother? Not a married uncle. Jeesh."

We laughed, and she grabbed some of the veggies I had washed and moved them to the cutting board for me to start chopping. She left to go and pick up Lucy at day care. Working from home, she liked having Lucy go to a place where she could play with kids her own age, and she found a great spot only a few blocks away. Lucy went three days a week. In the fall, she would start kindergarten and be gone every day. Paige often remarked she wasn't ready for that to happen yet.

I kept watching as Evan spoke to Van. Their conversation seemed to focus on his leg, and Evan demonstrated how he used his crutches and patted his hip and thigh as if showing them where the lingering damage was. Van did a lot of talking and, I assumed, asked a lot of questions, although at times, Ronan would add something in. Evan was surprisingly relaxed and talkative. He normally refused to discuss his injuries, especially to a stranger.

Eventually, Van stood, placed his hand on Evan's shoulder, and spoke directly to him. Evan nodded, then turned and headed to the front door. He came inside, waved in hello, then went to his room to get rid of his book bag.

Van spoke to Ronan, his gaze flickering to the window, catching me staring at them. He smiled, clapped Ronan's shoulders, shaking them slightly, and spoke seriously. Ronan followed his gaze, then nodded. He waved as Van pulled out of the driveway then disappeared. A few moments later, Ronan came into the kitchen.

"What smells so good? Is that…homemade tacos?" he asked, looking at the piles of fixings and sniffing the aroma of the ground chicken I had cooking with the spices.

"Yes. I know you love them, and so do the kids. I thought you'd enjoy them."

"I was going to order in for us," he protested as he snagged a slice of red pepper off the pile. "I said I would."

"Well, consider this payment for the door."

He stepped behind me as I stirred the filling, switching off the heat. He wrapped his arms around me, burying his face into my neck and kissing the skin. "I prefer my form of payment," he muttered.

I shivered at his words. "We can split the payments," I joked.

"Maybe we can try out the effectiveness of the door later," he whispered, his breath hot on my neck and his tongue tracing the shell of my ear.

I never got to answer since Evan came into the kitchen, a huge smile on his face.

"Ronan—is the box on my bed from you?"

"Yeah, bud. Those were my Lego sets when I was a kid. I thought you'd enjoying building with them. There are a few kits you can't get anymore."

I was touched by his gesture. His thoughtfulness knew no bounds, whether it was for me, my kid brother, or the small group of people in my life. Paige had told me when he arrived earlier, he had noticed her chair was wobbly, and in ten minutes, had tightened the bolts, oiled it so it no longer squeaked, and gotten rid of a virus her computer had picked up. He seemed too good to be true.

"I'll take really good care of them, Ronan."

Ronan laughed, his white teeth flashing. "Lego bricks are almost indestructible. I'm not in any hurry to have them back, so build to your heart's content."

"Do you wanna come build with me?"

Ronan met my gaze, and I nodded imperceptibly. I wanted him to stay in the kitchen with me, but I knew how much Evan would enjoy his company.

"You guys go and build. I'm going to finish this and grab a shower. We'll eat about five thirty, so Paige can join us before she leaves for her meeting."

Evan and Ronan high-fived each other. Evan turned and left, and Ronan grabbed me, hauling me in for a fast kiss.

"Goddammit," he swore. "Your mouth is addictive." He tilted up my chin and kissed me again. A long, slow, lingering one. He shook his head. "Addictive."

He left the kitchen to follow Evan, and I touched my mouth, feeling the possession left behind of his.

Addictive, he'd said.

I had to agree.

Dinner was one of the most fun meals we'd ever had in this house. Ronan was droll, teasing everyone, consuming tacos like a starving man. Evan was fascinated watching him, determined to match him taco for taco. He gave up after three. I lost count after six for Ronan. Somehow, Lucy ended up on his lap, and he held her easily with one arm, only releasing her to quickly roll another taco. She looked at Paige, wide-eyed with wonder.

"Momma," she whispered. "Is he a giant?"

Ronan chuckled as he finished another taco. "Not a giant, Lucy-loo, just hungry." He winked at me before he lifted her arm, studying it. "If I were a giant, though, you look good enough to eat." Then he pretended to chomp on her, causing loud shrieks of laughter to escape her mouth. We all laughed, and even Evan looked amused. He'd smiled more tonight than I could recall him smiling in a long time, and I was grateful to Ronan for that.

When I had gone to get them for supper, I found all three of them on the floor, a building happening between them. Ronan was showing Lucy how to put some pieces together, his voice patient, his big hands helping guide her smaller fingers that fumbled. He was amazing with children. I'd watched them in silence for a moment before Ronan noticed me in the doorway, and our gazes locked for a long minute, causing my breathing to pick up. How he said so much with his intense green eyes, without uttering a word, was astounding. It was as if I knew exactly what he was saying. He wanted me. Alone.

And God help me, I wanted the same thing.

Paige left after we finished. She paused before leaving, her voice low. "If the basement door is shut, I'll just head to bed when I get home." Then she nudged me. "And it will be, so don't even try with me."

I didn't say anything.

Ronan helped me clean up while the kids returned to the creation of the Lego building.

"How busy is your weekend?"

I hesitated and he smiled. "I was thinking of a picnic on Sunday. Bring Evan, Lucy, and Paige. I know a great spot. A storm is supposed to move in later in the afternoon, so we might see some clouds. I could pick you up around eleven?"

"I'd like that." Then I frowned. "Do you have a car seat?"

"Not an issue."

"Okay. That sounds fun." I smiled. "How about I provide dessert?"

He waggled his eyebrows, and laughing, I slapped his arm. "I meant a cake."

He wrapped his arm around my waist, dragging me close. "I'd rather have you."

"Maybe later," I whispered breathlessly.

He kissed me, hard and fast.

"I'll hold you to that."

I tucked in an already-sleeping Lucy, making sure the covers were loose the way she liked them. After dishes, Ronan had disappeared, coming back with ice cream from a local shop he had asked me about. He brought a sampler and opened it in the middle of the table, handing us all tiny spoons so we could try the various flavors he had picked out.

"Which is your favorite?" I asked.

He paused with a frown. "The blueberry cheesecake is awesome. So is the white chocolate raspberry. I like those the best."

"Mine too. The triple chocolate is delicious." I dipped my spoon into it and held it out. "You haven't tried it yet."

He covered my wrist with his large hand, pulling it close to his mouth. I stared, fascinated, as his lips wrapped around the spoon, and his tongue flicked out over my finger, catching the tiny amount on my skin.

"Decadent," he hummed, once again his eyes locking on mine.

I had to look away before I jumped him in front of my little brother and Lucy.

He grinned and dug back into the ice cream. "I don't usually like the type with nuts. My mom always bought strawberry and butter pecan ice cream. Sometimes maple walnut. I was never as big a fan as my brothers."

"She didn't buy your favorite?" I asked.

He shrugged. "I never said anything. They liked those flavors, so I just went along with it."

I studied him, wondering what else in his life he simply "went along with."

Before I could ask, he made Lucy laugh, and I filed that question away for later.

He'd built Lego with Evan then helped him with homework as I bathed and got Lucy ready for bed. I could hear them talking while I washed her hair, their voices low. I had a feeling they weren't talking about other Lego projects, and I wondered what Evan was saying to Ronan.

After Lucy's bath, Ronan read her a story, and she fell asleep. He carried her into her room and watched as I tucked her in.

Ronan followed me down the hall. I stopped at Evan's door and peeked in. He was busy with his books, concentrating on homework.

"Need anything?" I asked.

He looked up. "No, I'm good. I'm going to study a bit and read."

I smiled. He loved to read as much as I did. We went to the library a lot to pick up books for all of us.

"You figured out that math thing?"

He nodded. "Ronan explained it to me, and now I get it."

"Okay."

"Can you shut my door?"

"Sure." He liked his privacy, and I always knew when the door was shut not to bother him.

"Night, bud," Ronan said behind me.

"Thanks, Ronan. For the Lego and…and the talk."

"Anytime."

I shut Evan's door, and we went to the living room. I sat down, Ronan beside me on the sofa.

"Is he being bullied?" I asked quietly.

"He's having a hard time."

"I don't know what to do," I admitted.

He exhaled hard. "Maybe I can help."

"How?"

"Give me a few days. Just…just trust me."

"I do," I whispered, surprised to hear myself say those words. "I do trust you."

"Good."

"What were you and your uncle talking to Evan about?"

"Oh. Van's son, Reed, is adopted. When he was little and first came to live with them, he had a bad limp. Van and my dad helped build up the strength in his muscles. Reed overcame the limp, and I thought Van might have a few ideas on how I could help Evan. He asked Evan some questions about his leg to better understand what we're dealing with."

"Your dad?" I asked, surprised. "Is he a doctor?"

"No. But he's taken countless courses about therapy. He does massage, acupuncture, and knows all about the body. He's really into fitness and strength."

"I see."

"I think we could help Evan, Beth. I want to try if you'll let me."

"Why?" I asked, unable to stop myself. "Why do you care?"

He frowned as if searching for words. "He's a good kid and I like him. He matters to you." He paused, picking up my hand. "You matter to me."

"I don't want to bother——"

He stopped my words by shaking his head. "It's not a bother. I like him," he stressed again. "Let me try. All we asked was what he was doing so we could see if we could add something to it that might help."

I sighed. "I have no supplemental insurance, so his therapy is mostly what we do at home. The place we went was good and gave him bands and exercises, and when I can, he goes in for an assessment..." I trailed off as Ronan nodded in sympathy.

"Let me try."

I would do anything for my little brother. Seeing how determined Ronan was to try to help touched my heart.

"Thank you," I breathed out.

He stroked my cheek. "You're welcome. Now, how are your intersession classes going?"

I smiled at him. He remembered everything I told him on our date. He'd asked so many questions, I'd lost track of all that we'd discussed. He didn't, though.

"Fine."

"You work too hard."

I shrugged. "By taking two now, I can work all summer and save more money. With tourists, the diner will be busy, and I can get full-time hours. My schedule is lighter than usual for the next while with only two courses."

"I did the same thing when I was going to school. I took summer classes too."

"Then you know how busy I am."

"I didn't have the responsibilities you do. You amaze me, little bird." He played with one of my curls, twirling it around his finger, looking thoughtful. "I want to make your life easier," he said with a frown.

"My life is fine," I responded, touched by his sincere words. He seemed so concerned about me. About us. It was an odd feeling to have someone be worried about me anymore, aside from Paige.

I met his eyes. "Especially now you're part of it."

With a low groan, he hauled me onto his lap and covered my mouth with his. He kissed me until I was breathless. Until I was clutching his shoulders as need and desire twisted inside me so tightly, it felt as if my nerves were on the outside of my body, stretched and taut. I wanted him more than I had ever wanted another man. I felt his desire trapped between us. I twisted so I straddled his lap, and he groaned as I moved over him.

"I want you," I whispered into his ear as I nipped at his lobe. "Ronan, I want you so much. What are you doing to me?"

"The feeling is mutual," he hissed as I undulated over him. "How fast does Evan fall asleep?"

I eased back, meeting his eyes. "What?"

"I can't—we can't—" he sputtered, his cheeks darkening. "I can't make love to you with your brother listening."

His obvious discomfort caught me off guard. To see this big man flustered and embarrassed was touching. Amusing. I turned my head, trying not to laugh.

I cleared my throat. "You build things, Ronan?"

"Yes."

"Then you should have realized my brother's bedroom is at the back of the house. My room downstairs is at the front." I nuzzled his neck, flicking out my tongue and tasting him. "And I have a nice new door."

He was on his feet fast. "Let's go."

CHAPTER TEN
RONAN

Beth checked the front door, then peeked in on Lucy and Evan. Both were asleep. She smiled when I was surprised to see Evan had crashed already.

"He had a long day." She squeezed my hand. "A good one, thanks to you."

She pulled me to the stairs, and I went ahead of her. She paused for a moment, then pushed the door shut behind her and followed me.

I looked at her, and she grinned. "It's like a sock on the door in dorms."

I waited until she walked into her room and shut the new door I had installed. I pulled her into my arms. "You use that sock a lot?"

"Never," she admitted. "It's been a long time for me, Ronan. In fact, it's been so long, I don't remember who gets tied up anymore."

I threw back my head in laughter, managing not to be too loud. I hugged her tight. "We'll figure that one out as we go along, little bird. Tonight, I want to be able to touch you." I laid her hands on my chest. "And God, I want to feel these little hands all over me."

She gazed up at me, her dark eyes wide with desire. I saw a glimmer of fear in their warm depths—a hint of vulnerability she kept hidden.

"Tell me what you want, Beth," I murmured. "I'll give you anything."

"Kiss me."

I covered her mouth with mine, lifting her up and wrapping her in my arms. I walked backward to the bed, kissing her the whole time. Her mouth was hot, her tongue like silk against mine. She tasted of ice cream, sweet and tangy. Like chocolate, rich and decadent. Like Beth. I slid my hands under her loose shirt, spreading them across the smooth skin of her back. She whimpered as I sat down, my erection pressed between us. I kissed her until she trembled, until I felt her desire overtake any fear or misgiving she harbored. I dragged my mouth across her cheek to her ear, tugging on the lobe. "Tell me."

"I want to feel you."

I stood and turned, laying her on the bed. I tugged my shirt over my head, letting her look. Her gaze roamed over my chest, down my abs, and lingered on my crotch.

"More?" I asked, my fingers hovering over the waistband of the sweats I was wearing.

She nodded, her breath catching in her throat as I pushed the sweats down, my cock springing free, hard and aching for her.

"Oh God," she whimpered.

I stroked myself as I watched her. I stepped between her legs and slipped my fingers under her T-shirt. "My turn."

She caught my hand. "I'm not, ah, pretty, like you."

I shook my head. "I know. You're beautiful."

"You haven't seen—"

I cut her off. "*You. Are. Beautiful.*"

Seconds later, she was naked. Her breasts were heavy, tipped with rose-colored nipples that begged for my mouth. Her hips were full, showing off the sweet indent of her waist. Her legs were long for someone so short, her calves shapely and toned. I lifted one foot, studying it.

"Little feet to match your little hands." I kissed the high arch, trailing my fingers upward. "Perfect hips for me to grab. An ass I can't take my eyes off." I bent, nuzzling her breasts, pulling a nipple into my mouth and sucking. "I have fantasized about your breasts." I switched to the other one, sucking and licking at the hard nub. "The fantasy didn't do them justice."

I let my hand smooth down her body until I cupped her. The heat of her blazed against my palm. She whimpered as I stared down at her.

"Beautiful," I whispered.

She pulled my head down to kiss me. I let her lead, her tongue playing with mine. I slid my finger through her slick center, touching her, claiming her. She moaned low in her throat as I explored her. Learned what made her gasp, arch into my touch, whimper, and moan. I kissed her mouth, suckled her earlobes, licked her neck, gathered her curls in my fist and turned her head, nuzzled at the juncture where her shoulder and neck met, drawing the skin between my teeth and biting down. She ran her hand over my back, clutched at my shoulders, yanked on my hair, and wrapped her legs around my waist, pleading. I slid one finger inside her heat, pumping. I added a second, pressing on her clit with my thumb, making sure to apply the right pressure. She gasped and lifted her hips, moving in tandem with my fingers until she came. Her eyes wide and open, her neck straining, the arch of her back so high it was a graceful bow in the air. I covered her mouth, swallowing her scream, working her until she collapsed, her muscles fluttering around my fingers like small kisses on the digits. I eased back, looking down at her. Her chest was flushed, the skin pink and glowing. Her nipples were red and hard from my mouth. My fingers were still inside her, and as she watched, I withdrew them, then lifted them to my mouth and sucked. "Perfect," I murmured.

"I'm on the pill," she said, breathless.

I reached over to her nightstand and lifted a string of condoms lying on the wood. For a moment, she frowned in confusion, then a grin lit her face.

"Paige."

I held them up. "Six," I mused. "She has a lot of confidence in me."

"How about you use one and get in me?" Beth asked, reaching for them.

I held them higher. "Tell me."

"I want you inside me, Ronan. I want to feel that huge cock of yours." Her breath stuttered. "Please."

"Since you said the magic word." I tore open a package, rolling on the condom. Beth pushed herself toward the middle of the bed, and I crawled up the mattress, settling between her legs. "Show me."

She wrapped her hand around my cock, guiding me to her entrance. I groaned at her touch, the feel of her stroking me before she notched the head to her heat.

"Please," she whispered again. Our eyes locked and held as I slid in. She was tight, warm, and perfect. I took my time, slowly inching forward, feeling the heat and perfection of her fist around me. She exhaled when I was seated deep within her, our bodies flush. I braced myself on my elbows, hovering above her.

"Okay, little bird?"

"More."

I began to move. She tightened her legs around me, meeting my thrusts. I wanted to take it slow. Be gentle with her. But it was impossible. She felt too good, and I wanted her too much. I took her powerfully, my hips moving of their own accord. Deeper, harder, faster. She whimpered and moaned, grabbing my arms, digging her nails into my back, kissing me with a passion that made me dizzy. I slid my arms under her and sat up on my heels, sinking even deeper. She let her head fall back, and I ravished her neck, sucked her breasts, and rode her until she came. Pulsating around me, setting off my own orgasm. It exploded like a storm, obliterating everything in its path. I cursed and shook with the force of it. Gripped her to me as I rode it out. Fisted the curls I found so alluring on her head and kissed her mouth with a fury I didn't know I possessed. She gripped me back, her nails sinking deeper, her pussy milking me for everything I had, closing around me like a vise until we were panting, exhausted, and sated.

I held her close. Felt her rapid heartbeat against my own. I kissed her head and mumbled words of warmth, worship, and affirmation. There was no doubt if I adored her prior to making love to her, my affection had grown tenfold.

I drew back, meeting her sleepy gaze. I kissed her once, twice, three times, then again. I kissed the end of her upturned, adorable nose and along the line of freckles. Then I laid her back on the mattress and withdrew, my body already objecting to being removed from hers.

I disposed of the condom and returned to the bed.

"Should I go?" I asked.

She lifted the blanket. "No."

I slid in beside her, pulling her into my arms.

"Good."

She nuzzled my chest and shut her eyes. In seconds, she was asleep.

It didn't take me long to follow her.

BETH

I toweled my hair dry, using the damp fabric to wipe off my shoulders. I studied my reflection in the mirror, recalling last night.

Ronan's passion. His gentleness. His demands. How it felt when he touched me. Kissed me. The way he felt moving inside me. The whispered, fervent word he repeated all night.

Beautiful.

He made me feel that way. I wasn't too short. Too chubby. Too hippy. Too much effort. Too anything except—his.

We'd dozed for a while, then he'd made love to me again, this time slowly. Then again as the early light began outside my small window. This time, he took me from behind, easing into me, teasing my clit with his fingers as he pulled my head back to his, kissing me hard, swallowing my moans.

He slipped away while I was sleeping, but on his pillow, he left a piece of paper with a heart drawn on it. Somewhere in my sleep-riddled mind, I recalled the press of his lips on my forehead and low murmured words before the sound of my door closing.

I smiled at the memories. Ran my fingers over my lips, still feeling his mouth. Touched the small purple mark at the juncture of my neck that he had left. He'd seen it as well, grinning and touching his mouth to it in a soft kiss.

"Marked as taken," he murmured.

Upstairs, I heard multiple footsteps, and I knew I had to get going. Evan had to go to school, I had studying to do, and Paige would have a million and one questions. I was grateful Lucy would be home today. I couldn't talk much with her around. Plus, I was going into the restaurant early today. There was another large order for cakes, and I wanted to get ahead if I could. Mike promised there would be one free oven so I could at least get a few done. That would save me from some of the inquisition.

I was afraid the smile on my face would only encourage her, yet I didn't seem able to stop it from happening.

———

It was almost closing when I carried in a tray of utensils from the kitchen to the dining area. It had been steady all night but not crazy. Jane had cleaned the restaurant, and once the last couple of tables left, I would close up and head home. I had heard the bell and had to force a smile to my face. We stopped taking orders fifteen minutes before we closed, and whoever had walked in was cutting it close. I hoped they wanted an order to go.

I wasn't expecting to see Ronan sitting in the booth. He had sent a couple of messages during the day and left a voice mail that caused a blush to settle under my skin.

"I can still taste you, little bird," he murmured into the phone. *"Leaving you today was hard. Sort of like my cock has been all day every time I think of you. I'll see you soon."*

He stood, meeting me halfway across the diner, taking the heavy tray from my hands.

"Hey, pretty girl." He smiled and bent down, brushing my cheek with his lips.

"What are you doing here?"

He frowned. "I came to drive you home. It's raining," he added, as if that would explain everything.

"Ronan, I go home in the rain all the time. I don't melt."

He shook his head. "Not on my watch."

Before I could argue, a customer approached the cash register, and I hurried over to settle the bill. When I went back to the booth, Ronan was busy wrapping the utensils as if he had done it a hundred times before.

I slid in and picked up a pile of the napkins. "You're doing my job now, too?" I asked wryly.

He shrugged. "I did this when I worked at a deli. It'll help you, plus, I get to have you close." He flashed a grin. "Then I'll drive you home."

"Are you hungry?"

He shook his head. "I ate."

"I don't expect you to be here every night to drive me," I said quietly.

"Good. I can't promise to be here every night. But when I can be, I will."

"Ronan, I can take care of myself."

He met my eyes, his gaze intense. "I know you can. It's one of the things I find so attractive about you—your independence. But I'm around, I have a car, and I felt like driving you. Nothing wrong with that." He hunched closer, dragging his fingers over my hand slowly. "I was hoping you'd let me kiss you when we were alone in the car."

I hooked my baby finger with his, holding tight. "I might."

"Excellent."

"I might invite you in."

"Even better."

"Still want to kiss me?"

"My cock wants to kiss you. Deeply. Repeatedly. Hard."

I blinked. "Well, that went in another direction fast."

He grinned. "Just saying. I think we're addicted."

The last customer approached the register, and I slid out of the booth and closed the tab for him. He was older, with silver hair. He slipped on his coat and helped his wife with hers, smiling as he buttoned it up as she shook her head.

"I can do that, Timothy."

He bent and kissed the end of her nose. "But I like to."

They left hand in hand, and I watched them with a smile. I locked the door behind them, pulling down the blinds after switching the sign to "Closed." Ronan was grinning as I got to the booth.

"Charmer."

"Remind you of anyone?" I asked. I could see Ronan in forty years, doing the same thing. He already acted that way with his courteous gestures.

He rolled the last of the utensils. "Done." He stood and lifted the tray. "Where does this go?"

I knew better than to argue with him. I pointed to the counter, and he carried it over. I quickly cleaned the last tables and took the dishes to the kitchen. When I returned, Ronan was waiting patiently.

"Any cakes tonight?"

"No, I got a bunch done earlier. That company from last week ordered six this week. Another place in the same building ordered four." I shook my head. "I have no idea how they found out."

"Good news travels fast. Someone must have eaten here and liked the cake. Made a call." He shrugged. "It's great cake." He smiled. "Can I take you home now, Beth?"

I returned his smile, grateful he was here. It was raining hard outside, and I really didn't want to have to run to the corner in the deluge.

I took his proffered hand, letting him lead me. "Yes."

We pulled into the driveway. The outside light was on, and I could see the soft light from the kitchen burning inside, but the rest of the house was in darkness. I unclipped my seat belt and glanced at Ronan. He was already turned toward me, his gaze intense.

"Thanks for the ride." I swallowed, the air in the car suddenly thick. "Did you—did you want to come in?"

He stroked my cheek with the backs of his fingers. "Are you tired, little bird?"

I shook my head.

He grinned and leaned close, brushing his mouth where his fingers had just been. "Fibber. I can see you are. I kept you up most of the night."

"I liked being up with you."

He groaned at my words. "Don't make this harder."

I edged closer, sliding my hand up his thigh, feeling him thick and solid beneath my fingers. I squeezed him gently.

"Too late, I'd say."

He yanked me close, kissing me. His tongue played over mine, stroking and fierce. I whimpered as he delved his hand into my hair, stroking my scalp. He seemed to love the curls I despised since I was never able to do anything to them. They had a mind of their own, and the more I tried to control them, the wilder they became. Ronan was constantly playing with them, burying his nose into them and inhaling. Staring at them.

"Come in with me," I pleaded against his mouth.

He shut off the car.

CHAPTER ELEVEN
BETH

He followed me inside, a silent shadow behind me. I indicated the stairs, and he went down ahead of me while I checked on Evan and Lucy. Paige was asleep, the sounds of her even breathing indicating she had settled for the night. I shut the door behind me and went to my room where Ronan was waiting. Without a word, he drew me into his arms and kissed me. All too soon, I forgot about everything and everyone but him. Me. Us. The roar of desire in my head grew louder, obliterating everything else in my mind. Impatiently, I tugged at his shirt, and laughing low in his chest, he stepped back, pulling it over his head and dropping it on the floor.

"I need a shower," I blurted.

He stopped, a grin crossing his face. "Oh?"

"I smell like the diner."

"I could come wash your back."

"My shower is pretty small."

He sat on my bed. "Then I'll wait here for you."

I hurried away, glancing over my shoulder. "Don't go away."

"Trust me," he replied. "I'll be right here."

"Lose the pants," I added before leaving.

His deep laughter made me shiver with want.

After the fastest shower of my life, I walked back into my room, my breath catching at the sight waiting for me.

Ronan, on my bed, leaning back on his hands, his shoulders broad, his chest and abs pronounced and taut with the position. His pants were gone, his thick thighs and long legs stretched out before him. He looked at home and at ease. Except I saw the pulse beating erratically at the base of his neck. The way his hands gripped the sheets beside him. His deep, uneven breathing. His black boxers were tight, his erection straining against the material. His intense green eyes were focused on me, and he smiled.

"Lose the towel."

I walked to the edge of the bed and let the fabric fall. Ronan's breath caught as he stared at me. "Beautiful."

Bravely, I leaned one knee on the mattress and ran my hands up his legs. I teased his skin with my fingers until I reached the dark cotton on his thighs. "These are in the way."

He lifted his hips without a word, and I slipped my fingers under the waistband and pulled them off, tossing them over my shoulder.

His erection, heavy and thick, slapped against his stomach. I crawled up the mattress, never breaking our gaze. He looked oddly vulnerable as I wrapped my hand around him. His eyes drifted shut as I marveled at the feel of him. Silk over steel. Hot, pulsating flesh that jumped under my touch. A low groan left his mouth, my name a sigh in the air as I stroked him. I crawled up farther, his torso too much to resist. I traced over taut muscles that contracted under my touch. I ran my tongue along the path my fingers drew, teasing his flat brown nipples, feeling the light smattering of hair on his chest. I kissed my way across his shoulders, up his neck, and tugged his earlobe into my mouth. When he turned his head, capturing my lips, I kissed him with everything in me. All the passion he made me feel. All the longing I had kept locked inside me for so long. The whole while, I stroked him, feeling the wetness growing under my fingers. I pulled back from his mouth, retracing my journey of discovery until I hovered over him, kneeling between his thighs. He lifted his head, the green of his irises eclipsed by the black pupils wide with frantic desire.

"You want my mouth on you, Ronan?"

"More than my next breath."

"Keep breathing, big boy. I need you with me." I lowered my mouth, engulfing him with my lips. His entire body stiffened, and then he groaned in satisfaction.

"*Yes.*" He choked out.

I licked and sucked, taking in as much of him as I could. I cupped his balls, teased the crown, and lapped at the length of him. He groaned and gasped. Fisted my hair and arched into my mouth. He wasn't rough, and he didn't try to go deeper, letting me set the pace. He murmured my name, praised my efforts, and watched me. I discovered a sensitive area just below his belly button that made him whimper and strain to get closer when I brushed my fingers over it. I teased him endlessly, working him into a frenzy. I had never been big on blow jobs, but with Ronan, it was different. He was different. Doing this for him turned me on as much as it did him, and I ached for him, my body yearning for what only he could give me. He tugged at my hair, his voice deep and pleading.

"I need to be inside you."

I lifted my head, slowly pulling my mouth away. "How do you want me?"

He reached for a condom. "On top. *Please* get on top of me."

I rolled the condom on him and hovered over him. He was so large, my legs were stretched to their limit. I felt the soft stroke of his fingers, and I moaned.

"Jesus, baby, you're soaked," he whispered, amazed. "You liked my cock in your mouth?"

I nodded, throwing back my head as he guided himself inside me, flexing his hips. I opened my eyes as his girth and size filled me, gasping in pleasure.

"Ride me," he demanded. "Move on me, Beth. Take whatever you need from me."

I began to move, the feel of him already bringing me to the edge. He gripped my hips, guiding me, and I rested my hands on his strong chest. We moved together, the pleasure spiking fast. My breathing quickened and I whispered his name, tightening around him. He rode through my orgasm, gripping my hands.

"You're going to give me another."

And I did. He sat up, enveloping me, driving himself deeper. He wrapped me close, covering my mouth with his as he moved, hard and fast, his body like a tidal wave that surged against mine. He controlled our movements, and all I could do was cling to him and take what he was giving me. His mouth was hot and wet, his tongue relentless as he kissed me. His body was rigid, his grip tight, and his touch possessive. I felt the stirrings of another orgasm, and I clutched at his shoulders, whimpering.

"Give it to me, little bird," he whispered in my ear as he came, his arms becoming bands of steel around me, his breathing harsh, and he groaned and gasped.

I exploded, every nerve in my body on fire. I felt him everywhere. Sensation after sensation rolled through me. Ecstasy so intense it brought tears to my eyes rippled under my skin. My orgasm went on and on, until I collapsed in his arms, too weak to lift my head.

He kissed my hair, sliding his hands down and cupping my face, lifting it from his chest. He rained kisses over my face, tiny little brushes of his mouth, then settled his lips on mine, kissing me slowly. Softly. His tongue lingering and lavish.

"Look at me, little bird."

I opened my eyes and met his verdant green.

"You are amazing."

I blinked.

"We are amazing together."

I managed to smile.

"I'm going to tuck you into bed now."

"Stay," I mumbled.

He kissed me again. "Beth, I'm not going anywhere."

The last thing I heard before I fell asleep was one other word.

"Ever."

RONAN

I glanced at my phone, wondering what Beth was doing. How she was feeling. I couldn't stop thinking about her.

Last night had been unbelievably erotic. The sight of her, my cock in her mouth, the vision of her riding me, the sounds of her pleasure as she shattered were all I could think about.

She was all I could think about.

I hated leaving her this morning. I woke about four, her draped over me, asleep on my chest, our legs entwined. I had noticed that the other night I had stayed. She liked to be close when she slept, held tight. I didn't mind, finding comfort in her closeness as well. But unlike the previous morning, I didn't wake her, instead carefully slipping out from under her and dressing quietly before heading up the stairs. I paused for a moment, watching her sleep. Her hair was a mass of curls around her face, her long eyelashes resting on her cheeks as she slumbered. Her lips pursed as she shifted, her hand reaching for something. I slid the pillow I'd been sleeping on toward her, and with a sigh, she buried her face into it and kept on sleeping. I was unable to resist bending to kiss her cheek and stroking my hand through the curls. I loved her hair. It suited her—wild and beautiful—just like her.

I had left my shoes by the front door, and I stopped in shock when I discovered Paige sitting at the small table in the kitchen having a cup of coffee. For a moment, I froze, and our eyes locked. She smirked then waved at the empty chair across from her.

"Coffee?"

I sat down and poured a cup.

"You always up this early?" I asked.

"For future reference, you mean?" She teased. "Generally, no. But I had a headache last night, so I went to bed early. So here I am at four a.m." She looked mischievous. "What's your excuse?"

"Um—"

She laughed. "I'm teasing. You should put your shoes by the side door and go out that way. It locks behind you. No chance of the kids seeing you. I'm sure neither of you is ready for that conversation."

"I'll keep that in mind." I took a sip of coffee.

"You serious about her, Ronan?"

I set down my cup. "It's early in the relationship, but I'd say yes."

"She comes as a package."

"I'm aware."

"I've never seen her react to someone the way she does to you. Or the way Evan has warmed to you." She frowned. "Don't hurt them, okay?"

"I have no plans on hurting them."

She patted my hand. "Then we'll get along just fine."

Her words seemed to be on repeat in my head. I cared deeply about Beth and Evan already. I wanted to get to know both of them more. I wanted them to know me. Just me.

I knew I would have to tell her about my family. Who I really was. My occupation. Everything. But for now, I relished just being Ronan. No one special, just a guy she liked.

I liked being the guy Beth liked.

A throat clearing interrupted my musings.

Paul and Jeremy entered my office and sat in front of my desk. Paul shut the door behind himself before he took a seat. I saved the design I'd been working on and shut the lid of the laptop. It hadn't changed much—I was too distracted.

"What's up?" I asked casually, lacing my fingers on the desk. I studied them closely. It wasn't unusual for them to shut the door, but it was strange to see the serious looks on their faces. The two of them were usually jokesters. When the three of us were together with our family, we were all boisterous, but often it was the two of them who started whatever mischief we landed in.

When they glanced at each other, neither speaking, I shook my head. "What's wrong?"

"You weren't at brunch on Sunday."

I threw up my hands. "I have missed brunch before."

"You never said you weren't coming."

I blinked, then laughed. "Is that what has everyone all distraught? I forgot, guys. I had other plans, and I just forgot."

I shook my head. "When Mom texted me, I said I wouldn't be there."

"We were just surprised, Ronan." Jeremy leaned forward. "We wanted you there when we introduced Diane and Kim to the family."

I laughed lightly. "That sort of happened last weekend, didn't it?"

Paul huffed an impatient sigh. "That wasn't planned. They were only supposed to meet Mom and Dad, Liam, and Ava. The rest sort of showed up."

"They usually do," I reminded them.

"It wasn't everyone, and it wasn't official. Sunday was all the cousins, uncles, and aunts. They think you're upset."

"Well, let me clear up that misconception. You've met women you both like, and I'm thrilled. I'm sorry I missed it. But it wasn't intentional, and I'm not upset. I just had a lot on my mind, and I forgot." I smiled, trying to lighten the air. "I know you think I'm perfect, but I'm not."

That broke the ice, and they relaxed a little. I picked up my thermos and drank deeply before continuing. "Listen, I know things are changing. I know we're not together as much." I tilted my head. "Maybe it's about time, though."

They shared another glance, and I slapped the desk. "What the hell is this a lead-up to? I may not be around as much, but I still know you better than anyone. What aren't you saying?"

Paul straightened his shoulders. "So, you know we're not moving to Port Albany."

"Yep. I already figured that out. What else?"

"We're going to divide our time between here and the other office. Bentley thinks we should keep both offices going for a while until the new office is settled and functioning."

It made sense for now. "All right."

"He wants the three of us to be together a couple days a week. He says we feed off one another when we're in design mode."

"He's right," I agreed. "Together anytime, we're a force to be reckoned with. Design-wise, we blow everyone out of the water." I rubbed my chin, suddenly knowing why they were so uncomfortable. "I assume this was discussed at brunch?"

"Yes."

"And you would prefer if I were here on those two days rather than you come to Port Albany."

"We'll come out there too, but for now, we want to stay here," Paul stated firmly.

"To be close to your girls."

They exchanged another look, and I laughed. Three weeks ago, I would have been pissed off. I would have done it because they asked, but I wouldn't have been happy. But now, I wanted to stay close to Beth and Evan.

"It's fine. We knew we'd have to do this slowly." I crossed my arms on the desk. "I know you two don't have the love for Port Albany that I do. I mean, I know you like it there, but you prefer the bustle of the city. Like Maddox. We're not always going to be together. We all know that. And I'm not upset about your girls. Let's be clear on that. I want you happy. If living here and commuting to the other office is what you do, it's all cool. At least you can set your hours and you're always traveling in the opposite way of the commuters." I grimaced. "Dad hated that part, but he loved Port Albany. So do I."

"Things are changing so quickly," Jeremy spoke. "I—we—just worry."

"They are. They will. But one thing that isn't going to change is my love for you two clowns."

I saw them visibly relax. I sat back, studying them. "We have a unique bond most people don't understand," I said quietly. "We shared heartbeats and blood for nine months. Mom loves to tell people how we couldn't be separated for the first few months."

They nodded, not speaking. That, in itself, was a rarity with my brothers—they were always talking.

"We've been a unit our entire lives, guys. And we were treated that way by most people. Hell, we treated ourselves that way. But it's time to separate a little. Come on, admit it, doesn't it feel good just to be Jeremy or Paul when you're alone with your girl? Not part of a trio, or even a duo, but just yourself?"

They exchanged glances, and Paul spoke first. "I do like it. I like being the man Diane looks at, knowing she is only seeing me, not us, if that makes any sense. She says she feels the same."

Jeremy nodded in silent agreement.

"Your girls would understand better than anyone," I replied. "They've lived this too." I rested my elbows on the desk, earnest. "But we're still us. The Callaghan boys. The triplets. We're always going to be that. But it's okay to be Ronan, Jeremy, and Paul too."

I let my words sink in. Jeremy regarded me, his eyes narrow. "When did you get so wise?"

I barked out a laugh. "I've always been smarter than you two. Happens when you're the oldest."

They laughed with me, no longer tense. I shook my head. "Go get some work done. I need those specs of the roof garden on the BAM building ASAP. I need to make sure we've got the beams in to support it."

They stood. "On it," Paul assured me.

I watched them go, my smile fading. What I said was true, but I had held back again. I didn't tell my brothers about Beth. I still wasn't ready.

I swung my chair around, staring out the window, my thoughts chaotic.

I needed to sort this out.

I just wasn't sure how.

CHAPTER TWELVE

RONAN

The rest of the week flowed with a new rhythm. I worked during the day, being the Ronan my family knew. I designed and planned. Attended meetings, enjoying the give-and-take of the dynamics of our group. We all celebrated when Addi told us she was pregnant, confirming the little tableau I had witnessed not long ago.

"How did Bent and Maddox take it?" I asked.

Addi smiled softly. "They were both thrilled."

Brayden laughed. "That's an understatement. They were both more emotional than our moms. Dad called Richard to share the good news and wept like, well, a baby."

Everyone chuckled. The serious businessmen who ran BAM all had incredibly soft sides for their family. Richard VanRyan was part of our adopted clan and Maddox's best friend. He had been the first of them to become a grandparent when Gracie gave birth to Kylie, and he had gloated about it.

"No doubt he had lots of sage advice to offer."

That brought out more laughter, especially from Gracie. Her father was confident, brash, and to some people, arrogant. But like the others, when it came to his family, he was a total pushover.

I wanted to emulate them.

I picked up Beth every night after her shift and, on Thursday, stayed with her as she baked the last of the cakes needed.

"Could you do this instead of waitressing?" I asked, curious as I helped her carry some wrapped cakes into the walk-in refrigerator.

"I would have to bake a lot of cakes." She laughed. "I don't think there's a venue that needs as many cakes as I would have to bake to make up the difference." She smiled at me. "Stop worrying about me, Ronan. I'm fine. It's not forever. Once I'm done school, hopefully I'll get a job and I won't have to wait-ress or bake cakes anymore."

I pinned her to the counter, caging her in with my arms. "But you'll bake them for me."

She looked up at me, the expression in her eyes vulnerable. "If you're around," she whispered.

"I will be."

"Then you can have as many cakes as you want."

I bent my head and kissed her. "Good."

Friday night, she was done as soon as the diner closed. I was waiting in my booth as she came over, pulling on her coat.

Once again, there was a mist in the air, and the breeze was chilly.

"You tired?" I asked.

"No, actually. I had a nap this morning after Evan left. Lucy was at day care and Paige was out, and I took the opportunity of a quiet house."

"Would you like to come to my place for a drink?"

"A drink," she repeated.

"Yes. I don't want to go to a bar, but I'd like some alone time with you. Nothing more, I swear."

"Okay," she agreed.

At the condo, she was curious, and I watched her walk around. It was pretty sparse and, of the three places we had in the building, the smallest. A sofa and a TV that I rarely watched in the living room. A couple of high stools at the bar separating the kitchen from the living space. My bedroom had a king-sized bed and nightstands. That was it. There was a walk-in closet that held most of my clothes, but I made sure the doors were shut. My custom-made suits and dress shirts hung in there, and I wasn't ready to have that conversation about my wardrobe or the need for it. The bathroom was simple. It was an older BAM building, not as luxurious as some of the newer builds, but still well-appointed. There was a small pool and workout room in the basement, and the security was good. It was an easy drive to the office and suited our needs. It wasn't the place I considered home. It was modern and clean, and I was good with that. As I looked around and saw it with different eyes, I realized how un-homey it was. Paul's and Jeremy's places were both settled, well-furnished, and personalized. While going to school, we'd shared a larger unit on a different floor, but once we graduated, we'd moved in to our own condos. The difference I could see now was that I never planned to stay and they had. This was their home, whereas I was still looking for mine.

"No roommate?"

"Not anymore. I had two going through university. Now I like having my own space."

"It's a nice place," Beth said.

I laughed. "Needs work. I'm rarely here."

"These places are expensive, aren't they?" she asked. "I mean, it's downtown, in a nice area…" She paused. "Paige and I looked at a couple around here, but even pooling our resources, we couldn't afford one."

This was a good time to tell her about my family. That they were wealthy. That I was well-off. Instead, I deflected. "It's an older building, and I guess I got lucky. All condos are expensive in Toronto. It's only one bedroom and pretty small at that."

"Oh."

She waited for me to elaborate, but instead, I steered her to the sofa and went to pour her a glass of wine, then sat beside her. Luckily, she let the subject drop. She drew her legs underneath her and sipped the cold liquid. She hummed and ran her fingers through her hair. "Delicious." She licked her lips, unconsciously sultry in her actions.

"Jesus, you're sexy." I spoke without thinking.

"Me?" she asked, sounding incredulous.

"Yes. Your curls, your curves, your smile. You're so beautiful, and you have no idea, which makes you even more so in my books."

She blinked, looking startled. "I had no idea you felt that way."

I leaned forward, taking her glass from her fingers, setting it on the table, then dragging her onto my lap. I covered her mouth with mine and kissed her. I plunged one hand into her curls I loved so much, smoothing the silky strands between my fingers, and used my other arm to hold her tight. She opened for me, and I explored her, the crisp taste of the wine still lingering on her tongue. I only meant to kiss her once and let her return to her corner, but now that I had her in my arms, I didn't want to let her go. I kissed her harder, delving my tongue into her mouth and finding all the sweet ridges, the smoothness of her teeth, the velvet feel of her tongue in my quest. She returned my caresses with enthusiasm, pressing herself closer, her legs splaying over mine so she straddled me. She wove her fingers into my hair, tugging and pulling, teasing the nape of my neck, making me hiss in pleasure. I was hard with desire for her, and I let her feel it. I wanted her to know how much she turned me on. When our mouths separated, I dragged my lips to her ear, after worshiping the smooth skin of her cheek and neck. "Beautiful," I stated firmly.

She blinked at me, her dark eyes wide in her face. "I think you're the sexiest man I have ever seen." She ran her hands over my arms. "I have never met anyone like you. So strong and masculine, yet so sweet and amazing." She swallowed. "You make me feel safe, Ronan."

"You are always safe with me. Always."

She bit her lip, glancing down between us. "You're, ah, large everywhere."

I chuckled. "All to make you smile, little bird."

"Well, you do that just fine," she responded.

Regretfully, I lifted her back to the corner and handed her the glass of wine.

"I don't know how you do that."

"Do what?"

"Lift me like I weigh nothing."

"Do I need to strip you and show you with my mouth just how perfect your curves are? Happy to do so, but you'll be here all night." I paused. "And most of tomorrow."

Her eyes widened to the point of hilarity. "Um…"

I leaned over and kissed her gently. "Whatever and whoever put those doubts in your head—forget them. I like your curves. They're sexy as hell. I like how your hips feel in my hands. How fucking gorgeous your breasts are. Thinking of how you looked riding me, I can't wait to see you ride me again and watch them. Touch them." I lowered my voice. "Suck them."

"Oh, ah…"

"Are we clear?"

"Yep." Her head bobbed, her voice slightly higher than normal. "Curves good. Mouth standing by, ready. Big dick. Sucking…" She swallowed. "Good God, I'm rambling."

Laughing, I kissed her nose.

"Another thing I find highly attractive. Now, drink your wine and tell me in detail about the weather system around us. I want to hear every weather-related word you got."

She grinned, her color still high and her eyes bright. I was thrilled I made her look like that.

It was worth the aching balls.

At least for now.

On Sunday, I packed a picnic. I went to my favorite place in Port Albany on Saturday and picked up fried chicken. Then to the deli where I had them make up some sandwiches. Beth was bringing dessert—there was no point in even pretending to think about getting anything else.

I added some chips and snacks and filled a cooler with ice and drinks. I even remembered to add napkins.

After my errands, I stopped by my parents' for a visit. We sat on the deck looking over the water. My dad and I talked about a new project they were thinking of undertaking, and he asked me to go over the building plans with him on Monday.

"Or tomorrow if you're around," he said casually.

"Oh, um, no. I have plans."

My mom looked at me. "Again? With your friend?" she asked pointedly.

I shrugged. "A few people, actually."

"You're awfully secretive, Ronan," she admonished.

Luckily, my dad stuck up for me. "Give him a break, Sunshine. He's got a life. Let him live it. He doesn't have to tell us everything." He threw me a wink. "Does a man good to have some secrets."

She tapped her fingers on the table. "Is that right?"

I tried not to laugh as he backpedaled. "When you're young and single, I meant. Not when you're happily married to the most beautiful woman in the world. Nope." He shook his head. "No secrets then."

She harrumphed and I chuckled. Luckily, she dropped the subject, and I left not long after, tamping down my guilt once again.

I was smiling as I headed to Beth's. It was a warm day, although the weather report had indicated a change later today. I was hoping we would see some cloud formations and Beth could name them for me. I found it sexy when she spoke "meteorologist" in her lovely voice. She became animated and used her hands to indicate the various parts of the cloud she was detailing to me. I loved it.

The trunk was full of the food I had brought. I had a car seat for Lucy. The weather was good. It promised to be a grand day.

The kids were excited when I arrived, and I let Beth and Paige deal with getting them strapped in. Not for the first time, I was glad I drove a spacious car. I had an SUV as well, but it was parked in Port Albany. Once everyone was ready, we headed back toward the place I felt really at home. Part of me felt guilty that I wasn't taking them to my house or the Hub, where my family would be hanging out—or at least some of them. I also felt guilty I hadn't told my family about Beth.

Then I shoved down all those feelings. Today was about them, enjoying some fresh air, spending time with all of them, and getting them out of the city. I would deal with my family and everything around it later.

I bypassed the entrance to the housing complex. The kids were so busy spotting the water and the open spaces no one noticed as we went by. I drove a short distance and turned on a barely visible road.

"Is it okay to be here?" Beth asked.

I squeezed her hand which had been on my thigh most of the drive. "It's private, but I have permission."

"You know the owner?"

"Good friend of the family. I've done a lot of work for them."

That statement wasn't a lie. Bentley was a very good friend of my family. And I had done lots of work for the company and in the houses on the property.

I pulled up as close as I could. "It's a short walk through the trees." I looked at Evan. "I can piggyback you if needed. My dad used to do that with us," I explained. "Sometimes more than one of us at a time." We all used to dogpile on him.

He smiled, letting me know he wasn't offended. "I'll see how it goes."

"Okay."

Slowly, we made our way through the mostly flat path. The trees around us hid the high wall that ran the perimeter of the property. The thick forest to the right protected the houses from view as well. I set down the coolers and basket I had brought and opened up the two camping chairs as Beth and Paige unfolded the large blanket I had bought just for today.

I stayed with Lucy and Evan as they explored. The view of the water in the distance and the stretch of rocky beach they could see fascinated them.

168

"What's around that bluff?" Evan asked, pointing to the right.

"Ah, private homes."

"Whoa," he breathed. "Do you think they can see the water?"

I nodded. "They have their own beach."

"That is so cool. I would sit and watch the waves."

I ruffled his hair. "Me too."

"That house looks lonely," he said, pointing to the house on the bluff in the distance on the left. Set apart from the main compound, the rocky cove was only accessible by foot over the jagged shoreline, walking through the trees and over this piece of land, or coming from the other direction to the driveway. It was the only piece of property around not owned by BAM. Not for lack of trying, but the old man living there refused to sell. The house was as remote as he was, although my family did check in on him, regardless of his rudeness. He tolerated the women a little better but hated all the men, so we stayed clear unless it was completely necessary. One day he fell, and I went to help my sister Ava get him inside. I carried him from the hard rocks into his little place, admiring the woodwork inside. He threw me out the instant his ungrateful ass touched the chair he instructed I place him in. I hadn't been back since.

"Yeah, it does." Evan had struck the nail on the head, and I felt another small tug of guilt. Maybe I should go back and try again. I didn't care about the land, although Mr. Owens thought that was my game. Mrs. Owens had died when I was a kid, but I remember her being kind. He was alone, and I needed to try harder to be a better neighbor—even if he was cantankerous. Loneliness did that to a person.

We ate the feast I had brought while sitting in the sun. I felt some sort of caveman-type satisfaction knowing I had brought the food and looked after all of them. After lunch and the best brownies I had ever eaten, plus a slice of rich vanilla cake, we lay on the blanket, looking up at the puffy white clouds. I had made Beth study the sky, but she assured me there was nothing exciting about the clouds. She did, however, check her phone and break down the weather report for me, adding in a few extra words. I kissed her when the kids weren't looking, in thanks.

"That's a bunny," Lucy said, her head on my chest.

Evan was beside her, and he shook his head. "That's not a bunny."

"What is it, then?" she demanded.

He pursed his lips. "It's a dragon."

She was silent. "I liked it better when it was a bunny."

I chuckled and met Beth's gaze. I patted my chest. "Plenty of room over here," I said, crooking my empty arm in invitation. Again, that feeling of satisfaction swelled as she curled beside me and we all looked at the clouds as they drifted by. We found lots of bunnies, kittens, and flowers in the sky. A few more dragons and an alligator. Beth found a shoe. I enjoyed listening to them all.

Paige wandered around, sitting near the edge, her sketchpad on her lap, and she was busy drawing. Beth told me Paige had been so excited to come and hoped to be able to do a little sketching.

"Not much scope for nature in Toronto," she explained. "Some pretty parks but they're usually overrun with people."

I was glad she was having a good time, and I had no problem spending time with the kids. They were highly entertaining, and I liked both of them a great deal.

They got quiet, and I realized I was now trapped under two sleeping bodies. Beth was silent, and I wondered if she had fallen asleep as well. I nuzzled her head, and she nestled closer, making me smile. The warmth of the sun sank into me, and I felt my eyes drifting shut.

A ten-minute nap wouldn't hurt any of us.

I woke up with a start, something tickling my nose. I batted it away, hearing Lucy's giggle. I reached over, lifting her high, opening my eyes to meet her excited face. She was holding a blade of grass, waving it. "I woke you!"

I pretended to lift her like a set of weights. "Yes, you did, Lucy-loo."

I sat up and set her on her feet. Beth and Evan were by the overhang, and Paige was across from me on the blanket, her legs crossed.

"Still sketching?" I asked, reaching for my thermos and taking a long drink.

"Just adding in a couple of details," she said, concentrating with a frown.

"Can I see?" I asked.

She held out the pad, and I flipped through a couple of pages. She was very talented, her eye for detail astounding. On the last page, my breath caught. It was a sketch of me sleeping, with the kids and Beth nestled against me. It wasn't finished, but already, it was awesome.

"I'll do some shading and filling in," she explained.

"Can I get a copy?"

She smiled. "Of course." She began to get up and stopped. "Oh. A lady was here."

My stomach sank. "A lady?"

"Yeah. She said she lived in the houses over there." She pointed in the direction of the compound. "I think she was shocked to see us, but she recognized you, so it was okay."

"Did she give you her name?" I asked, keeping my voice neutral.

"No. She was younger, with dark hair and purple highlights. She seemed curious about us, you especially, being here, but I said you'd brought us for a picnic and had permission to be here. That appeared to amuse her."

Ava. It had to be her.

Why the hell was she up here? She never came up this way—it was too rugged through the woods, which was one reason I loved the spot. I was guaranteed to find privacy.

What the hell were the odds that the one time I *needed* that privacy, she would show up?

I almost cursed out loud, but I managed to keep my frustration in check.

"She's the daughter of one of the owners," I said. "She is easily amused."

"Well, she seemed nice."

"Did she talk to Beth or the kids?"

"No, you were all asleep. I was sitting here sketching you when I heard a twig snap and looked up. She was standing there, looking confused and surprised. I went over and spoke to her for a moment, then she left."

"I'll speak with her soon." I smiled benignly, knowing full well soon would be today.

And knowing Ava, she wouldn't let this go.

I was busted.

CHAPTER THIRTEEN
RONAN

All too soon, the afternoon was over. I was surprised how the time had flown by, even with my forty-minute nap. I refused to let the knowledge of what Ava saw dampen my enjoyment of the day. We played a few games of I spy, ate some of the candy I had saved, then we packed up, and I drove them home. It had been a great day, aside from Ava, and I felt sad to leave them. But I knew they needed time without me as well and that I had monopolized Beth enough. I did kiss her senseless before I left, pressed against the brick of her house behind the bushes by the side door. I kissed her until she was breathless and wanting. Until I could barely see straight.

As if it were the last time I would kiss her.

Then I regretfully watched her walk away.

I pulled up to my house in Port Albany, not at all surprised to see Ava sitting on the deck. I knew she would be there and, no doubt, have a lot to say.

I climbed the steps, meeting her gaze. She looked so much like our mom with her dark hair and facial features. Her eyes weren't as green as all the boys—instead, they were a mixture of green, gold, and brown, the colors swirling and at times one color more prominent than the other. Usually when she was emotional, they looked green. When she was angry, they were brown. Right now, they were normal, although the gold flecks seemed brighter. She was tough and smart at her job, keeping everyone in line with her no-nonsense attitude. The staff called her the General at work, but with her family, she showed her softer side.

I had a feeling, though, that wouldn't be the case today.

"Ava."

She stood. "Ronan."

"Need to borrow some sugar?" I asked.

She crossed her arms. "Don't even start with me, little brother. We need to talk. We can do it here and risk being overheard, or we can go inside." She flipped her hair and glared at me, the color of her eyes now brown and dark. I had already pissed her off, which wasn't a good sign. "Given what I saw earlier, I know you like covert operations, so I'm assuming inside."

I rolled my eyes at her dig, but I unlocked the door and went inside the house. I kicked off my shoes and indicated the solitary chair. "Make yourself comfortable. I'll be back."

In the bathroom, I washed my hands and ran my damp fingers through my hair. Between the wind and Beth's impatient little fingers, it was a mess. I gripped the edge of the sink and drew in a long, calming breath. I had a feeling I was going to need it.

I headed back to the living room. Ava was by the window, looking at the vast expanse of water.

"What did I see today?"

"Why don't you tell me?"

She spun around. "I saw you with two women and a couple of kids that aren't yours—unless you are really good at this secret thing." She scowled. "Are you into dating two women at once, Ronan? Is that your thing?"

I had to laugh at her thoughts. I supposed what she saw was unusual.

I wiped my eyes. "No—dating one woman. The young boy is her brother. The other woman is her roommate, and that was her daughter. We were having a picnic and looking at the clouds." I shrugged. "We fell asleep."

"Who is she?" she asked. "The one you're dating?"

"Her name is Beth."

She tapped her foot. "And who is Beth to you?"

"Someone important."

Her shoulders dropped. "Then why don't we know about her, Ronan?" She frowned in confusion. "Are you ashamed of us? Your family?"

"What? Fuck *no*, Ava. It's not like that at all."

"What is it like, then? Explain it to me, because I'm confused." She stepped closer, tilting her head to one side and studying me. "This isn't like you."

I met her eyes, grateful to see them more green than brown. "I'm not sure how to explain it so anyone can understand."

"Try me."

I walked around, feeling restless. "I met Beth a few weeks ago. We clicked. She's a waitress and is putting herself through school to become a meteorologist. She also looks after her brother, Evan, who you saw with us." I glanced over my shoulder. "She has a lot of responsibilities." I explained about Evan's accident and his continuing struggle. Then I told her about Paige and Lucy. I explained how we met and the cakes Beth made I had been buying to help her out. How much I enjoyed talking to her. How she made me feel. When I was done, I let out a long breath. It felt good to tell someone about Beth. About everything.

"You've been busy."

"Yeah, I guess so."

"And keeping it all to yourself."

I nodded.

"What were you doing there today? Up on the bluff?"

"I wanted to bring them for a picnic," I repeated. "Get them out of the city. That spot is one of my favorites on the property. I hang out up there a lot." I turned and faced her. "I've never seen anyone else there but me all these years, so I thought we'd be safe. What were you doing there?"

"Don't think you can turn this around on me, Ronan. I walk that way often. In fact, I've seen you there, but I know you rarely get to be on your own and I always assumed you were seeking solitude, so I didn't bother you." She crossed her arms and pursed her lips, looking just like Mom as she studied me. "I was walking that way to see if Mr. Owens was around. If I see him outside his house, I go talk to him, check up on him."

"See if he's ready to sell?" I guessed.

"One day, I'll catch him off guard, and he'll say yes. He won't talk to Dad or any BAM people. He threatened to shoot Dad last time he dropped by, even though Dad was only bringing him some soup."

I chuckled. Mr. Owens was the last holdout of all the properties around the compound. It was a small piece of real estate, on the very edge of all the land we owned and had a great view of the water. I was shocked when he'd refused the last offer—they proposed over market value with the condition he could live there until he died. He'd only threatened to get out his shotgun if they didn't leave. Still, my dad and the other BAM men liked him, and someone checked on him regularly. The only one he ever seemed to like was Ava, and even that was hit or miss.

Ava narrowed her eyes. "Stop trying to change the subject."

"I'm not. I was just asking."

"You were just avoiding my question. What is going on with you? Why haven't we met Beth? Or even heard about her?"

"I'm not ready to introduce her to the family."

"Why?"

"Why? *Why?*" I laughed. "Do I have to have a reason?"

She frowned. "Yes."

I paced for a minute and finally spoke. "Because I'm not ready to share her yet."

"Explain that to me."

I turned and faced her fully, gripping the back of the armchair, feeling a flare of anger. "Because once I do, they'll be all over her. All over us. Sunday brunches, interfering with plans. Hanging out with Paul and Jeremy. For the first time in my life, I have something of my own. Something I don't have to share. When I'm with her, I'm just Ronan. Not one of the triplets. Not one of 'the kids.'" I shook my head. "She makes me eggs the way I like. She asks me how I want something. And I get to choose. I don't have to think of my brothers. I don't have to worry they won't like it. She looks at me and sees *me*. Nobody else. She knows I dislike lettuce on a sandwich. Mom still adds it because it's what Paul and Jeremy prefer. I'm the odd man out so often there. But not with her. Not with Beth." I hung my head. "I'm not ready to give that up."

For a moment, there was silence.

"Keep going. What else? Talk to me."

I looked at her, her gaze understanding. Once again, I had to avert my eyes, but her look of sympathy was enough and it was like a dam burst. "I don't like nuts in my ice cream, and Mom never remembers. And mustard. I hate that shit." I was rambling, but I didn't care. "Or last year when Paul and Jeremy decided to try stock car racing and I wasn't interested. They did it on their own, not even thinking maybe we could find something to do together, and no one questioned it or thought about the fact that they were doing something without me. But when I did that windsurfing course by myself, they got their noses all out of joint about not being included. It's fine for me to be alone because, you know, it's good ole Ronan."

I stopped and ran a hand through my hair. I sounded like an idiot, but I didn't care.

"But with Beth, I'm not alone," I concluded, mumbling.

"That was hard for you to admit," Ava stated softly.

I nodded, not looking up. "I feel guilty."

She laughed and knelt on the chair, looking up at me. She tickled my chin the way she used to when I was little, making me lift my head. I looked down at her, expecting to see anger, but there was none. Caring and understanding were in her expression.

"Ah, Ronan. You've always been the leader for your little pack, haven't you? Always looking out for Paul and Jeremy."

"Someone had to," I mumbled.

"You have no idea, do you?" She smiled and patted my cheek.

"No idea about what?"

"They know it. Liam and I know it. So do Mom and Dad. You think no one sees you for you, but we do. We know you're the strongest. The smartest. The leader. We know you step back and make sure Paul and Jeremy come first. The other two-thirds of your little pack adore you beyond reason and look up to you, even if they don't tell you." She dropped her voice. "I'll tell you another secret, little brother. You're the favorite. Of everyone. Not just Gracie."

"I am not."

"You are," she confirmed. "And I'll tell you something else. You're wrong. You don't have to give up anything with your girl. What you have to do is learn to say no."

I furrowed my brow in confusion. "What?"

"You can set the boundaries. You can say no to invitations. You can tell people to call before they drop over. You can say no if you want to." She met my eyes, her gaze steady and serious. "You say it to yourself often enough. Now you have to learn to say it to other people."

I didn't say anything for a moment, and she kept talking. "Gracie and Jaxson set boundaries. So did Addi and Bray. Even I have some. Think about it. So do Paul and Jeremy. They have chosen to stay close to their girls rather than live here all the time." She smiled. "It's called being grown up, Ronan. Making our own choices."

I let her words sink in.

"We all want you to be happy, Ronan. From what I saw today, this girl makes you happy. How does she feel about meeting the family?"

I shuffled my feet. "I haven't told her about our family."

She stood, frowning. "How does that work, exactly?"

Her words were so similar to Gracie's, I had to smile.

"You find this funny?"

"No."

I began to pace again. "She thinks I'm just a regular guy. She has no idea of my connections, my family, what I do, how much money I have, nothing."

"So, you're lying to her."

"I'm letting her get to know me."

"How can she know you, Ronan, if you're hiding part of yourself?"

Her words brought me up short.

"We are a part of you. A huge part. Why would you hide all the love we feel for you? That you have an amazing support system?"

"Beth doesn't have that."

"Maybe she would benefit, then."

I blinked at her.

"What does she think you do for a living?"

"Um…construction, sort of."

She shook her head. "You are one of the most honest people I know. I'm shocked at your behavior." Then her eyes widened. "Is this because of that tramp? That Loni creature?"

I held back my smile at her description. It was pretty accurate.

"It's nice to know Beth likes me for me, not my money or my connections." I paused, looking down. "It feels good to know she isn't pretending."

"But you are."

I opened my mouth to protest, but she held up her hand.

"You are Ronan Adam Callaghan. Son of Aiden and Cami. Brother to all of us. Friend. Architect. Godfather to Kylie. Successful in your own right. Independent. And yes, wealthy. How many of those facts does she know?"

"She knows I have a family. Just not the details."

She narrowed her eyes. "The guilt you're feeling isn't because you're not ready to introduce her to us. It's because you want to, but you're letting your fears override your judgment. If you really care about this girl, think about it, Ronan. Think of what would happen."

"What do you mean?"

"We *are* loud. Interfering. In one another's lives and business. We're also incredibly close. We work together, play together, live near to one another. If one of us is down, the others rally. You say Beth carries a lot of responsibilities. That her brother needs help. That she works too hard. Now think what would happen once the family knew about her. Dad would help her brother. You know no one is better than he is with healing. Think of the equipment you have access to that might help him. Uncle Richard would talk to Evan—encourage him with his story. All of us would figure out a way of making Beth's life easier. Be it looking after Evan so she has more free time, having her grass mowed, buying more of her cakes—whatever it took, we would all pitch in because she means something to you. Something very important, I think."

"Yes," I affirmed without hesitation.

"Then stop hiding. Show her who you really are and let her know all about you. Otherwise, the longer you hold back, the more she will feel you are lying and question everything you say to her. Is that what you want?"

"No."

She stepped closer, laying her hand on my arm. "I want to know the woman who made my brother look so relaxed today he was napping and covered in children. Who thought so much of someone else, he wanted to make her happy. Bring her someplace that meant so much to him. Don't hide, Ronan. Show her. Show us."

I pondered her words.

"Do you trust her?"

"Beth?" I asked. "Completely. She's genuine and real."

"Then you need to show her. Prove it and be the same with her. Before you dig yourself a hole you will never get out of. You could lose her."

She pulled my head down and kissed my forehead the way she always did when I was a child and smiled. "I'm proud to be your sister. Be proud to be my brother."

"I am."

"Then you know what you have to do."

And she left me alone with my thoughts.

CHAPTER FOURTEEN
RONAN

Tuesday afternoon, I was restless. Edgy. I hadn't seen Beth since Sunday, and although I spoke with her, I missed her. It felt strange to miss someone—my family was always so close, it was a rare feeling. It was different from the cut-off feeling of missing my brothers. This was more an ache—a longing. I felt incomplete in a way I had never experienced until now. It shocked me to realize, in the short time I had known Beth, how important she had become to me. I was falling for her quickly. I shook my head at my internal thoughts. I had already fallen for her.

A knock at my door broke through my musings, and I looked up, surprised to see my elder brother, Liam. He waited for me to invite him in, and I waved to the chairs in front of my desk.

"Hey, stranger."

He walked in and sat down heavily. He was tall—in fact, he was an inch taller than me. We shared the same dark hair and similar features, but his eyes were a brilliant hazel that glittered under the lights. And he was built, as our mom would say, like a "brick shithouse." Solid. Massive shoulders, a barrel chest, and a thick waist. Heavy legs. Large hands and feet. He preferred a short beard. Plaid shirts and jeans. His skin was tanned from all the time he spent outdoors. When you first met him, you might step back at his sheer size, worried about the type of man he was.

But his eyes showed his true nature. Gentle and kind. He had a low voice, and he was quieter than some of us. Namely, my two other brothers. He loved anything to do with the outdoors, plants, and nature. Seeing him in the setting of the office was unusual, and he looked as uncomfortable as I was with him sitting across from me.

He smiled, the similarity between us evident. We looked like my dad, but we all inherited our mother's smile. When we were little, our dad called us his sunbeams. His nickname for my mom was "Sunshine" and he always said she beamed when she smiled, and we took after her.

"What are you doing here?" I asked.

"I was meeting with Bent. He wants a new garden at the Towers. He never liked the landscaping they did, and he wants me to redesign and change it." He rubbed a hand over his beard. "I need to figure out how to move some things and save them."

Liam always saved everything he could. The grounds at the compound were home to many transplants. He constantly worked on the gardens, and every season they were spectacular.

"So, you just dropped by?" I asked, knowing full well why he was here. He and Ava were close, and I had no doubt she shared with him what was going on.

He grinned widely, his eyes crinkling. "Something like that." He leaned back, crossing his arms behind his head, the muscles stretching the fabric tight over his biceps. The chair creaked under his weight.

"I hear you got yourself in a bit of a pickle there, little bro."

"Our sister has a big mouth." I scowled.

He shook his head. "Nope. She's concerned."

"There is no reason for her to be."

He regarded me in silence, stroking his beard. "Let's see," he said quietly. "You've met a girl you've got strong feelings for who has a whole lotta baggage——"

I leaned forward, almost snarling. "Evan is *not* baggage."

He lifted one eyebrow, and I sat back, muttering, "He's a good kid."

"Again, I'll say, strong feelings not only for her, but her kid brother. You're keeping it to yourself because you don't want to share yet—which, by the way, I understand. But the confusing part to me is that you haven't been honest with her about us. Your family. I don't understand how you think this is not going to blow up in your face?" He frowned. "Frankly, you're going to hurt a lot of people, Ronan. I'm surprised you can't see that."

I sighed and scrubbed my face.

"I didn't mean to hide my family or who I am," I confessed. "It was just nice to be liked for me for a change. Just me. It felt good to be Ronan." I sighed.

"So basically, it's not that you didn't want her to meet us, but rather us meet her? You wanted to keep her to yourself for a while?"

"Yes," I said. "In a nutshell."

"Better ways of handling it, my brother. That skank you were seeing really messed you up, didn't she?"

I didn't answer, and he reached behind him and shut the door. "You never told me what she did. I want to know."

I knew he was serious and wouldn't leave until I told him.

"I met her at a fund raiser I went to with Dad. She was gorgeous, funny, and sexy."

"Until you got to know her," Liam stated.

"I know none of you liked her." I laughed dryly. "That should have been my first clue. I thought you were all wrong. I thought Paul and Jeremy were jealous."

"She was an expert manipulator."

"I figured that out too late. I only saw what she wanted me to see. I thought I had found the one."

"What happened, Ronan? It seemed one day you were together, then suddenly you broke up, and you retreated and hid away."

"I found out everything she told me was a lie. She was using me. Using our family name. She wanted my connections and my money, not me. I believe her words were '*I don't even like you. You're too much. Too loud. Too—too everything. Embarrassing.*'"

"I'd take that from the dubious source it came from and forget it."

I nodded in silence.

"Did this have something to do with Dave?"

Dave Meadows had been a friend all through university. He'd hung out with the three of us triplets, but he and I were close. He'd known how I'd felt about Loni.

Finding them in bed together had been the biggest betrayal of the entire fucked-up situation.

I didn't meet Liam's eyes. "Turns out, he wasn't as good a friend as I thought either. He liked and hated the fact that I came from money. Liked it because I was generous and he took advantage of that fact, and hated it because he resented me for it. He and Loni planned and schemed behind my back." I laughed again, the sound bitter. "Loni planned on my bankrolling her business idea. Dave would ride along on her coattails. They'd suck me dry and disappear."

"How did you find out?"

"She was at my place all the time—we were basically living together. Loni couldn't find her bank card one morning, and I was running late. I gave her mine and told her to take what she needed. She gave it back and paid me the hundred bucks a day later. I tucked the cash and the card into the drawer and never thought about it again. I always use my credit card, rarely the debit since I like the cash back thing."

"We all do." Liam chuckled. "Dad drummed that into our heads. 'Free money,' he'd say."

I nodded. "A couple weeks later, I got a call from the bank manager, saying he'd been trying to get a hold of me. There was some weird activity on my account. A lot of cash withdrawals. He told me he'd left several voice mails and left messages with my wife. I told him I didn't have a wife. Loni had been deleting the voice mails at home and intercepting the calls." I sucked in a deep breath. "She had the password to the account and changed my cell phone number in my profile so I wouldn't get the calls. He'd gone a step further and called the office to speak directly to me."

"What a bitch," Liam snarled.

I lifted one shoulder. "I went to the condo and found her in bed with Dave. We had a huge fight, and it all came out. Her plans. Her scathing opinion of me. How useless I really was. Dave called me a few choice names."

"What did you do?"

"I punched him, threw her out, and filed charges."

"You never said a word."

I met his puzzled gaze. "I was embarrassed."

"You had no reason to be."

"My supposed best friend and the woman I thought I loved both *hated* me. Only wanted me for my money and my connections. Stole from me. And I never noticed."

"As you say, you were in love."

"No, I was in lust. And stupid."

"What happened to the charges?"

"She paid back some of the money and left town. So did Dave. I dropped the charges. I wasn't going to get money out of a stone, and I just wanted to move past it."

"She might do it again."

"Ah, well, I did tell one person about what happened. At least part of it."

"Who?"

"Reid. He hacked in to her personal profile and is still tracking her in the background."

"I see."

"She's working at a casino in Alberta. Alone. I have no idea where Dave is, and I don't care. Without me, they had nothing together."

"I'm sorry you went through that. I'm even more sorry that you never told us, and that you went through that alone." He shook his head. "Don't ever do that again, do you understand? We all love you, Ronan. We're here. For you. You need to understand that." He jabbed the top of the desk with his finger. "Never again."

I was surprised by his vehemence. "Got it."

He was quiet.

"So, by not telling Beth who you are, you felt what— protected? You were making sure she wasn't like Loni?"

"To be honest, I never compared them. Beth is so different. But I liked just being Ronan with her." I stared at the top of my desk, the plans covering the surface, files open and waiting for my attention. "But you're right. I have to tell her and hope she'll understand and forgive me. And then I'll bring her out to meet Mom and Dad if she does." I paused. "Just Mom and Dad and my siblings. I don't want to scare her."

He smiled wide, his eyes crinkling. "I can understand. But you need to do it soon."

"I will. This weekend."

"Ronan," he began. "I know you feel a responsibility toward Paul and Jeremy. You've always been the watcher. The peacemaker. I know how often you put aside your own wants and likes for them. Ava sees it, so do I." He paused. "Mom and Dad see it as well—to a point. But I know. It's okay for you to have something they don't. To keep part of your life just for you. We all need that. But don't hide who you are because of what that woman did. She was the exception, not the rule." He met my eyes. "You deserve to be happy. If Beth makes you happy, grab it."

"She does. I feel differently when I'm with her."

"Then later we're going to sit down and you're going to tell me all about her. Deal?"

The thought of sharing my feelings about Beth made me smile. "Yeah, deal."

He stood. "And remember, I'm here if you need me. Anytime."

"Thanks, Liam. But I'm still giving Ava shit for telling you."

"You do what you gotta do, little bro. Piss her off, though, and you'll end up in a headlock faster than you can blink."

I laughed, knowing he was right. Our sister was strong, and she didn't take any shit. Especially from us. I'd have to tell her off across the table so I could run if I had to.

"Okay, enough brother talk for now. I think it's cake time."

"Cake?" I asked.

He nodded. "Bent ordered a couple of those cakes you've been getting. It's Wanda's birthday in accounting. We're having them in the boardroom upstairs at BAM. He invited me to stay, and who am I to turn down cake?"

That was news, but I was pleased. It meant extra money for Beth. We walked out of the office, meeting up with Paul and Jeremy and my dad. He grinned, throwing his arms open wide.

"Me and my boys!" He clapped Liam on the shoulder. "I didn't know you were here!"

"I was talking to Bent, then came to see Ronan."

Dad frowned. "Everything okay?" he asked, his eyes darting between us.

"Everything is good," Liam assured him. "I hear there's cake upstairs."

"The best cake in the world," I added.

"It's pretty damn awesome," Dad agreed.

Paul pushed the elevator button, and we stepped in.

"Hope this can hold us all," Liam quipped.

"No one move," Paul deadpanned, pushing Jeremy. Jeremy, in turn, jostled Liam, who pulled at me good-naturedly. We were all laughing as we filed out of the elevator, my dad leading the way.

I stopped laughing at the sudden sound of a startled gasp. It was familiar, and I turned my head, meeting the dark, shocked eyes of Beth. She stared at us, realization dawning on her face. She paled as the secret I'd been hiding unfolded in front of her. She whispered my name, her breathing harsh.

"Ronan?"

I stepped toward her, knowing it was too late. "Beth," I pleaded quietly. "I can explain."

She looked around, her eyes widening more as they landed on the picture on the wall of Bentley Ridge, Aiden Callaghan, and Maddox Riley. BAM. Her gaze flew to my dad, who was watching us closely, and she instantly saw the connection.

I moved closer. "Please," I murmured, holding out my hand. "Come with me."

She shook her head, pressing the elevator button repeatedly.

"Don't." I stepped closer.

Her hand flew up, and I stopped.

She got in the elevator, her expression devastated. Her tormented eyes, filled with tears, tears I had caused, were the last thing I saw before the doors closed.

I hung my head, defeated.

I had left it too late, and now I had lost her.

CHAPTER FIFTEEN
BETH

I breathed in the scent of summer approaching. The storm yesterday had cleared the air, and as I walked along the street, I smiled at the blooms starting to appear on the flowers, the new green leaves in the trees. Even with the trace of the traffic and the city, underneath was the aroma of the new season approaching. I felt different these days. Lighter. Happier. And I knew why.

Ronan.

He had somehow become incredibly important to me. A part of my life. We spoke on the phone, and he texted regularly. We saw each other whenever we could, whether he picked me up and drove me home after work, hung out with me while I baked cakes, played with Evan and Lucy, any and all of it was great. He was open and honest. Affectionate. When we were alone, he showed his feelings openly, his lovemaking thorough and passionate. I worried about him getting enough sleep with the odd hours we were keeping, but he assured me he was fine. Paige liked him, Lucy adored him, and to Evan, he was a big brother. He had somehow lit a fire in Evan, who was now faithfully doing the exercises Ronan showed him. It was as if Ronan had given him back his hope.

Even though it had only been a matter of weeks, Ronan had influenced all of us. I stopped at the corner, waiting for the traffic light to change as I thought about him with a smile.

I was falling in love with him.

I huffed a small impatient sigh when those words hit me. I hadn't planned on it or wanted it to happen, but it did.

I crossed the street, one person among the crowd, still lost in thought. There was so much I still didn't know about him. I had the basics. His name, birthday, favorite color, favorite food. I knew he had four siblings and his parents were alive. He worked in the construction field. Somehow, though, whenever the topic turned personal, he became evasive. He was good at distraction. Kissing me until I forgot what I had asked. Teasing me until I laughed and he changed the subject. I was determined to find out more about his family. More about him. My feelings were already strong, and I needed to know we were on the same wavelength and for him to know he could trust me and tell me anything.

I walked into Nifty Fifty, hoping to get a cup of coffee and a sandwich. It had been a busy morning with class, and I had a project due. I wanted to grab something to eat on the way to the library, then I would start back to work. My boss Mike looked up, relief flashing across his face when he saw me. My heart sank, worried he was going to ask me to cover a shift for someone who hadn't shown up, and I hated the fact that I was going to have to say no. I needed to get this project done.

He smiled. "Just the girl I need."

I shook my head. "Mike, I—"

He laughed. "No, I don't need you to work, but I have a favor."

"What is it?" I asked, relieved.

"We got a last-minute order for two large cakes. I have no one to deliver them. I'll cover a taxi if you take them and drop them off."

"Where are they going?"

"The company is called BAM. They've ordered before. They're in the same building as the ABC Corp that has ordered a lot of your cakes. They're a few blocks away."

"I can walk them over."

He shook his head. "They ordered the big ones. Two are heavy. You can take a cab, and I'll pay your way home too. They were happy to pay the extra fees."

I laughed, the mystery of how another company had heard of the cakes explained. They must somehow be connected or a staff member had mentioned the cakes.

"I can do that. But no need for a cab home. I'm heading to the library. I'll take a sandwich in exchange. I'm starving."

"Great. I'll box them up, and you eat."

"Perfect."

———

I slipped from the cab and carefully took out the large box, grateful for the wooden board in the bottom supporting the

197

cakes. I glanced up at the structure, taking in the well-kept appearance of the building. I paused on the steps, admiring the landscaped garden starting to bloom and manicured bushes. It was nice to see in downtown Toronto. The building spoke of wealth and an understated elegance. Different from many in the area that were plain concrete edifices.

Inside, I was given directions to BAM, and I rode the elevator to the top floor. I stepped out into a welcoming area, hearing the hushed sounds of voices down the halls. I made my way to the reception desk, and the woman there looked up with a smile.

"Oh, the cakes!" she gushed. "That is wonderful."

"Would you like me to take them somewhere?"

Her phone rang, and she grimaced. "Would you mind setting them on the boardroom table?" She indicated the glassed-in room across the hall.

"No problem."

I carried in the box and slid it on the table, where a pile of plates and forks was already set up. I looked around curiously. I had no idea what BAM stood for, but there were pictures on the walls of various buildings. Large houses. An aerial view of a community of homes set by the water. I cocked my head to the side as I peered at that one. It looked familiar, but why, I wasn't sure. The boardroom held a huge wooden table, the rich oak gleaming in the light. I counted twenty chairs around the slab of wood, all upholstered and comfortable-looking. There was a large-screen TV on one end and in the corner a door that I assumed led to a private office. As I turned to leave, I spied a neat kitchen tucked to one side. It all spoke of the same understated elegance as the outside, and I wondered if

BAM was an upscale real estate firm. I would have to look it up when I got home.

A tall, silver-haired man walked in and eyed me speculatively. "Hello?" he said.

I indicated the table. "Hello. I was delivering the cakes."

A smile broke out on his face. "Ah. Great."

"Nice, um, room," I sputtered.

He chuckled. "We like it."

"Okay, well, enjoy."

"You work for the diner?"

"Um, yes. I, ah, I bake the cakes," I offered.

"Really?" he asked, sounding delighted. "They've become a favorite here. Aiden had a piece downstairs and raved, so we ordered a couple." He glanced over my shoulder. "Bent, this lovely young lady is the baker of our new favorite treat."

I turned and met the intense blue gaze of "Bent." He was tall, with broad shoulders and a severe, unsmiling expression. Both men were in their early sixties, I assumed, and wore suits I was certain cost more than what I paid for a year in rent. Bent's face changed as he smiled.

"Well hello, cake lady. I think we need to put you on retainer."

I laughed and edged toward the door. "Glad you enjoy them."

"We do." He smiled. "Thank you for bringing them."

"You're welcome."

The silver-haired man opened the door, and I stepped into the hall, waving to the woman who was still on the phone. I peeked at a few of the other pictures on the walls. I pushed the button for the elevator and waited for it. Another picture caught my attention, and I moved over to look at it as I waited. The elevator opened, drawing my attention as a group of men, all laughing and talking, filed out. I startled as I looked at the first man, his face familiar. He was an older version of Ronan. He was dressed in a crisp white shirt and dress pants, a silk tie loose around his throat. He was tall and well built. Two younger men followed, dressed in high-priced suits, their green eyes verdant, their dark hair and build eerily similar. The fourth man in the group was bigger—his shoulders wider, stockier—and slightly dangerous-looking, although he was laughing. He was dressed more casually, but his leather coat appeared expensive.

But it was the fifth man who grabbed my attention. His dark hair gleamed under the lights, the width of his shoulders, his imposing height, and the sound of his laughter easily identifying him. I gasped as I took him in.

It was Ronan. But a Ronan I never dreamed existed. He was dressed in an expensive suit, obviously custom tailored to his large form. A striped tie hung around his neck, perfectly knotted with a glittering pin holding it in place against his snowy shirt. Loafers encased his large feet, polished to a high gloss. An oversized silver watch was clasped around his wrist. His face was smooth, none of the scruff I was used to showing on his chin.

All the men looked too alike to be anything but brothers. The older man obviously their father. Even the more casually dressed one shouted money.

His name escaped my lips in a painful sound. "Ronan."

They all stopped, looking my way. When he saw me, Ronan's face drained of color, and his eyes grew round.

He stepped forward, and I pushed at the elevator button as my breathing picked up in my panic.

"Beth," he pleaded quietly. "I can explain."

I looked at the picture behind him.

BAM.

Bentley Ridge, Aiden Callaghan, Maddox Riley, it read under the frame.

Callaghan.

Ronan's father. He was part of this wealthy company. From the looks of it, the entire family was.

I looked at him again. Construction workers didn't dress in three-thousand-dollar suits. They didn't work in fancy offices and wear watches that would pay for a car.

He'd been hiding his identity.

I felt the flicker of shame and anxiety when the obvious conclusion as to why became apparent.

A sense of déjà vu hit me. He was hiding *me.* I wasn't good enough for him. Hurt and betrayal rolled through me.

He moved closer. "Please," he murmured, holding out his hand. "Come with me."

I shook my head, unable to talk, only needing to get away.

He stepped closer.

"Don't."

My hand flew up, and he stopped, his eyes beseeching. The other men stared at us, the one wearing the leather jacket shaking his head and looking upset.

I stumbled into the elevator, unable to think clearly. To process what was happening. Tears filled my eyes as pain lanced through my chest. I met his pleading gaze as the door shut.

I had been fooled again.

I hung my head, letting the tears fall.

I ran across the lobby, pushing open the door. I could barely see the steps through my tears, but I made it down, and for a moment, I stood, confused. I had to go to the library—I had work to do. But I wanted to go home. Lock myself in my room and figure this out before Evan got home.

Oh God, *Evan*. How was I going to tell him? It would break his heart.

With a sob, I turned to the right, heading toward the house. I needed time to think, so I would walk. I'd go in through the side door so Paige didn't see me, and by the time she did, I would be calmer.

Except the sound of running footsteps and my name being shouted came from behind me. I began to hurry, trying to rush away from that voice. *His voice.*

A large hand closed around my elbow, forcing me to stop.

"Beth. Little bird, *please*."

I spun, jerking my arm from his touch. "Don't call me that," I snarled. "Don't you ever call me that again. I don't want to talk to you, Ronan Callaghan. If that's even your real name," I spat.

"It is."

"It's the only thing that was real, wasn't it?"

"No. Everything was real," he insisted, his voice sounding thick and odd.

"Oh. Really?" I looked at him, blinking away the tears, ignoring the looks we were getting.

"So, you're a construction worker?" I indicated his clothing. "Dressed like that?"

"I design buildings."

"At your father's company."

"No. I work for ABC, not BAM. Well, not directly."

I rolled my eyes. "Trying to figure out the lies, Ronan?"

He stepped closer. "Beth, come with me. I'll tell you everything. Answer any question you want."

"As if I could believe you?"

"Please," he murmured. "I'm begging you. I'm so sorry."

"Sorry because you got caught, you mean."

"No. I was going to tell you. To explain. Give me a chance."

I laughed, wiping my cheeks. "So you can lie some more?" I indicated the building behind us. "How are you going to explain me to your rich family, Ronan? Your little piece on the side? A joke?" I looked at him, suddenly feeling ill thinking of the odd times he would appear. "Oh God, you're not married, are you? Was that your little fuck pad you took me to?"

"No!" He wrapped his hands around my upper arms. "Jesus, *no*, I'm not married. That is my condo." He looked horrified. "I'm not hiding you away. *Please*, I need to explain it to you."

I stepped back and shook off his hold. "There is nothing you can say to explain this away. You had plenty of opportunities to tell me. That night at your condo, you could have said something. I asked you questions—you could have told me! Any of the times we were alone making cakes. You've been lying to me for weeks. Worst of all, I let you. I should have pushed, but I was waiting for you to trust me." I wiped my face. "My brother adores you, and you've been lying to him too." A sob caught in my throat. "Now I have to go home and tell him the person I let into our home was nothing but a liar. Someone using us for whatever the hell reason." I clapped my hand over my mouth. "I slept with you. And you were lying about your life the whole time."

"I wasn't using you. I swear to God, everything I told you about how I was feeling, every touch, was real." He lifted his arm, his hand shaking. "I'm falling in love with you, Beth. I need you in my life. Please come with me, and we can talk."

"You're falling in love with me?" I laughed, the sound brittle. "Another nice lie. Good try, Ronan, but I'm not buying it. You think you can take me somewhere, lie some more, fill my head with your sweet words and I'll fall for them again? That I'll fuck you again?"

He narrowed his eyes. "It wasn't fucking. Don't say that."

"Don't bother denying it." I exhaled hard, my chest aching with the need to scream. "I have nothing else to say to you but this. Leave me alone. Don't come to the house. To the diner. Lose my number. I don't ever want to see you again."

I turned and hurried away. At the corner, I looked back. He was standing in the same place, his head hanging down, his shoulders dropped. I felt a pang in my chest and something stirred inside me, but I ignored it.

He meant nothing.

I just had to keep reminding myself of that.

CHAPTER SIXTEEN
BETH

I knew there was no point in going to the library. I walked home in a daze, my thoughts on a continuous loop in my head. I had been such a fool. Again. I had fallen for Ronan's act. The sweet, helpful guy. Just the average Joe.

Except he was anything but.

I slipped in the side door, hoping Paige would be on the phone, but she was coming down the hall, looking surprised to see me.

"I thought you were heading to the library?" she asked, a laundry basket perched on her hip.

My sunglasses hid my eyes, and I cleared my throat before I spoke, hoping my voice sounded normal.

"I got a wicked headache. I'm going to lie down for a while," I croaked, but it was easily explained by the headache pain. Paige seemed to buy it anyway.

"Oh shit, I'm sorry. Want a cup of tea or something?"

"No, just some quiet and dark."

"You take all the time you need. We'll have an easy supper—unless you're seeing Ronan later?"

Hearing his name made my heart lurch. "No," I managed to get out.

"Okay. Go rest. I'll make sure Evan is doing his homework." She shooed me downstairs, and I shut the door behind me, dropping my bag and burying my face into my hands. I summoned my strength and stumbled to the bed, falling in. The scent of Ronan hit me as I rolled—his masculine and rich cologne clinging to the sheets.

I buried my face into the linens and let the tears come. Ronan would never lie beside me again. I would never feel his strong body moving with mine, hear his whispered words of adoration. Feel his protective embrace or listen to the steady beat of his heart under my ear as I fell asleep.

It had all been a lie—one I'd fallen for, hook, line, and sinker. And now I had to start again.

———

I woke up, my eyes burning and dry. I washed my face and used some Visine to clear the red still lingering in my eyes. I couldn't do anything about the weariness I could see in my face, but I hoped it would be explained by the headache. I brushed my hair, trying not to think about the fact that Ronan loved to run his fingers through my curls. I was surprised to find it was past seven and I had slept for four hours.

It was quiet upstairs. Paige was on the phone, and she waved as I peeked around the corner then went to check on Evan. He was in his room, Lucy sitting beside him. They were building something, using the kits Ronan had brought over. I wasn't sure how I was going to tell Evan he had to pack them up so they could be returned, but I decided not to say anything just yet. Given what I had seen today, Ronan could easily afford to replace any amount of Lego he wanted.

"Hey, munchkins," I said, trying to sound cheerful.

They looked up, happy to see me, but Evan frowned. "You okay, Beth? Paige said you were sick."

I ruffled his hair. "Just a headache. Too much time on the computer and poring over books. It's better."

"You look, um, tired."

Tired, I could work with. I was glad he hadn't identified the real reason for my pale face and red eyes. "Headaches wear me out. I'll be good as gold in the morning. Did you have supper?"

He nodded, and Lucy piped up. "Grill cheese!"

"Mmm," I hummed.

"You gonna eat?" asked Evan, looking at me far too closely.

"Yep. I'm starving," I fibbed. "You guys keep building."

He nodded. "I can hardly wait to show Ronan. I combined three sets and made something totally new. He is gonna freak out."

My heart lurched. "Ah, he got called out of town," I lied again. "He won't be back until next week."

"Oh." He frowned then shrugged. "You can take a picture and send it to him, right?"

I swallowed and stood. "Sure."

That satisfied him. "He'll still like it. I might have to tell him everything I did, so let me know before you send the text."

"I'll do that."

In the kitchen, I looked at the plate in the refrigerator, knowing I wouldn't be able to eat the grilled cheese Paige had ready for me to cook. I wasn't sure it would stay down. She came into the kitchen, looking at me critically.

"Headache still there?"

"A bit."

"I was going to go grab some milk at the corner store. Want me to get you anything?"

"Shit, I forgot." I was supposed to pick up milk earlier.

"No biggie."

"I'll go. The fresh air will do me good."

And it would get me away from Paige's watchful gaze. She knew me too well, and I wasn't up to talking to her about what happened. I hadn't assimilated it all yet.

"Okay. I'll give Lucy her bath. Maybe you'll feel like eating when you get home."

I forced a smile. "I'm sure I will."

———

The next night, I wiped down the last table. The diner had been busy, which I was grateful for. I had avoided Paige the night before, talking to Evan and helping him with his homework. While she was putting Lucy to bed, I slipped downstairs and shut my door, and she didn't bother me at all, no doubt thinking I had gone back to bed.

I sat up most of the night, going through everything in my head. All the signs I had missed. The evasion of my questions. Ronan's lack of sharing about his job or the company he worked for. I had seen the signs and ignored them. Paige had questioned his clothes and the car he drove. I felt like a fool as I looked up the make on the internet and saw the price tab. He always had lots of money in his wallet. I looked up BAM, shocked at how easily I had been fooled. Ronan's family was one of the wealthiest in the city. The company he said he worked for, ABC, was owned by BAM. There was a picture of the business partners online. Ronan was one-third of a set of triplets. He stood beside his brothers, and I could easily pick him out. He was slightly taller and broader than the other two, and even in my anger, I could see a difference in his expression. He was more serious-looking than the other two. The rest of the company varied in ages, but I guessed them all between mid-twenties and early thirties. The article talked about the vast talent of the group and their already impressive resumé of holdings and businesses.

What else could one expect from the offspring of the BAM boys? the article stated.

I looked at the group picture, then like a martyr, scrolled through other pictures I found on the web. I recognized the silver-haired man I had seen as Maddox Riley and the stern-looking one as Bentley Ridge. I had no problem picking out Ronan's dad. He was large and imposing, usually standing next to Bentley in all the pictures. Unable to help myself, I read their history and all about the company. It was fascinating, and I found myself wishing I had heard it directly from Ronan. Tears coursed down my face as I looked at some pictures of him. There were surprisingly few. He had told me once he wasn't big on social media. He had no Facebook, Instagram, or Twitter accounts. The pictures I found were related to the company and a few of him with his parents or business partners at charity functions. I couldn't help but notice he was always a step or two away from the group, and I wondered why, then shook my head. It was none of my business anymore.

I took a deep breath to clear my thoughts, wiping the errant tear that ran down my cheek. I needed to stop thinking about him. I finished tidying up and headed to the kitchen. We had been especially busy with cake sales in the diner, and I needed to make some to keep up with demand. I tried not to think about the fact that the past few weeks Ronan had been with me while I made them, making the process easier and fun. There would be no singing helper tonight, no drugging kisses, and no slumbering car ride home with a large hand wrapped around mine.

Sighing, I got to work, measuring, mixing, and baking. I slid the first batch into the oven and prepped the second batch. I checked the time, shaking my head. I was slow tonight, and I would be here late. I went to the front and checked the book where Mike kept the outside cake orders. Unable to help myself, I checked the older ones, seeing the big burst in sales had been because of Ronan. ABC Corp and BAM had bought a lot of cakes the past few weeks, although there were a few other orders. There was an order from ABC for Friday, and I assumed Ronan hadn't gotten around to canceling it yet, but I was sure he would. Except his love of the cakes was real, and perhaps he still planned on ordering them. I shut the book, half tempted to tell Mike the cakes weren't available to anyone at ABC, but I resisted. The extra money let me buy Evan new sneakers and jeans. He was outgrowing his pants and shoes fast these days, and I didn't want him to wear ill-fitting clothes. I knew he already had enough to contend with at school without giving the kids more ammunition.

It was past two when I left the diner. It was cool with a slight drizzle outside, and I shivered. Outside, a car waited, its engine running. For a moment, my heart was in my throat, thinking it was Ronan, but an older man climbed out of the driver's seat.

"Beth Jones?"

"Yes?" I responded apprehensively.

"I'm Wayne. I was hired to drive you home."

"Hired?" Suspicion clouded my mind. "By whom?"

"Mike Chalmers—your boss. Did he forget to tell you? He assured me he had texted you."

I checked my phone, scrolling through messages. Sure enough, a text had come through a few hours ago from Mike that I had missed, telling me from now on I would get driven home on any night I stayed late to bake cakes and my driver's name was Wayne. Why he had decided this, I had no idea, and I shook off my doubt—I was too tired to question it tonight.

"Great," I said, smiling as he opened the back door. I slid into the warm car gratefully.

"Have you been waiting long?" I asked as he pulled away from the curb.

"I got here about one. I saw the lights on, so I knew you were there."

"I'm sorry I kept you waiting. I had more cakes to make than usual."

He waved off my concern. "I have coffee and puzzles. I'm used to it. I'll give you my cell number, and you can call me tomorrow about half an hour before you're ready to go."

I hummed in agreement and watched as the streetlights flashed through the windows. I tucked my coat collar a little closer, fighting back the wave of disappointment. Of course Ronan wouldn't be here to drive me home. I told him to stay away. That was what I wanted.

I ignored the little voice of disappointment in my head that questioned my decision.

It was Friday morning before Paige confronted me. Evan had left, Lucy was off to day care, and Paige sat across from me. "What's going on?" she asked, her blue eyes concerned. "Don't tell me you're busy or studying too hard. Something is up."

I looked at the table and my hands that seemed to tremble all the time. "Ronan," I began, my voice cracking. I cleared my throat. "We're done."

She reached across the table and covered my hands. "Oh, sweetie. What happened?"

"He lied."

"About?"

"Everything." With a sigh, I told her what happened. By the end of my short story, she was shaking her head.

"He seemed so honest. So open."

I laughed. "I know. And the bottom line is, I should have pushed more. Made him talk to me. But I let him divert my attention. I was nothing but a distraction."

"Did he say that?"

"No. But it reeks of Carson. Rich family. Not being good enough," I confessed.

"He never came across that way. But I'm sorry he hurt you."

I wiped at the tears that kept coming, no matter how hard I tried to stop them.

"You miss him."

"It doesn't matter. I'll get over it."

"He meant something to you."

"Yes, he did. But if I can't trust him, it means nothing."

"You don't want to give him a chance to explain?"

"I'm not sure. I need time."

"I get that. But think about it, Beth. You both seemed so happy. I can't believe that wasn't real—for either of you."

"That's why it hurts so much," I admitted.

She stood and hugged me. "I know. I'm here if you need me. You should talk about it. About him. It might help."

"Maybe in a couple of days."

"Okay. I'm here anytime."

I smiled. "Thanks."

"Have you told Evan?"

"I will on Sunday. He is going to be upset. Lucy will too."

She tilted her head, studying me. "Funny how quickly we all fell for him."

"Yeah, he had that effect."

She frowned and nodded. "Yes, he did."

———

Evan looked confused. "You broke up?"

I nodded, tamping down my reaction. I was shocked how emotional I was still. I couldn't stop thinking about Ronan. All the wonderful things he did. His touch. His laugh. The way he would watch me. His terrible, off-key but enthusiastic singing voice.

"It just didn't work out, Evan."

"I liked him."

"I know. He liked you a lot."

"You too," he insisted. "He told me how much he liked you. Did you have a fight? Maybe you could just say sorry and it would be okay?"

My heart ached, and I felt the anger I had been looking for flare a little. I hated the fact that Evan was going to hurt now as well.

"It's more complicated than that. I'm sorry."

He looked down, and I was shocked to see tears in his eyes when he glanced back up. "Are you okay, Beth?"

"I will be."

"I guess I have to give back his Lego stuff. I'll pack them up." He sighed. "He'll never see what I made with them."

"I will take them to his office next week. You can use them for a few more days."

"Maybe—if it's okay—maybe you can take a picture? He might want to see it."

I ruffled his hair and bent to kiss his forehead. "Sure, I can do that."

I couldn't promise him Ronan would look at it. But if it made Evan happy, I would do that for him.

"Want to go for ice cream later?" I asked.

He shook his head, his voice subdued. "Maybe another time."

"Okay." I paused at his bedroom room. "Hey, Evan. It's going to be fine. We were good before, and we'll be good again."

He nodded, offering me a small smile before he turned away.

I had a feeling neither of us believed those words.

CHAPTER SEVENTEEN
BETH

By the following Saturday, I was dragging my ass. I was drained. I couldn't sleep, and my appetite was nonexistent. I was tired of trying to pretend everything was okay at home. Evan was withdrawn and had stopped his exercises. More than once, I had heard Lucy ask Paige if Ronan was coming back yet. Paige herself looked sad. I felt sad. Depressed. Everything seemed to remind me of him. Even the diner. I couldn't escape it. Despite my anger and the pain he caused me, every time the bell would ring over the door later in the evening, I would look up, half hoping it would be Ronan striding in. I hadn't heard from him at all, and there had been no reaction to the Lego sets being sent back. Paige had taken them, not saying a word after she dropped them off except a shake of her head when I asked if she had seen Ronan.

Surprisingly, the cake orders hadn't stopped. I considered refusing to make them, then decided that would be foolish. Evan needed things, and the income helped me supply them.

Mike told me his wife insisted on the rides home any night I stayed so late to make cakes, and I accepted his explanation, too weary to question the sudden interest in my safety.

I was picking up an order when I heard the bell over the door. I was grateful I only had an hour left in my shift. As I walked out of the kitchen, I saw a couple of women seated in the booth where Ronan always sat, and I quelled the silly notion of telling them to move. Lots of people sat in that booth. I carried the loaded plates to the table waiting for them, filled their coffees, then, with a deep breath, walked to the booth.

"Welcome to Nifty Fifty. May I get you something to drink?"

One woman glanced up, observing me carefully. She was small with bright-blue eyes and a warm smile. "Coffee, please. For both of us. Cream as well."

She looked familiar, but I couldn't place her. I got the coffees and carried them to the table. The other woman at the table looked up, and I froze.

The cup I was holding paused midair as I stared at the other woman, who was regarding me steadily. Her hair was a rich brown with purple highlights. I judged her to be average height and slim. She had unusual eyes and delicate features, but her smile was the same as Ronan's. It had to be his sister.

She reached up, taking the coffee cup from my hand. "I'll take that," she murmured.

"What do you want?" I asked.

"I'll have a burger," she said.

"I don't think she meant our order, Ava," the other woman murmured.

"That is *all* I want," I responded. "Your food order."

She pursed her lips. "I'll have the house salad. Ava will have the burger. We'll share the fries."

Ava huffed. "I don't think so, Gracie. You'll eat them all. We'll each have an order."

Gracie shrugged. "Fine." She met my gaze. "And ten minutes of your time, please."

"That isn't happening. I have no desire to hear whatever Ronan sent you to tell me."

They shook their heads. "Ronan has no idea we're here."

"He'd be furious if he did," Ava added.

Gracie looked at me beseechingly. "Please, Beth. Ten minutes of your time. Then if you want, we'll leave and never bother you again."

"Give me one reason why."

Ava leaned close. "If you ever had feelings for my brother, please."

Something in her voice stopped me. My chest felt strangely tight. "Is Ronan all right?"

"Please," she repeated.

"I'm off in an hour."

She nodded. "We'll eat and wait."

"Fine."

I hurried away, wondering what they were going to tell me.

And why I wanted to hear it.

I carried over a cup of coffee and sat beside Gracie. She was talking on her phone but hung up as I sat down.

"Everything okay at home?" Ava asked with a smirk.

"Jaxson told me to take my time." Gracie smiled at me. "He's at home with our baby girl. I wanted to make sure they were doing all right."

Ava snorted. "I'm sure he was eager to kick you out of the house so he'd have Kylie to himself."

Gracie laughed but didn't deny it. "She is a bit of a daddy's girl," she murmured. She turned to me and held out her hand. "I think we should start with proper introductions. I'm Gracie Richards—Ronan's cousin."

Ava extended her hand across the table. "I'm Ava Callaghan. Ronan's sister."

I shook them both. "I'm Beth Jones."

For a moment, there was silence, so I cleared my throat. "Your ten minutes is going to go fast if you don't say anything."

Ava sighed and flipped her hair over her shoulder. "Ronan is my younger brother. He's part of a set of triplets."

I waited, lifting my eyebrow.

"He's complex and smart. He's been struggling lately and…" She huffed. "Okay, he's been a jackass about how he handled this, all right?"

"Handled what exactly?"

"You. Him. Having a relationship. Shit," she muttered. "I'm usually a far better speaker." She looked at Gracie, who smiled and turned to face me.

"Ronan," she began, "he's the oldest of the three boys. He's always been the leader. The peacemaker. He looked out for the other two all the time. The three of them are jokesters, but Ronan has a deeper sense of..." She paused, looking for a word.

"Responsibility," I finished for her.

"Yes," she agreed. "He always made sure the other two were happier."

"Even if it meant he wasn't," I stated.

They looked at me. "How did you know that?" Ava asked.

I shrugged. "His mannerisms. He was shocked when I asked him how he wanted his eggs. He was thrilled to pick his favorite ice cream—little things most people wouldn't think of or notice, I noticed about him."

Gracie nodded. "Yes. That's Ronan."

"It doesn't explain anything," I pointed out.

She sighed. "Give me a minute." She paused. "The three boys have always been incredibly close. I think, at times, Ronan felt lost in the shuffle. He was always part of a group. One of the triplets. He rarely was just Ronan. But when he met you, that was what he got to be. Just Ronan."

"So, he hid his identity?" I laughed dryly. "Convenient. More like he didn't tell anyone about me because of who I am."

Gracie frowned. "What do you mean?"

"I'm nobody. A student struggling to pay her bills. To look after her brother. I have no place in the world Ronan inhabits. He knew that, so he let me think he was just a normal guy. He didn't want his family to know about me."

"You're wrong," Ava said. "I know it looks that way, but it isn't. You let him be just a regular guy." She held up her hand. "I'm not saying what he did wasn't wrong, or pretty stupid, but the fact is, I think he was more Ronan when he was with you than ever."

Gracie chimed in. "He shouldn't have hidden his family, but Ronan wasn't ashamed of you. Why would he be? You're strong and independent. He likes that."

Ava spoke. "Our aunt Emmy put herself through school as a waitress and baking scones for a coffee shop. My mom and her sister worked their way through school with odd jobs and tight budgets. The three of them were friends. They pooled clothing, food, and resources to get by. Uncle Bentley—one of the wealthiest men in the city—met Emmy and fell for her. Because she was real. My dad and mom fell in love for the same reason. Dee and Maddox were from two different worlds, but they found what they needed with each other. Money doesn't dictate where your heart lies."

"I'm grateful for the family history lesson, but what does that have to do with Ronan lying to me?" I asked. "If he was so proud of me, why wouldn't he tell me who his family was?"

Ava smiled. "Simple. It wasn't you he was hiding. It was us. He didn't want to share *you*. For the first time in his life, he put what he wanted above everyone else."

I wanted to believe her, but I couldn't.

"Why are you here?"

Ava leaned close. "Paul and Jeremy—the other two-thirds of the triplets—met a set of twins and started dating them. Ronan was left out of the loop for the first time in his life. He struggled with it. Everything he'd known all his life had changed. It wasn't the three of them anymore. He was on his own, and they were together."

"I'm sure that was hard for him."

A frown crossed her face. "Something happened to him last year. Liam knows more about it than I do. It involved a woman who wanted him only for his money and his best friend who betrayed him, so I think we can all guess what it was. Neither of them is in his life anymore. It affected him deeply. We were all worried about him."

I felt the stirrings of sympathy. "I see."

"But as much as those things affected him, they didn't hit him as hard as you walking away from him did. He's devastated. I've never seen him like this."

I swallowed. "Like what?"

"Serious. Sad. Cut off," Ava whispered. "He isn't Ronan. He goes through the motions, but he isn't there. His heart is missing."

"Are you sure that is because of me?"

Gracie smiled sadly. "When he broke up with Loni, he refused to talk about her. He wanted to put her in the past. But this time, it's entirely different. It's as if he doesn't want to forget you. He wants to relive every moment he had with you. Well, the ones he can share." She waggled her eyebrows, the gesture reminding me so much of Ronan, I had to smile. "I know you think we don't know about you, Beth, but since you walked away, you are all he talks about. How amazing you are. How much you mean to him. How you saw him for *him*. For Ronan. How much he misses you. Misses Evan. He beats himself up all the time about not being honest with you. He knows he handled it badly."

"He talks about me?" I asked, shocked. "To you?"

Ava laughed. "To Gracie, to me. To our brothers—especially Liam. To our parents. He admits he was stupid. He shocked us all when he said why he didn't tell you. Why he hid his identity from you. He admitted he liked just being Ronan. *Beth's* Ronan and not Ronan Callaghan." She met my gaze. "He is suffering more losing you than he did when Loni betrayed him or he was trying to find his place when Paul and Jeremy met their girls and he was on his own."

I blinked, trying to take it all in. I meant that much to him?

Was it possible?

Gracie patted my hand. "You mean more to him than you know. He is truly lost without you."

I realized I must have spoken out loud.

"We've only been seeing each other a few weeks."

Ava shrugged. "Fast in my family isn't unusual. Bentley said he knew he was going to marry Emmy not long after he met her. My mom said she knew my dad was the one the first day she met him." She grinned. "It took him a little longer to come to the same conclusion." Then she tilted her chin at Gracie. "She married her boss after seeing him secretly for months. They eloped, and we all found out on Christmas Day." She winked. "Talk about drama."

I tried not to laugh, but a smile made my lips quirk.

"I see."

"Talk to him, Beth. Please. Let him explain. If you can't forgive him—well, dammit, you have to. He's in love with you," Gracie insisted. "And I can't stand to see him so unhappy."

I gaped at Gracie. "In love?"

"I know him. He is. He told me once that being loved for yourself would be the most wonderful thing he could imagine. You did that for him. He wants you. He wants to be part of your life."

"He hasn't reached out."

"He's respecting your wishes. Trying to give you space. But he's still around."

I pursed my lips. "The car driving me home is from him, isn't it?"

"Yes."

"And the tips I keep finding in my jar?"

"He sends someone over every day to buy lunch and bring cake to the office. He wants to take care of you, and it's the only way he can right now." Ava paused. "He wants to look after you so much."

"I don't need to be looked after."

Gracie laughed. "We all need to be looked after, one way or another. Let's face it. Ronan fucked up. He can't drive you home, so the car was the only way he could make sure you were safe. He can't eat here, so he feeds others and makes sure you are rewarded. He is desperate to talk to you but terrified you'll refuse and send him away. He's trying to give you space. He's hoping you'll let him talk to you. But I am worried about him. He's in pain, and I can't help him. His hope is fading. That's why we came."

"To get me to talk to him."

"Yes."

I sighed. "I have to think about it."

They looked disappointed, but neither of them argued. Ava wrote a number on the back of a business card. "This is my cell. If you call me, I'll get you to Ronan. He's out in Port Albany at his house."

I frowned. "Port Albany? Where he took us for a picnic?"

"Yes. Our family owns that land. He has a house there." She hesitated before speaking again. "He was going to move there permanently until he met you. He changed his mind because he wanted to be close to you. But he's been staying there because he can't stand to be in Toronto and not be with you."

I took the card she offered me. I looked at the logo on the front.

"ABC Corp. You all work there. Together."

"Some of us." Gracie patted my hand. "If you move forward with Ronan, there are lots of us. We're a huge, blended family. You might wish Ronan kept us a secret forever."

I smiled sadly and stood. Evan always wanted a big family. He thought it would be cool.

I slipped the card into my pocket. "Whatever happens, I'm glad Ronan has you," I said with a smile. "He is very lucky to have two women standing up for him."

Ava met my gaze. "He would rather have you."

I picked up my cup and headed back to the kitchen. I had no words to offer her.

CHAPTER EIGHTEEN
BETH

The kids were in bed, and Paige and I lounged on the sofa with a bottle of wine and a bucket of popcorn. I chewed the buttery goodness, licking the salt off my fingers.

"So, they were there without Ronan knowing?" she asked.

"That's what they said."

"I assume his best friend slept with the other girl."

"Reading between the lines, yes."

"Were they nice?"

I sipped my wine and nibbled on more popcorn. "Yes, they were."

"Did you believe them?"

I sighed. "They had no reason to lie to me. Although, neither did Ronan, so I have no idea."

"So, they said Ronan lied because he wanted to keep you to himself. Because he liked just being Ronan. A regular guy."

"In a nutshell."

"Huh." She inhaled, and I braced myself for her next words.

"If I read between the lines, I'd say since that other girl used him for his money, he decided to downplay that part of his life. Maybe it was a test—I don't know. He seemed so genuine, I can't imagine him enjoying keeping things from you. Maybe he was, as his sister and cousin said, enjoying being just one guy—not part of a trio. I remember thinking how odd it was he was unsure about his favorite kind of eggs."

"Or ice cream," I added without thinking.

"Yes!" she exclaimed.

"What are you trying to say?"

"Just playing devil's advocate here, Beth, but is it the worst thing in the world finding out your boyfriend, who is crazy about you, is rich and has a big family that is dying to meet you?"

"I don't like him for his money."

"That is a fact he will forever be sure of."

"So, you think I should forgive him?"

"I'm going to be honest. I know you weren't ready before, but I think you should talk to him. You're miserable. I've never known you to cry, and you do it all the time now. Evan is sad. Hell, even Lucy asks about him." She huffed. "I kinda miss the big lug, too." She nudged my foot. "I think you miss him terribly. It sounds as if he is pining for you. Maybe you need to talk and clear the air. Decide if you can trust him again. You can start again with no secrets."

She was right. I did miss him. More than I admitted. I missed his smile and laugh. The way it felt when he hugged me. Kissed me. I longed for his touch. To watch him inhale something I had cooked and praise it while filling his plate again.

"I'll call Ava."

Paige smiled. "Good plan." She refilled our glasses again and lifted hers in a mock toast. "To secretly rich boyfriends. Maybe your luck will rub off and I'll find one too."

We both began to laugh, and I had to admit—it felt good.

The next morning, Paige appeared in my doorway. "My God, Beth. Your ride is here."

I had called Ava the night before, and she had asked if I could go to Port Albany the next morning. She promised to arrange a driver for me, and I had assumed it would be her. Paige had encouraged me to go, saying she would take Evan and Lucy out for breakfast and they'd go to the park.

"Okay. Is it Ava or Gracie?"

She clutched my arm. "It's his brother. The non-triplet one. Heavens, he is enormous. And incredibly sexy." She fanned her face. "I want to climb him like a tree."

I followed her upstairs, where Ronan's brother waited. It was the man from that fateful day who had been with Ronan. The one who wore the leather jacket. He looked bigger than I remembered, which, as Paige said, was enormous. His broad shoulders filled the hallway, but his expression was calm and his eyes gentle. His mouth was curved into a smile as I approached.

"Hi," I said, holding out my hand. "I'm Beth."

He enclosed it in his grip, shaking it. "Hi, Beth. I'm Liam. Ronan's other brother." He winked, looking directly at Paige. "The non-triplet one."

I heard her squeak, and I tried not to laugh. There was no doubt he had heard everything she said. His eyes danced, and the smile that broke through was the equivalent of a thousand-watt bulb.

"Considering I'm a landscape architect, the tree reference was particularly pleasing." His gaze never left her face. "Climbing can be arranged. I'll make sure Beth has my cell number."

I glanced over my shoulder. Paige's face was flushed, her eyes locked on Liam.

"Okay, then," she responded. "I'll, ah, I'll be leaving now."

She turned and hurried away.

Looking back, I caught him ogling her ass, and I lifted one eyebrow in a silent question.

"Single, right?" he said quietly.

"Yes." I paused. "With a daughter."

"Lucy," he confirmed. "Ronan thinks she's adorable."

"She is."

"I'll give you my number in the car."

"Okay, then."

"Now—" he grinned "—let's get you to my idiot brother. He has no idea his miserable little existence is about to take an upswing."

"I only agreed to talk to him."

He leaned close, mischief once again dancing in his eyes. "I've got a good feeling. And, Beth? I am never wrong."

RONAN

My feet pounded on the sand, and the only sound aside from my heavy breathing was the water lapping at the shore. I headed toward the trail in the woods, the heavy overhang of the trees casting shadows, the change in temperature immediately cooling my overheated skin. I stopped by an overturned trunk, stretched, then sat down. I grabbed the water bottle from my waistband clip and drank deeply. All around me were the signs of new growth, signaling that summer was fast approaching. The trees were budding, new shoots of green peeking up through the forest floor.

I had seen Liam yesterday, walking around the complex. No doubt he was planning, mentally calculating what spots needed filling, already mapping out what bloomed when and how the gardens would all look once he was done. Every year, he added and changed, thinned out and replanted. He had flowers and plants blooming from early spring until late fall. We all helped with the maintenance, and all the women had their preferences for their own private gardens by their houses, and Liam made sure each one was met. He loved working in the dirt and spent many hours bent over the neatly laid-out landscapes. His own garden was filled with fruit trees, and there was a large vegetable patch we all took care of and had access to.

I sighed and rubbed my eyes. I had promised him I would help work on turning over the dirt in the vegetable garden later this afternoon. It would keep me busy—at least, my hands and body. My mind, however, seemed stuck in the same place, no matter how hard I tried to move forward.

I was still standing on that street, watching the hurt fill Beth's eyes. Desperate to erase it. Frozen as she walked away, refusing to listen.

Not that I blamed her.

Selfishly, I had tried playing a game, not thinking of the consequences, and I had lost. I had made her feel as if I were keeping her hidden, as if I were ashamed of her, when in fact, it was myself I was ashamed of. My actions caused her pain. I had hoped if I gave her space, she would cool down and at least let me talk to her. But my phone remained silent, and there was no attempt to reach out.

And the chickenshit I was, I never reached out to her.

I hung my head, a long exhale of air leaving my mouth. I could recall, with finite detail, the look on her face when she saw me with my father and brothers in the hall. The way the color drained from her face. How her dark eyes widened, the pain and insecurity filling them as she stared at me. The conclusions her mind made. As soon as the elevator doors closed, I ignored the shocked, curious stares of my family and headed to the stairwell, taking the steps two at a time. I caught up to her on the street, my long legs easily closing the distance as soon as I spotted her.

The agony in her eyes, the emotion in her voice, destroyed me. She was distraught, unable to process the depth of what she had discovered. What I had hidden from her. She refused to listen, thinking the very worst of me. Thinking she had meant nothing, when in fact, she had meant more than I had even realized.

After she walked away, leaving me staring after her, I had stood, frozen, unable to comprehend how my life had taken such a vast downturn in the space of only a few moments. How long I stood there, staring, hoping she would come back around the corner and let me explain, I had no idea. Liam had appeared beside me, his voice quiet.

"Come on, Ronan. Let's go."

My feet propelled me forward, but I didn't speak. I followed him to his truck, not saying a word as we headed toward Port Albany. At my house, he watched as I walked around, too edgy and upset to sit. He made coffee, sipping a cup as the one he pushed my way went cold.

Finally, he stood in front of me. "Talk. Tell me everything from the beginning."

So, I did. And since then, I hadn't shut up. I talked to my parents, my sister, my brothers. Nan and Pops. Gracie had listened to me for hours. Jaxson had shaken his head when I talked to him, offering his counsel.

"You need to tell her, Ronan. Even if it makes no difference. Even if your relationship isn't able to go forward. You need to tell her." He sighed as he rocked Kylie, his big hand running up and down her back in gentle passes. *"Don't let her think she wasn't worthy. That will eat at her the rest of her life."*

"I don't think she can forgive me," I admitted.

"It's a lot to forgive." He glanced at Gracie, the two of them sharing a look saturated in love and understanding. "But if she cares about you, if she's the kind of person you say she is, there is a chance she will. And if you care about her the way you say you do, she is worth that risk."

He smiled. "Trust me, I know about risk. But this is worth it."

My entire family now knew about Beth. And Evan. I had gone on about Paige and Lucy as well. It was as if now that I had turned on the tap, I couldn't stop the words from flowing.

I had confessed to what happened with Loni and Dave, letting my family voice their anger over the situation and their distress that I had remained silent. Paul and Jeremy had been distraught over my silence and had listened to me go on for hours, their sympathy and companionship appreciated. They wanted to help, but I told them I had to work this out on my own with Beth. They understood and offered their support. I was grateful but knew this was something I had to fix.

I scrubbed my face roughly and stood, having made a decision. Beth was off today. I had to go to see her. Beg her to let me explain. Jaxson was right. Even if she decided she couldn't trust me again. If she never wanted to see me—I had to try. I had to make sure she knew how incredible she was, how much she meant to me. I had to make sure she knew the blame rested entirely with me and she was innocent. I never meant to hide her.

She was far too special to hide.

———————

I walked in the door, weariness saturating my body. I had run a long distance, farther than I normally did. But it only cemented the fact that I couldn't outrun my demons. I had to face them. Face Beth and let the chips fall where they may.

I had to admit, that terrified me the most.

She might agree to listen, then dismiss me. Decide I wasn't worth the effort to get past the pain I had caused.

I was so lost in my thoughts, I almost missed her.

Something, some sense of not being alone, hit me, and I stopped on my way to the shower and spun on my heel to find Beth sitting in the large chair by the window. She looked small and vulnerable in the big piece of furniture. She was pale and nervous-looking, her hands twisting in an unending pattern of finger gymnastics. Her legs were crossed and tucked underneath her. How she got here, I had no idea, and I didn't really care.

She was here.

I crossed the room and dropped to the floor in front of her, our gazes locked. There were faint smudges of purple under her eyes, and her lips looked as if she'd been biting them constantly.

"I'm sorry, Beth. I'm so fucking sorry."

She offered me a shaky smile. "I thought you might ask how I got in your house, first."

"My sister?" I guessed.

"She had a hand in it. But Liam brought me here. He let me in and assured me you'd be home soon. He said you were probably out for a run."

I nodded, unable to believe she was here. Sitting in my house. "I was. I run a lot these days. It helps calm me down."

"You look tired," she whispered.

"I miss you." I dropped my head to her leg. "Fuck, little bird. I missed you so much." I started at the feel of her fingers, light and soft, running along the base of my neck and up into my damp hair. Unable to stop myself, I crowded closer to her. Wrapped my arms around her legs and waist and held her tight. She didn't pull back or push me away. For a moment, I basked in the feel of her. The rightness of being this close. I lifted my head, meeting her watery gaze.

"I want to tell you everything. I want to answer every question you have. Will you let me?" I swallowed. "Can I ask that of you, Beth?"

"Yes," she replied.

Hope, a small bubble of anticipation, pushed at my chest. "I need to have a shower. If I go do that, will you be here when I come out?"

"Yes, I'm not leaving."

I took her hands in mine and kissed the insides of her wrists. I felt the rapid pulse beat under the delicate skin, her veins faint blue lines of life that led to her heart. Her forgiving, beautiful heart.

I stood. "Promise me."

"I'll be right here."

I walked backward from the room, never breaking our gaze.

CHAPTER NINETEEN
RONAN

I rushed through my shower, pulling on a pair of sweats and a Henley, and hurried back to the living room. Beth wasn't in the chair, and panicked, I spun on my heel, only to find her standing in the kitchen. I realized I could smell the delicious aroma of breakfast, and I shook my head as I headed toward her.

"You don't have to cook."

"Liam says you haven't been eating. Your face is thin." She frowned. "I don't like it."

I slid onto the seat at the island. "I haven't been hungry," I admitted.

"You're going to eat now. You need to go grocery shopping too," she admonished.

I captured her hand as she slid a plate my way. "You'll eat with me?" She looked as if she'd lost weight as well. Her cheeks weren't as full as they normally were. I preferred them rounded and soft under my touch.

She picked up another plate. "Yes. We'll eat, then talk."

She pulled herself up onto the stool beside me, muttering about giants and chairs. I felt the first honest laugh I'd had since that awful day escape my lips. "I'll get a table and normal-sized chairs."

She pursed her lips. "Let's not get ahead of ourselves."

It was a sobering reminder that I had a long way to go. Feeling grim, I looked down at my plate, my fleeting appetite gone once again.

She put her hand on my arm and waited until I met her eyes. "It's fine, Ronan. Eat, please."

I picked up my fork because she asked me to. I knew right then I would do anything she asked, because it was her. I cut into the omelet and chewed slowly. It was full of cheese and ham, with onions and peppers added to it. I regarded her curiously.

"I had this in my fridge?"

"No. When Liam said you hadn't been eating, I asked him to stop at a store."

"It's delicious."

"Then eat it before it gets cold."

I tucked in, watching as she nibbled on toast and pushed a small piece of the omelet around on her plate. I wanted to pull her closer and feed her from my plate, make her eat, but I decided to hold back for now. I finished my breakfast, then took her plate and ate hers.

"I'll be feeding you later," I informed her, unable to keep quiet.

She only smiled. She looked exhausted, and I hated that. She already walked a thin line of permanent weariness, and the fact that I had pushed her over the edge didn't sit well with me.

I drained my coffee and turned to her.

"My name is Ronan Adam Callaghan. I'm one-third of a set of triplets, and I have an older brother and sister."

"Your poor mother," she murmured.

I grinned. "That's not the worst of it. Wait until you meet my dad. He's the biggest handful."

"So, the apple doesn't fall far from the tree."

I lifted her hand and kissed the knuckles, holding her palm to my chest. "Beth, I have so much to tell you, but I'm not sure where to start. I think maybe it might be easier for me if you asked me any questions you want." I huffed out a long sigh. "Otherwise, I feel as if I'm just going to spit out facts. I have no idea how to do this. What you want."

"I want to know you, Ronan. All of you. Why did you hide part of yourself?"

I played with her fingers, then lifted my head and met her gaze. "I liked how you looked at me. How you treated me. I was just Ronan. I wasn't attached to a name or a family. I wasn't part of a group. I was just me."

"You don't like being a triplet?"

"No. I mean, yes, I do. I love my brothers. But people tend to treat us like one person, and we're not. You only saw me. You made me poached eggs," I finished, sounding lame, but unsure how to explain it. "You asked me what *I* wanted, what *I* liked, and for the first time in a long while, I could tell someone. I didn't have to defer."

"I can understand that, but…" She trailed off.

"I also liked the fact that you liked me for me. Not my money, my connections, or who my family was."

"Why?" she asked. "Tell me."

I slid from the stool and walked to the window. She didn't interrupt me as I told her about Loni. How shocked I'd been to discover her betrayal. How much more upset I had been over Dave's disloyalty. The hateful things Loni had said to me. How shaken I had been.

"It's not that I compared you to her. Not at all," I assured her. "You couldn't be more different. It just—it really shook my self-confidence."

She stood behind me when I fell quiet and wrapped her arms around me. I could feel her warmth at my back. She was so small that her arms barely reached around my torso, but she gripped me tight.

"I'm sorry," she whispered. "I understand hurt like that. That fear."

I turned and slid my arms around her, gazing down at her sad face. "Who did that to you?"

"His name was Carson. He told me I was nothing but a fling. I wasn't the right sort of girl to be part of his real world. I wasn't good enough, basically."

Bending, I leaned my forehead to hers. "And you thought I was doing the same thing." I shook my head, pressing harder. "I'm sorry, little bird. I fucked that up so badly."

For a moment, we stood, holding each other. "I think we both have suffered in the past. The question is, can we move forward?" I asked, a strange hitch to my voice. I had to swallow before I could speak again. "Can you forgive me?"

"I need you to tell me everything, Ronan. All the things you've kept from me."

I slipped my fingers under her chin, lifting her face to me. "Can I show you, little bird?"

"Show me?"

"Come with me, and I'll show you my life. You can ask me anything." Then I frowned. "Or do you have to go home?"

"No, Paige is spending the day with the kids. She wants me to spend the time with you." She paused. "They all miss you too. Especially Evan."

"I miss them. Evan the most. I liked spending time with my little bud."

"He made some Lego things with your kits. He had me take pictures."

"I want to see them. See him." I dragged her to my chest, holding her close. "I want to work this out with you."

She let me hold her, and I felt a sense of peace that had been elusive since she'd walked away from me. For a moment, everything was right with my world. Then she stepped back.

"Show me."

I smiled down at her.

"You're standing in my house in the BAM compound."

She lifted one eyebrow. "Is that like a cult?" she asked, her eyes dancing.

I laughed. "My family—BAM—owns this land. A lot of it. Originally, it was purchased to be made into a resort. But my father and Bentley both loved it here and decided to keep it for themselves. They gradually bought up all the land around it they could, and a lot of the family lives here. I grew up here." I tugged her to the window. "I will never tire of this view. The water, the clouds." I pointed to the sky. "Is a storm coming?"

She peered up, cocking her head. "No, those are just cumulus. There are no cumulonimbus clouds forming that I see."

Unable to help myself, I bent and kissed her neck. "I love it when you talk cloud."

She laughed, and I felt the shiver that ran through her when I touched my mouth to her skin. It was a good sign.

"So, you live here?" she asked. "Not the condo you showed me?"

"No, the condo is mine. I've lived there the past few years. We're all given a piece of land here for a house if we want one. I love it here—I feel different when I'm out here than in the city. ABC is building its head office here and will open soon. I'll go between the two for a while, but I do plan on settling here."

"Oh." There was a sad sound to the single word, and I felt her stiffen in my arms.

"Not for a bit, Beth. And we'll work it out, if you want us to. I can commute." I rested my chin on her shoulder. "I can arrange to commute you to and from school. Port Albany has great schools for Evan."

She startled. "You're getting way ahead of yourself."

"Just wanted you to know I was already thinking it. Making plans."

"Oh," she said again. But this time, the word was breathed out in wonder.

I stepped back and held out my hand. "Come with me."

We walked on the beach, and I showed her the houses. "Bentley and Emmy. She was the waitress." I indicated the other large house. "That's my parents' place. Aiden and Cami."

"And that one?"

"Nan and Pops. Sandy was the assistant at BAM until she retired. Pops is her second husband. He worked there too."

"I love how all the houses have a view of the water or the woods."

"It was designed that way. Bentley and my dad had a whole vision for this place. When everyone is here, the place is hopping. None of us has huge yards—we share the land. There's a pool and games area in the middle we all have access to." I pointed to the Hub. "That large building is our gathering place. We celebrate holidays and special occasions there. We all use it the rest of the time like a recreation center. There's a gym and a small indoor pool. A library. Lots of places to sit and read or visit. Tons of games." I grinned at her. "Evan and Lucy would have a field day."

"And your whole family lives here?"

"No. Some use their places like vacation homes. A few, like Bentley's son, Thomas, or Maddox's daughter, Shelby, don't want a place. Thomas lives in BC, and Shelby has a condo in Toronto." I pointed to a house close to the woods. "That's the guest house. It has lots of bedrooms, so they can come stay whenever they want. Shelby usually stays with her parents, but Thomas likes his privacy when he visits. It's used for other guests too."

"And you all get along?"

"Yeah, we do." I held her hand, stroking my fingers over her knuckles. "I grew up with all of them. We're a huge, blended family. Everyone has their own lives, their own passions and pursuits. Some of us work together. We all have our little circles within the family, but we all also get along."

"That is amazing. And unusual."

"I know. I'm incredibly blessed." I smiled down at her. "I know I am. Despite my actions to the contrary, I know that."

She shrugged. "I can also see needing your own space."

I nodded. "We give that to one another as well—at least, most of the time. We're a family, and we squabble and bicker. But we do love one another."

I tugged on her hand. "If you're ready, I'll show you more." I met her gaze. "Brace yourself. We'll be driving around in the golf cart, and we're bound to run into my family. Are you ready for that?"

"Are you?" she asked.

"Yes," I said with a smile. "I am so ready."

"Then let's go."

I pointed out houses as I drove the cart slowly around the property, answering Beth's questions as they came up. Liam was on his deck, drinking coffee. He waved, and I gave him the finger. Beth slapped my hand, and he laughed, making an obscene gesture back at me. I stopped by Gracie's house as she came out, holding Kylie. She hugged Beth and met my gaze, her eyebrows lifted. I winked so she knew I wasn't angry with her. I could never be angry with Gracie. Jaxson followed and shook Beth's hand.

"Heard a lot about you, Beth. Looking forward to getting to know you more. Ronan says you're one in a million."

Beth blushed, which made me smile. She watched me holding Kylie with a strange look on her face. I only got Kylie for a few moments. She was too impatient these days to be held long, and she pointed to the beach, wanting to play on the sand. Laughing, Jaxson took her from me, heading to the sun-filled area. Gracie smiled. "The parents are in the Hub, having coffee."

"All of them?" I asked.

"Yes. I was there a few moments ago to borrow some cream. They were sitting around, talking about next weekend." Her gaze flitted to Beth then back to me. "Not sure if you want to avoid that today or not."

She waved and hurried to join Jaxson and Kylie. Jaxson wrapped an arm around her shoulder, pulling her in close. She looked tiny beside his towering height. Beth watched them with a smile. "What a lovely family."

"They are."

We continued our drive. I showed her Ava's place, not surprised to see the blinds still drawn. "She likes to sleep late on Sundays," I explained. I showed her the pool and outdoor area, and all the other houses.

"Your house isn't beside Paul's and Jeremy's?" she asked. "I'm a little surprised, given what you told me."

"That piece of land was always my favorite. I loved the bluff and the unobstructed view." I paused. "Paul and Jeremy aren't as big on Port Albany as I am. They each have half of that semi attached over there, by the woods. There was only room there for two houses. My mom knew how much I loved the other spot and that I wanted to live here more than they did." I was quiet for a moment. "I guess that was the first time I picked what I wanted over what they wanted."

She slipped her hand into mine and squeezed. We pulled up in front of the Hub, and I looked over at her. "I would like to introduce you to my parents, Beth. Bentley and Maddox are in there as well. Nan and Pops, probably. If you don't want to meet them today, I'll take you back to my place and we can do it another time." I took in a deep breath. "Or not, if that's what you prefer."

"You want me to meet your parents?"

"Yes."

"Are you sure about that, Ronan?"

I turned to her. "I know we have a lot of talking to do. I know I have to earn back your trust. I have a long road ahead of me before you forgive me. But I want to show you everything. Show you who I am." I shook my head. "I am *not* ashamed of you. I'm *not* hiding you. I want you to be clear on that. I am so fucking proud of you—of everything you do. How you look after Evan. All the responsibilities you carry with such grace and fortitude. Your selfless nature. All of it."

Her eyes widened, tears forming in the corners. "Really?" she whispered.

"Don't," I begged. "I hate that I hurt you. I hate knowing I made you cry. That I'm still making you cry." I wiped at the moisture on her cheeks. "Please give me a chance."

She sniffed and smiled. "These are good tears, Ronan." She pulled a tissue from her pocket and dabbed her face. "Yes, I would love to meet your parents." She glanced down. "I would have dressed up more, though. Maybe brought flowers or a cake if I'd known."

"You look beautiful. And they would much rather meet you than have flowers," I assured her. "It's time."

CHAPTER TWENTY
BETH

Ronan hesitated as I got out of the cart. There was an odd look on his face, and I stopped. "We could leave," I offered. "You can introduce me to them another day." I sucked in a fast breath as a thought hit me. "Unless you've changed your mind," I whispered.

"*No.* No, I want you to meet them. Even more important, I want *them* to meet you. It's just now I'll have to share you."

I reached up and cupped his face, something in his expression telling me he needed my touch right now. "What if I'm not ready to share *you* yet? What if I want all your time when we're together to be with me?"

My words sank in, and the worry eased from his face. He covered my hand with his, pressing it into his skin. The scruff on his face was back, and it rasped against my palm as he smiled. "Oh, yeah, little bird? You don't want to share me either?"

"I share you at my house already." I sighed. "Evan and Lucy want you all the time. Now, I'll have to share you with your family. I suppose it's only fair."

"I have the condo. We can hide out there on occasion. Just us." His smile was wide now, the tension eased from his shoulders. "You wanna hide away with me there sometimes? Have me at your mercy?"

I leaned up on my tiptoes and kissed him. "Yes."

He wrapped me in his huge arms, elevating me off the ground in a tight hug. "Thank you."

I laughed. He made me feel tiny and delicate the way he lifted me effortlessly. I liked being held in his arms, and I had missed it.

He set me down and held out his hands. "Let me introduce you to my parents."

At the door, he looked down at me. "Take a deep breath. Brace yourself."

"I'm ready."

He grinned. "They're not."

Ronan was right—they weren't prepared.

We walked into a large, sunlit, multi-level area. To one side was a living room, filled with sofas and chairs, well-worn and comfortable-looking. There was a massive dining area and open kitchen. A large table was set with coffee, mugs, and a platter of pastries. Four couples sat around it, and I recognized the men from the other day, and their wives from pictures I had seen online and that Ronan had shown me earlier in his house.

Bentley Ridge, the serious-looking man from the other day sat next to his wife, Emmy. Today, his face was wreathed in smiles, his posture relaxed. He had his arm draped across the shoulders of his pretty wife. Her honey-colored hair was shot with silver and her expression sweet. She wore a shawl wrapped around her frame and looked tiny tucked beside Bentley. Maddox Riley sat across from them, laughing, his silver hair gleaming in the sun. He was relaxed and casual, his long legs crossed at the ankles. His wife, Dee, sipped coffee, shaking her head at whatever had just been said, her smile wide. Her free hand rested on Maddox's leg, and his large one covered it, holding it to him. The oldest couple had to be Sandy and Jordan, Ronan's grandparents in the blended family. They were a lovely couple, sitting close, fingers entwined on the table. Sandy was scolding Ronan's dad, who was laughing loudly. He was an older version of Ronan, as tall and wide, his muscles rippling as he gestured. His wife, Cami, had shoulder-length dark hair, stylishly woven with gray and purple highlights. When she glanced over and saw us, she laid a hand on her husband's arm, her eyes going wide.

The entire table stopped. The laughter ceased as they all stared at us. Instinctively, I moved closer to Ronan, who drew me to his side.

"Hey," he muttered. "I, ah—" He cleared his throat. "I have someone I'd like you to meet."

"Well, well." Aiden smiled. "Isn't this a nice surprise."

Ronan led me closer, introducing every person to me. Maddox called me the "beautiful treat girl." Bentley shocked me by winking and asking if I had brought any of my amazing cakes with me.

I shook my head. "Sorry, it was sort of a spontaneous visit."

Sandy stood with a smile. "The best kind. I'll get a couple more coffee cups."

Aiden stood and shook my hand. His grip was gentle, his smile kind. "Hello, Beth. We've heard a lot about you." He laid a hand on his wife's shoulder. "This is Cami, Ronan's mom."

She stood, elegant and lovely. Her eyes were the same verdant color as Ronan's. He had her smile. I swallowed my nerves and extended my hand. "Mr. and Mrs. Callaghan, it's lovely to meet you."

His mom laughed, waved away my hand, and embraced me. She smelled of jasmine—light, floral, and exotic. She hugged me hard, squeezing my shoulders, then stood back. "Welcome, Beth. And it's Cami and Aiden. We don't stand on formality here."

Aiden grinned and moved closer. "If my wife gets a hug, so do I." Before I could move, I was swept into a bear hug. He lifted me off my feet, laughing. "She's a little thing, Ronan! I could carry her in my pocket like I used to with Emmy!"

Everyone laughed, and Ronan grabbed his dad's arm. "Put her down, Dad. She isn't a new plaything."

"For you, anyway," Maddox quipped.

I blushed as everyone laughed again.

Sandy set down some cups. "Behave, all of you. She'll never come back."

I sat next to Ronan, grateful when he slipped his hand over mine.

"It's fine," I assured them. "I can take it."

"That's what she said," muttered Aiden, chuckling despite Cami elbowing him in the ribs and Bentley rolling his eyes.

"What? I couldn't let that one slip."

"Too good to pass on," I agreed.

Aiden grinned. "I like her, Ronan. Let's keep her around."

Ronan met my gaze, the heat in his stare making me blush.

"I intend to."

If it was possible to fall in love that fast, I was in love with Ronan's family. They were down-to-earth and funny. It was easy to see the connection between the three older men. Despite the teasing and the jabs, there was an underlying affection and respect. Sandy and Jordan were the matriarch and patriarch of them all. A while later, Liam joined us, and soon, Ronan's sister, Ava, showed up, her hair pulled into a messy ponytail, demanding coffee and yelling at her dad for eating all the lemon Danishes. Gracie and Jaxson arrived with their daughter Kylie, and the place buzzed. Soon after, I was introduced to Addi and Brayden, and my head swam trying to remember names and relationships.

Cami leaned over, patting my hand. "You'll figure it all out," she assured me. "There's more to come, but you'll get it. You just need a little more time."

"Oh, ah…" I trailed off, unsure how to respond.

She smiled. "You'll have lots of time, sweetheart. I see how my son looks at you. I've never seen him look at a woman that way."

I bit my lip, holding back wanting to ask her how he had looked at Loni. She must have read my mind because she shook her head and met my eyes.

"Never."

I felt a small glow of satisfaction in that fact. She smiled back at me and leaned closer. "Thank you for giving him another chance. He's worth it. I promise you."

I looked at him across the table from me, holding Kylie in his embrace, listening to Gracie. He glanced my way, smiling and lifting one eyebrow in a silent question.

"You okay?"

I nodded reassuringly, and he returned his attention to Gracie, stroking along Kylie's forehead in gentle passes. My heart beat faster watching him with her, and in that moment, I saw a future I'd never expected to see.

Ronan, children—and happiness.

As I returned my attention to his mom, I had a feeling she was right.

He was going to be worth it.

Aiden sat beside me, moving his chair back so he could face me fully. "Ronan told me about your little brother. Evan, right?"

"Yes."

"He said there'd been an accident. Can I ask you about it?"

I took in a deep breath and told him about the incident. The man who fell asleep at the wheel and plowed into a group of people waiting on the corner to cross the road. The horrendous impact the vehicle had on the crowd.

"My parents were killed, and Evan was severely injured."

He was quiet for a moment, resting his large hand on my shoulder. "I'm sorry."

I nodded, unable to speak. Behind me, Ronan moved closer. "Dad—"

I shook my head. "It's fine. Why are you asking me, Mr.—I mean, Aiden?"

"I'm not sure if Ronan told you, but I've studied therapy all my life. I believe in the benefits of exercise and massage. Acupuncture."

Gracie leaned over Aiden's shoulder. "He helped my dad walk again."

At my quizzical glance, she explained. "When I was little, Dad was in a bad accident. He was paralyzed for a time. Aiden worked with him. He says, without Aiden, he never would have gotten out of that wheelchair."

Aiden smiled. "I helped him find his drive and belief that he could walk again. Without that, he wasn't ever getting out of that chair. Mad Dog and I played good cop, bad cop." He leaned forward. "I'd like to meet Evan. Would you allow me to look at his records? Ronan says you keep a very detailed file on him."

"I don't want—"

He waved aside my words. "Don't even finish that sentence. You're part of my son's life—therefore, you are part of mine. There might be nothing I can do. There may be something. I can try, though. Ronan said he thought he'd seen a difference with the exercises he was doing that I suggested."

"I saw it too before…" I trailed off, unsure how to finish.

Aiden bent close. "I was an ass with Cami too. Even more so than my son here. She forgave me a lot, and I will forever be grateful for her open heart. You remind me of her." He smiled, his eyes crinkling in the corners. "That is one of the highest compliments I can give a person, Beth. I'm glad you're with us today." He squeezed my hand. "Thank you."

Ronan cleared his throat, and Aiden sat back, picking up his coffee cup.

"We should go," Ronan said. "You ladies have your book club, and I need to get Beth back to Toronto."

"Book club?" I asked.

Gracie grinned. "Do you like to read?"

"I love it. I don't have much time anymore, but I love getting lost in a book."

"We have a book club, and we meet once a month—the second Sunday—and discuss. The men disappear because they can't handle it."

I laughed.

Addi came over and sat down. "You should join us. Do you like historical romance?"

"My favorite genre."

"We're reading Scarlet Scott. Still." She laughed. "We're all so busy, we can only do a book a month. We tried a couple other authors, but she is our favorite so far. Gracie introduced us to her."

"Oh, mine too. And Paige, my roommate. We trade and reread her all the time."

"Then it's settled. You both have to join us."

I hedged a little. "I'll ask her."

Cami leaned over the back of her chair. "Next Sunday is family brunch. We'd love it if you joined us."

"Oh, um, Sundays, I usually spend with Evan, Paige, and Lucy. I don't think—"

She didn't let me finish. "They are, of course, included. Make sure the kids bring their suits. You and Paige too if you want. You can swim in the pool here. The one outside is still too cold."

I glanced at Ronan, who looked at me, nodding eagerly. Now he'd introduced me, it seemed it was full steam ahead. Even more fascinating was the fact that Liam looked as interested in my response as Ronan did. I had a feeling Paige would like that little tidbit of information.

"I'll pick you up," Ronan assured me.

"I have a car seat in the truck," Liam offered unexpectedly. "I could bring Paige and Lucy. I'll be in town Sunday morning."

I looked at him, confused and wondering why he had a car seat. He laughed. "It's built in to the truck," he explained. "One of the features I never needed until now."

"Then I'll bring Beth and Evan. You can talk to the ladies about the book club, and Dad and Evan can chat," Ronan confirmed.

"It's settled, then," Liam said, sounding satisfied.

"Yep," Ronan agreed.

I guessed it was.

We left, and I was hugged and kissed, exclaimed over and hugged again. Ronan steered the golf cart away but didn't head in the direction of his house. Instead, he took me on a tour of the grounds, pointing out everyone's house and explaining more of the dynamics of the family.

"We all have our own lives, but we come together here."

"You have such a large family. Won't you run out of room?"

He laughed. "Mine is the last generation to get a house. It's up to us to decide if we leave the house to our kids or turn it back to the company. This property will stay within the family until such time as they decide to sell it all. It can't be broken up. We have a trust that oversees it and a very strict set of guidelines that exist to protect everyone."

"Wow."

He pulled over and parked. He turned my way with a wink. "I guess it does sound like a cult, doesn't it?" He chuckled. "Many think that, I believe. But we're a family. I'm so grateful my dad loved this place so much he couldn't bear to sell it. Bentley felt the same way. Maddox wasn't as big on the idea, but even he grew to love it here." He climbed out of the golf cart and took my hand. He turned and swept out his arm, indicating the area of houses. We had been climbing elevation in the cart, and below us, the houses looked like a little village spread out with the water and trees a lovely backdrop. "They made this place so we'd have roots. It's my favorite spot in the world. It's not for everyone, and many come and go, but it's our nucleus, and we all find our way back for important times. Family times."

"I see why you love it." I paused. "Your house…" I trailed off, unsure how to say what I was thinking.

"Is sort of empty?"

I thought about the layout. The sparse décor. One chair and a still-in-the-box TV in the living room. When I'd peeked in, his bedroom held only a bed and a dresser. All the other rooms were vacant. The kitchen cupboards had the basics, but that was it. When I thought about it, his condo in Toronto was much the same. It looked as if he were either just moving in or getting ready to move out. As if he were in limbo.

"Rather," I said.

"I've been in between the two spots for so long," he admitted. "The condo was easier to stay at for work, but my heart was here. Yet, when I was here, I couldn't put down roots, as if I wasn't ready. I've been living half lives in both spots."

"You'll move here now the company is opening up?" I asked, feeling sad he would be so far away and wondering what that meant for us. I certainly wouldn't see him very much. I was shocked how distressed that made me feel.

"Not right away. We're doing a slow transition until everything is set and running. We're working on a schedule." He gripped my hand. "I'll still be around. I'm not going anywhere, little bird. We're going to work this out. I promise."

His words made me feel better.

He tugged on my hand. "Come with me."

We walked through the trees, the area familiar. When we broke through the woods, I knew why.

"This is where we came for the picnic!"

"Yes. I come here because it's right at the edge of the property. BAM owns everything behind us and as far as the water's edge. This bluff is the last of it. We leave it undeveloped for many reasons. Privacy, wildlife, and the fact that it's so beautiful. I don't think they had the heart to disturb it. I always came here when I was younger. When Paul and Jeremy drove me crazy and I needed to be alone. I could see the water, feel the wind on my face, and hear the silence. I was the only one who ever did, for the most part. It felt like my special spot." He paused before confessing. "We came from the other direction when I brought you. We parked just beyond those trees."

"So your family wouldn't know."

He sighed. "Yes."

He sat down on a huge boulder, his legs splayed. He gripped his thighs, meeting my eyes. "I shouldn't have kept who I am from you. Who my family is. I kept telling myself, by not saying anything, I wasn't lying. But I was. I was hiding. Partly to protect myself, even though I knew you were nothing like Loni, and partly because I didn't want to have to share." He laughed. "Then today, they meet you and fall as hard as I did. And I realized what an idiot I had been. It doesn't matter if we're in a room full of my family or alone—you still make me feel like *Ronan*. Just me. All you have to do is look at me, and I am more me than I have ever been." He shook his head in wonder. "I risked you, us, because I was stupid." He reached out his hand. "I will never lie to you again, Beth. I promise. Give me a chance. Let me be Ronan with you."

I slipped my hand into his and let him pull me close. I stood between his legs and wrapped my arms around his shoulders. With a sigh, he buried his face into my chest, pulling me close. I felt the weariness in him, the need of his huge body melding to mine. I ran my fingers through his thick hair, smiling at the groan of satisfaction that escaped his lips. He nuzzled closer, and I loved how he felt next to me.

"Forgive me," he murmured, the sound muffled but the plea clear.

I knew we had more talking to do. There were a lot of things we had to say. Questions I needed answers to. But the fact was that I had missed him so much. I understood what he meant about being Ronan with me. I felt I was Beth with him. He saw through my brave front to the worry I carried inside. His arms were the safe place I had been longing for. His touch was a healing balm, and his smile made my world brighter.

I pressed a kiss to his hair. "I have forgiven you."

He lifted his head, his eyes glassy. "I'll do better."

"I know."

"Kiss me, Beth."

I lowered my head and pressed my mouth to his. Instantly, the world faded away. He pulled me tight, moving his legs and lifting me to his lap. He kissed me with an intensity and passion that made me shiver. His tongue stroked along mine, possessive and deep. He splayed his hand over my back, holding me close. The other hand, he slid into my hair, fisting it as he dragged his mouth across my cheek and down my neck, licking, nipping, kissing, and teasing.

"I missed you. Your taste, the feel of you," he groaned. "How your hair feels in my hand. I love your curls." He captured my mouth again. "How you feel pressed against me."

The heat of his body soaked into mine. My breasts ached from the feel of his firm chest, my nipples hard peaks. I gasped as he moved his hand, cupping and stroking my nipple.

"God, Beth—"

I whimpered, the breeze picking up my hair and the cool air hitting my skin. It reminded me that we were outside, and although this was a relatively private place, anyone could show up. I eased back, Ronan following my body, his mouth seeking mine, protesting his displeasure with a little grunt. I cupped his face.

"Too fast," I whispered.

He opened his eyes. "I know. I was getting as much of you as possible before you stopped me."

I couldn't help kissing his full mouth again. His lips were red and swollen, damp from my tongue. "Incorrigible."

He grinned. "Yep."

"I have to go home."

"Can I come in and see Evan? I want to talk to him."

"He would love that. Lucy will want some Ronan snuggles."

"I'm up for that."

"Okay." I slid from his lap, trying not to notice the huge bulge in the front of his sweats. We weren't ready for that.

Yet.

But it didn't mean I couldn't look.

CHAPTER TWENTY-ONE
RONAN

Lucy's little arm squeezed my neck, her fingers digging into my skin. "I miss you!" she exclaimed.

"I missed you, Lucy-loo."

She met my eyes, her gaze surprisingly intense for such a little girl. "I habdn't had ice cream in forevah."

I threw back my head in laughter even as Paige groaned and Beth laughed.

"I'll take you later," I promised.

"Okay."

I set her down and met Evan's gaze. He looked between me and Beth suspiciously.

"So, you're back?" he asked.

"How about you show me what you've been doing with your Lego stuff, and we can talk?" I offered.

He glanced at Beth, and she nodded, smiling softly at him.

"Okay."

I followed him to his room, and he sat down on the bed but didn't offer me a seat. I kept standing, waiting for him to talk.

"You made Beth cry."

"I know, and I regret it."

"Are you going to do that again?"

I ran a hand through my hair and crouched down to his level. "Not intentionally. I really like your sister, Evan. I did something that upset her, and she was angry. I will never do it again, but I can't promise to never make her cry. Men do that a lot, unfortunately."

"Why?" he asked.

I shrugged. "Basically, we're idiots."

He puckered his lips, regarding me, obviously torn between his loyalty to his sister and his fondness for me. "She's okay with you?"

"I think so. We're moving forward."

"What did you do?"

I sat on the floor, and I told him. At least the CliffsNotes. He listened to me, his head cocked, never interrupting.

"So, let me get this straight," he said. "You're really rich, live in a house by the water, you have a really, *really* big family, and you like my sister?"

"I like you too, bud."

"So, I'm not in the way?" he asked, lowering his voice. "You didn't break up with her because of me?"

I was horrified. "Why would you think that?"

He shrugged. "She does everything for me, Ronan. She works hard so I can go to therapy. She makes extra cakes to get me more treatment. She uses her tip money to buy me Lego kits. I thought maybe you'd broken up because she was spending time with me that she should spend with you. I didn't know how to tell her it was okay. Because I liked you," he added. "And she was happy." His voice quivered. "Then you were gone, and we were both sad. But she was extra sad."

I rose up on my knees and wrapped him in my arms. His body felt so little, so vulnerable in my embrace. But like Lucy, he held on tight, and I knew right then I was done. I was as in love with him as I was with Beth, and I would be there for both of them. Going forward, they would be part of my life.

After a minute, he pulled back and surreptitiously wiped his eyes. "Don't hurt her," he whispered.

"I won't," I replied, my voice sounding thick and raspy. I cleared my throat. "My dad wants to meet you, talk to you about your leg. He wants to try to help if you would let him."

"Really?"

"Yeah. We're having a brunch next Sunday, and Beth is going to bring you to meet my family. If you want to," I added.

"Yeah. Wicked cool! The BAM people? I read things about them all the time on the internet. All their buildings and stuff. We talk about them in school."

"Really?"

He nodded enthusiastically. "My teacher, Mr. Humphries, likes to talk about current affairs. He loves entrepreneurs, and he is passionate about sustainability. We were discussing a new building that BAM was working on and their environmental design for it. I have to write a paper on it. Do you think—" he swallowed "—do you think they'd let me ask them some questions?"

I grinned. "My brother Paul is heading that up for them. You can talk to him about it on Sunday. He loves to talk environmental issues." I paused. "And you can talk to my dad about your leg and have a swim in the pool if you want."

His eyes grew round. "You have an indoor pool?"

I clapped my hand on his shoulder. "Bud, we got everything."

———

I sat beside Beth on the front step, loath to leave her. I knew she was tired. I knew she had a long week ahead of her. I wanted to see her—as much as possible—but I also knew she needed some sleep. She sat with her head resting on my shoulder, the late evening descending around us. I had played video games with Evan. Helped him build another structure with Lego and took pictures to show my dad. We all went for a walk, Lucy perched on my shoulders. I kept one arm firmly wrapped around her as we walked, and she clutched my hair for stability. I didn't breathe a word of discomfort when her little fist would tighten. I was too happy to care. Paige ever so subtly pumped me for information on Liam as we walked, and I made up lots of shit he would have to explain away. More than once, Beth slapped my arm, assuring Paige I was lying. I only shrugged and kept talking. They were both laughing, so I didn't care.

And the best part? Evan slipped his hand into mine as we strolled, letting me bear a little of his weight so he was able to keep up easily.

I insisted on ordering in pizza for dinner, and the kids were both zonked out by eight. Paige picked up a book and headed to her room, her yawns a little unbelievable, but I appreciated them, nonetheless.

But now it was time to say goodnight.

"Can I see you tomorrow?"

She hugged my arm. "If you want to."

"I do."

"And Tuesday?"

She hesitated, and I pressed a kiss to her head. "Tacos here? I'll bring the stuff, and we'll make them together."

"I'd love that." She hesitated. "Please cancel the car, Ronan."

I laughed under my breath. "Figured that out, did you?"

"Wasn't hard," she hummed.

"I will. I'll be there to drive you."

She inhaled. "And cancel the cake orders. I saw the standing order of four cakes a week. You can't keep buying my cakes to make sure I have enough money."

I shook my head. "That, I cannot do. There would be an uprising in the company. Besides, they are split between BAM and ABC. Addi would weep if there were no cake on Fridays."

"Is she pregnant?"

"Yeah, she told us last week."

"I thought so. I saw Bentley talking to her and saw him tap her stomach. He looked so excited and happy."

"He is looking forward to being a grandpa. So is Maddox."

"Is that odd for you? Them being married when they're family, so to speak?"

"No. They were always closer than anyone. Always together. It was as if they were meant to be together. Just like Reed and Heather—although that developed after she moved here when she was grown up. He's older, and they were friends..." I trailed off.

"Until they became more."

"Yeah."

"Anyone else?" she asked.

"Not that I know of." I nudged her. "You let me know if you spot anything."

She laughed and shifted to look at me. "Are you okay with us coming next Sunday? Meeting your family? Your brothers?"

"More than okay. Tomorrow, I'll talk to Paul and Jeremy. They've been very circumspect, which is surprising, but they'll be thrilled we worked it out. You'll meet them on Sunday."

"I have to bring something."

"Cake."

She laughed. "Aren't you tired... Forget I said that. I will bring a few. I have a chocolate fudge cake you haven't tried. And a spice cake with maple frosting."

"I vote for those."

"Okay."

"Only if you have time."

"I'll make time. I'm not showing up empty-handed."

I didn't argue with her. I knew there was no point. I stood and walked down the few steps, turning to look at her.

"I hate leaving you."

She hesitated. "You could stay."

"No. I want you to be sure. Completely sure."

"Thank you."

I rested one foot on the bottom step and leaned over. She stretched closer, and our mouths connected. Moved and brushed together. Softly. Sweetly. I cupped the back of her head and kissed her harder. Slid my tongue inside to taste her. She whimpered, cupping my jaw. I kissed her until I knew I had to stop or I would carry her back inside and make love to her. I eased back, dropping kisses on her brow, cheek, and nose.

"I'm calling you when I get home."

"Are we having phone sex?" she breathed, her eyes dancing.

I laughed and kissed her again. "Minx. I just want your voice to be the last thing I hear before I fall asleep."

"I'd like that."

I kissed her again, then forced myself to walk away.

It took everything in me to do so.

Monday morning, I headed straight to Paul's office. He was at his desk, looking over some plans. Jeremy was at the drafting table in the corner, bent over his task. I rapped on the door and walked in, shutting it behind me. They both looked up, each offering a smile.

"Hey. What's up?" Jeremy asked, his eyes dancing. "Coming to confess, big bro?"

I laughed. We were the exact same age, but those minutes between our births meant something to us. We always teased Paul for being the middle child in our group.

I sat down, and Paul joined us, nudging me with his knee. "Talked to Liam last night. I hear you and your girl have made up. That you took her to meet the family."

I was glad to see no anger in his expression. Curiosity, for sure, maybe a small hint of hurt, but not anger.

"We are back together," I stated simply. "Meeting the family wasn't planned. I didn't intentionally cut you out. Liam brought her out to see me, and I was showing her around. It just…happened."

Paul laughed. "Things usually do with this family."

"So, you're not hiding anymore?" Jeremy asked.

"No." I sat back with a sigh. "I didn't mean to hide. I was an idiot. I just didn't want to share."

"Were you ashamed of us?" Paul asked. "I mean, Ava said you weren't…" He frowned, looking worried.

"No, not at all." I sucked in a deep breath. "You guys were right. I was feeling left out. I knew we'd all find someone and lead separate lives, but I hadn't expected it to happen at the same time." I snorted. "And with twins."

"We sort of figured that out, but you wouldn't talk to us." Jeremy cocked his head to the side. "Still being the protective, selfless Ronan. Always deferring to us."

I was surprised Ava had been correct when she'd said they knew what I did. I didn't really think they had figured it out. "You knew that?"

They both laughed. "Everyone knew it, Ronan. You don't see yourself the way we do." Paul clasped my shoulder. "We both look up to you. We love you."

"So, you're not angry?"

"Because you were a selfish ass for a few weeks and hid part of yourself?" Jeremy shrugged. "Mildly annoyed, but we're over it. We knew you'd find your feet." He grinned. "Now, tell us about your girl. When can we meet her?"

An idea formed, and I smiled. "What are you doing tomorrow night?"

BETH

I lifted my face to the sunshine as I stepped off the bus. I was anxious to get home. Ronan and Evan were in charge of taco night. He had dropped by last night, spent more time with Evan and me, played with Lucy, and made Paige laugh. I wondered if he knew how his presence alone brightened all of our worlds. His smile and laughter. The way he teased and offered his affection so freely. It changed all of us.

I paused in front of the house. Ronan's car was parked in the small driveway, and behind it was another car—one I didn't recognize. I wondered if Paige had a client over. That happened on occasion, but she usually let me know in advance so I would look after Lucy for her.

I walked up the steps and into the house, stopping in the doorway at the sight before me. On the floor sat Evan and Ronan. Three Ronans, actually. They all looked up as I walked in, the same bright smile and green eyes greeting me. I blinked, unsure what I was seeing. My Ronan smiled wider. "Hey, little bird."

"Hi," I replied, still in shock. I met Paige's amused gaze. Looked at Lucy, who sat between Ronan's legs, a wide smile on her little face.

"Beth!" she exclaimed. "Ronan has brudders! They all look the same," she added, sounding delighted. "They big just like Ronan."

She was right. They all stood, their sheer size filling the room. I stepped forward, studying them, then held out my hand. "You must be Paul."

He grinned and shook my hand. "You're right."

I turned to Jeremy, who refused my hand and hugged me. "How did you tell?"

"Ronan told me Paul had a tiny scar above his right eyebrow from where you pushed him out of a tree."

Jeremy's eyes danced. "He slipped."

Paul laughed. "With your help."

"Whatever."

"You can tell us apart. It usually takes people a little while. That's awesome," Paul enthused. "People see three of us and immediately stop looking for variances, instead seeing the similarities."

I could understand that. They did all look alike with the same coloring, but all you had to do was really look at them to see the differences. Paul and Jeremy were a little shorter than Ronan. Jeremy was slighter leaner. His eyebrows were thicker. Paul's eyes were more deep set. His smile wider. His hair was longer.

And neither of them was as handsome as Ronan. Still holding Lucy, he stepped closer and pressed a kiss to my cheek. "My brothers wanted to meet you privately. We're making tacos for everyone. Our specialty. I asked Paige, and she said it was fine," he explained.

I turned with a grin. "I'm shocked she didn't tell you that you had to invite Liam."

"He'll be here shortly. He was picking up fresh tortillas at the place I took you."

I began to laugh. "I'm not sure the house can hold all four of you."

They all broke out in identical smiles.

"We can fix that," Jeremy offered. "We'll shore up the floor if we have to."

All I could do was smile.

CHAPTER TWENTY-TWO

BETH

I wasn't sure I had ever laughed as much as I did that night. Ronan and his brothers were a force unto themselves. When Liam arrived, he joined them building Lego creations, all of them arguing over pieces and ideas. Evan stayed close to Ronan, soaking it up like a sponge, the smile never leaving his face. I sat beside Paige on the sofa, sipping a glass of wine Ronan handed me after I had gone downstairs and changed. She and I exchanged glances, and I noticed how often Liam lifted his gaze to her, and I felt something pass between them. She never stopped smiling, and I couldn't resist teasing her when the men, including Evan, went into the kitchen to "finish our feast."

"I provided the single brother," I murmured. "Does that get me out of dishes now?"

She laughed under her breath. "Holy shit, their DNA needs to be bottled." She shook her head. "He is one hell of a man."

Liam walked in, Lucy on his wide shoulder, his arm anchoring her in place. He held the bottle of wine and filled our glasses. He noticed Paige's flushed cheeks and glanced up at Lucy with a wink, his voice teasing. "I think your momma was talking about me again."

Paige tossed her hair, the light shimmering on the dark strands. "I don't think so."

He laughed, not at all worried. "So Sunday, I'll be here about nine. We can have coffee before we head out."

"I don't recall inviting you," she retorted, a smile playing on her lips.

He turned and walked away. "You were planning on it. I was just saving you the trouble." He disappeared into the kitchen, and she huffed.

"Incorrigible."

"They all are," I assured her. "But so amazing."

"I already figured that out," she replied.

The mounds of tacos were delicious. The chips and salsa disappeared fast. Lucy didn't leave Liam's side, insisting on crawling up on his lap and eating there. He was entertaining, pulling her plate next to his and helping her make a taco she could handle. She watched him eat with huge eyes. In fact, we all watched the Callaghan boys eat with fascination. Evan tried to keep up again but stopped after four this time. There were forty tacos on the platter, plus the chips, guacamole, and all the fixings, and by the time we were finished, every plate and bowl was empty. The table was tight, but nobody cared. It was too much fun. The triplets exchanged stories, Liam added his own views and a few funny memories, and we laughed constantly. After dinner, they cleaned up while Paige got Lucy ready for bed and I made Evan do his homework. I wandered into the kitchen, picking up clean platters and bowls, putting them away, simply listening. They talked about work, the new office, the upcoming brunch.

"Our girls will be there Sunday, Ronan," Paul said. "You okay with that?" He glanced my way. "We don't want to steal your thunder or anything."

I answered before Ronan could. "I'm not thunder. I want to meet your girlfriends as well. Ronan has spoken highly of them."

That pleased them. "Oh yeah?" Paul grinned. "Cool."

Jeremy nudged Ronan. "Awesome."

Ronan looked at me and winked. "Yeah, she is."

I turned, lifting the last pile of plates into the cupboard, refusing to let him see my blush.

Once again, I sat between Ronan's legs on the front steps. The air was cooler now the sun had gone down, but I was warm and safe with him surrounding me. His brothers had departed after bear hugs and promises to see us on Sunday. The house seemed very quiet once they left.

"Thanks for making my brothers so welcome, little bird."

"I liked them. All of them."

He cleared his throat. "Paige is having quite the effect on Liam. I've never seen him so taken with someone."

"She thinks he is rather spectacular."

"Lucy likes him better than me," he groused.

I chuckled. "I think Lucy is rather intuitive. She knows he likes her mom." I patted his arm. "She still loves you."

"I'm Evan's favorite."

"That will never change."

"Good." He cleared his throat. "And thanks for saying what you did about Paul's and Jeremy's girls. It made them feel good."

I turned and looked at him. "I only spoke the truth, Ronan. Do you have any idea how much you've talked to me about your brothers since Sunday?"

He scratched his head. "Too much, I think?"

"No. You've told me so much about your family. Your life. It's exactly what I needed to help understand you."

"You think you understand me, Beth?" he asked, a hopeful note to his voice.

"I know one thing for certain. You don't see what everyone else sees about you."

He furrowed his forehead. "Which is?"

I tried to figure out how to say it. I turned even more, so his leg was over mine and I rested against his other thigh. I picked up his hand, marveling at the sheer size of it.

"You know I love historical romance."

He chuckled. "So I found out. The women in my family are crazy for it. They're looking forward to you joining in their book club."

"Your mom sent me the name of the book they're reading right now. I had already read it, but I started reading it again."

"It's by the Scarlett letter woman?"

I laughed. "Scarlett Scott. It's called *Her Virtuous Viscount*. It's part of her Wicked Husband series."

He grinned. "I am hardly virtuous, although wicked might be a good word."

I slapped his arm. "Shut up for a moment."

He pretended to lock his lips shut and looked so adorable doing so, I had to kiss him. He was all too happy to return the favor, so for a few minutes, I forgot what I was trying to say. I pushed at his shoulder, shaking my head. "Wicked is right."

He grinned. "You started it. Now, you were saying?"

"The hero in the story—Tom—has his heart broken by the woman he thinks he loves. In his mind, he is unworthy of real love. He is useful to people, but not loved. He feels invisible. He is a good man with a big heart, but in his mind, he wonders why he bothers. Good guys finish last sort of thing."

"Is this where he becomes wicked?"

"No, he meets a woman and decides to have an affair with her. No strings attached."

He frowned. "Was that allowed back then?"

I laughed. "That is why these books are so delicious. A hidden passionate affair? So scandalous and dangerous. Actually falling in love with your wife? Hard to believe and rare. Men who love so intensely that it changes them, changes their life? Trust me, the books are addictive."

"I see." He tucked a strand of hair behind my ear. "And this viscount of yours, he falls in love for real this time?"

"Yes. He falls for her hard. He realizes what he had in the past wasn't what he thought love was. She shows him how to love. How to believe in himself again. To move away from the past and begin to really live again. He lets people in, shocked to realize how many truly care. She lets him know he isn't invisible. *She* sees him, and he realizes if he has that, he has everything. He's finally able to accept his importance to people. It was hard for him to tell her, but he did."

He was quiet for a moment, then spoke. "Then I know how he feels, because knowing you see me has made all the difference in my life. I don't want to be without it, or you, again."

His words touched my heart. I cupped his cheek, unable to tear my gaze from his beautiful green eyes. His emotions were on full display, and I felt his adoration deep within my soul.

"What does he say to her?" he asked. "Do you remember?"

I could barely whisper the words. *"'You make my heart full, Hyacinth. Only, ever you. I was lost until I kissed you in the moonlight. Lost until I found you. I have been waiting for you. For this. For us. I just didn't know it until you were here, in my life, in my arms.'"* I cleared my throat. "Or something along those lines."

"Would you accept a kiss on the steps under the streetlight instead of the moonlight?" he asked. "I can't speak like that, but I can say this. I agree one hundred percent with everything he said or, at least, the sentiment. You healed me, Beth. You brought me back to my family. I hadn't realized how far I was drifting away. I want you in my life." He swallowed. "I love you."

"Ronan—" I breathed out, shocked.

"You don't have to say it back. I know you're not ready and we have a lot to work through. I thought maybe if you knew, then it would make you understand how important you are to me. I'm not going anywhere, unless you're with me."

"Evan—" I began, but he silenced me.

"He is part of you, so he will be part of me. Part of us. I don't expect you to abandon your brother. Or leave Paige and Lucy behind. We can figure it all out. Port Albany. My job, your school. All of it. If we do it together. If you want to move forward with me."

"Yes, I do," I responded without hesitation because I knew it was the truth. I wanted to be with him.

"Then let me kiss you, Beth, and know going forward that I do love you and I'll wait until you can tell me you feel the same way."

"How can you say that?"

"Because you'll be worth the wait. And I'll enjoy the journey because you're with me."

He bent and captured my mouth.

I decided right then streetlights were just as romantic as moonlight. Especially if the man kissing me was Ronan.

Ronan immersed himself in my life completely. He picked me up on Wednesday. Showed up on Thursday with his laptop and ordered enough food to feed three people and sat in his booth, eating as he worked. He did the same on Friday, and on Saturday, he appeared with Paige, Lucy, and Evan, ordering lunch and entertaining the three of them. Given our limited budget, going out to eat was a treat for us, and we were always careful about where we went. I heard Ronan telling the kids to order anything they wanted, and before I could protest, Liam walked in, joining them in the booth and seconding Ronan's words.

"After, we'll go to the park," he announced. "There's a little fair at the one not far from your place."

I had seen that but not mentioned it to the kids. It was expensive, and Evan found it hard to maneuver around the crowds. He must have said something to Liam because Liam shook his head and assured him he and Ronan had a plan. With the excited look on Evan's face, I didn't have the heart to say no.

They were a lively table, laughing and teasing. The restaurant was busy so I couldn't spend much time with them, but when I went over for refills and to check on them, Ronan watched me, his eyes seeing everything. When I left the diner at four, he was waiting outside, leaning against his car patiently.

I shook my head as I approached him. "You can't do this every day, Ronan."

"Why not?"

"You are a busy man and not my chauffeur. You don't have time to drive me home every day."

"It's not every day. And since I can only see you at the diner in the evenings, it works out great for both of us."

He held open the door, and I slid in, worrying my bottom lip.

"Why do you look so worried?" he asked as he joined the traffic heading down the street.

"I can't let myself get used to it," I confessed. "If something happens—" I swallowed. "If you get tired…" I couldn't even finish the sentence.

"Not going to happen. Get used to it. Get used to me being around. If I can make your life easier, it's going to happen, Beth." He lifted my hand, kissing the knuckles and resting our entwined fingers on his thigh. "I'm not going anywhere."

I wanted to believe those words more than anything. I smiled at him, squeezing his fingers.

"I hope not."

CHAPTER TWENTY-THREE
RONAN

We were quiet on the drive home, and I followed Beth into the house, still thinking about her words. Wondering how to assuage her worry. I knew it would take time, but I wanted her to know how serious I was about her.

Beth stopped in shock at the sight before us, and I walked into her, grabbing her against my chest to stop her from falling forward.

In the kitchen, Paige was sitting on the counter. Liam stood between her legs, his arms around her, kissing her passionately. Her hands were clinging to his shoulders, and her legs wrapped around his hips. Their dark heads were so close together, it was impossible to tell where he began and she ended. They were so focused on each other, they didn't even hear us come in. Beth looked up at me, looking as shocked as I was. I grinned and pulled her closer, lifting my hand and rapping on the doorframe.

Paige and Liam broke apart, both startled and breathing hard. Paige's cheeks were flushed, her lips swollen, and Liam looked annoyed at being interrupted.

I was unable to keep the enjoyment out of my voice. This was very un-Liam-like behavior. "Hey, what's up?"

Liam glowered at me. "Not much, thanks to you."

Paige flushed even darker and slid off the counter. "I have to go and check on Lucy." She hurried away, and Liam watched her go, frowning. He turned back to me, his eyes narrowed. Beth eased away, murmuring about going to see Evan. We were alone in the kitchen, and he crossed his arms.

"What?"

I stepped closer. "She's a single mom, Liam. That's sacred shit."

"I'm aware."

"I care about her a lot. She's Beth's best friend. Not to mention Lucy and her feelings. You don't trifle with that."

He stepped closer, intensity rolling off him. "*I'm not.* I care about both of them."

I met his eyes, his gaze steady and determined. "Wow. You're falling for her."

He lost his aggression and stepped back, shaking his head. "Yeah, I am. Both of them."

"You might want to tone down the kitchen groping. The kids like to wander around at times."

He chuckled low in his throat. "Evan is deep in Lego, and the hall floor squeaks. Lucy was in her room, and I could hear her singing away. I knew where they were."

"You didn't hear us."

"I can't listen for everything, Ronan. I thought you were taking Beth to your condo."

I shook my head. "She's exhausted. She needs a quiet night at home, not alone with me at my place. Not sure I could resist her there."

He nodded. "How about pizza for everyone, and we'll go? We can hang together tonight, and we'll be back in the morning to pick them up."

"You going to introduce Paige and Lucy as yours tomorrow?"

His eyebrows shot up, and I could see my question had taken him by surprise. "I think I need to check with Paige first. We're still figuring things out."

"With your tongues?" I asked mildly, grinning.

He grabbed me in a headlock, laughing.

"Shut up, little brother, or I'll tell Beth about the time you pissed your pants in the woods when you thought you saw a bear."

I grunted as I tried to escape. "I was five, for God's sake. You told me it was a bear that ate bad kids—I was scared for my life!"

Beth and Paige walked in, seeing our wrestling and hearing our conversation.

"Well, this I gotta hear," Paige said with a grin.

Liam released me with a smirk. "Happy to fill you in."

I groaned. This was going to be a long night.

Beth was nervous on Sunday when I picked her up. Evan was unusually quiet as well on the drive. As we approached the Hub, I assured them everything would be great. Liam pulled up beside me with Paige and Lucy. Of all of them, Lucy was the only one not apprehensive. She was excited about swimming, meeting new people, plus the fact that Liam had promised her she could help him plant some things in one of the many gardens.

I only hoped the others relaxed enough to enjoy the day. I helped Beth unload the truck, holding two large boxes of cakes. She held another box. I bent down and kissed her. "You've already met my parents. And my siblings. You'll be fine."

She glanced toward the windows. "There looks like a lot more of them."

I laughed. "There are. I won't leave your side. I promise."

"I'll hold you to that," she murmured.

I kissed her again. "They are gonna love you."

BETH

I had never seen anything like it in my life. There were people everywhere. More "uncles," "aunts," and "cousins" than I could count. Ronan laughed at my expression, informing me not everyone was there either.

"But for the most part, this is the usual crowd for special occasions."

"What's the special occasion?" I asked.

He stared at me with a grin. "You are."

He led me around, introducing me to his family. I was hugged by everyone. So was Evan. Ronan's family fussed over him the most, and he soaked it up like a sponge. Lucy won them all over with her smiles and curls, and I don't think her feet were on the floor for the first hour. Everyone wanted to pick her up and hold her. She loved it. Paige was as stunned as I was by the enthusiastic greetings. She was as warmly welcomed as I was. Liam made it clear she was there with him, not simply a friend of mine. If that surprised anyone, they didn't let on.

I helped Cami, Emmy, and Dee set out the food. They were all excited over my cakes, having heard from various people how delicious they were.

"Not that anyone thought to bring us home a slice," Emmy stated dryly.

Bentley, who was never far from his wife's side, reached over and tucked her shawl closer. "I tried, Freddy, but there's never any left." He kissed the side of her head. "Honest." He threw a wink my way, and I tried not to laugh. Ronan told me

Bentley took a massive slice every time a cake showed up and always went back for more.

I smiled at Emmy. "I can hook you up now."

She laughed. "See, Rigid, it's all about who you know."

"As usual, you are correct." He took a platter from her hands and set it on the table and pressed a kiss to her cheek. He smiled as he brushed past me, squeezing my shoulder gently. "I'll get the coffee."

She watched him, love in her gaze. I noticed the marked difference in him from the stern-faced man in the boardroom. He was gentle and loving with her and his family. His entire family, which, it seemed, included me now.

I cast my gaze over the huge amount of food. Platters of fresh scones and biscuits. Plates of ham, bacon, and sausage. Bowls of scrambled eggs. A large selection of frittatas. A massive dish of hash browns. On the side, there were toasters with boards of bread and bagels to make. They even had a waffle maker like you saw in hotels.

Evan was going to have a field day.

I carried the last two cakes over and set them in the dessert area. I had made five, and I hoped it was enough. I wasn't totally prepared for such a large number of people.

Cami clapped her hands. "Brunch is ready!" She turned to me. "We don't stand on ceremony here. But you and Evan, Paige and Lucy go first. The women follow, and then it's a free-for-all." She smiled. "By the time the boys are through their first go-round, we'll have to fill up the containers."

"You have *more* food?" I asked, shocked.

"Yep. All ready in the kitchen. The boys, all of them, can eat."
She winked. "You'll get used to it." She handed me a plate.
"We sit everywhere for brunch. Just help yourself and enjoy."

I sat beside Ronan's nan, Sandy, on one of the large sofas,
balancing my plate on my lap. Paige and Lucy sat across from
us. Evan sat with Ronan and his brothers, thrilled to be "one
of the boys" on the floor, gathered around one of the coffee
tables, their plates piled high. Aiden joined them, sitting next
to Evan, who looked thrilled to be between Ronan and his
dad. The atmosphere was relaxed and comfortable, but still,
every so often, Ronan glanced over to check on me. Diane and
Kim sat across from us on another sofa, and the rest of the
group scattered all around the vast room on sofas and chairs,
or some, like the boys, cross-legged on the floor, using whatever was close as a table.

The laughter was loud, the conversations around us never-
ending. I was fascinated watching Ronan. Not only did he eat
with his usual gusto, he was different from what I was used to
seeing him. He and his brothers were a comedy trio, loud and
funny, making everyone chuckle. Sandy smiled and tapped her
lips with her napkin.

"I'm sure you find this all rather overwhelming."

"Actually, I find it wonderful," I admitted. "I haven't seen Evan
smile like this since—" I swallowed "—since before our
parents died."

She patted my hand. "We're a close-knit bunch. None of my
boys had a family growing up—not one of them. They made
this place and this group their family, determined no one they
cared about would ever feel the way they did as children
growing up without love."

I sipped my coffee as I listened to her. Ronan had told me she was the assistant slash den mother to the BAM boys for years.

"Without her, they would have fallen apart. She became the glue that held them together. She means so much to everyone," he explained.

He had also told me some of the history of the family, especially that of his mom and dad, thinking that his father's upbringing and early childhood struggles might help him connect with Evan in order to help him. Seeing the way Evan was conversing with Aiden, I had the feeling he was right.

There was another burst of laughter from the group, making me smile when I could hear Evan's amusement mingle with theirs.

"They are quite the comedic tag team, aren't they?"

"Yes." I watched Ronan, fascinated by this side of him. He was always funny and charming, but this was different. Another layer of his already captivating character.

She smiled in understanding. "That's what everyone sees, you know. The fun, the laughter, when they're together." She met my eyes. "But those who know him best, know there is much more to Ronan than jokes."

"There is," I agreed.

"He doesn't let many see it. He feels he needs to play a part." She sighed as she watched him. "I am glad to know he found someone he can just be himself with."

Ronan lifted his gaze to me, tilting his head in silent question. I smiled his way with a nod, and he winked and turned his attention back to his dad and Evan. Sandy chuckled beside me.

"Ah, the protectiveness of a BAM man is strong with him." She picked up a scone, nibbling on the golden-brown edge. "He is smitten." She met my gaze. "And it does my heart good to see it."

Then she leaned closer. "And unless I am mistaken, so is Liam. Paige and that darling little girl have him spellbound."

I followed her gaze and saw what she was talking about. Liam was on the sofa, holding Lucy on his lap. He fed her tidbits, listening to her intently. His leg was pressed against Paige, her hand resting on his knee. She had her other hand on Lucy's leg. The three of them looked right together, like a small family unit. It struck me how much Lucy resembled Liam with her coloring—the dark hair and hazel eyes. As if she was meant to be his. I returned my gaze to Sandy's, surprised to find it bright with tears.

"I love this family," she admitted. "Seeing them happy brings me much joy." She reached for my hand and squeezed it. "Thank you."

I couldn't respond. I had no idea what to say.

But my heart felt full.

After the massive meal, the men cleaned up, making short work of the dishes. There were two of everything in the kitchen, including dishwashers, so they were stacked and running fast. Somehow, I wasn't surprised to see how little there was in the way of leftovers. All the food disappeared, including the cakes I brought. They were exclaimed over, praised, and it was determined that they needed to be procured for every brunch, which I gathered happened every month, plus any time deemed a special occasion.

People disbursed, the noise level dropping. Small groups sat conversing. Liam took Lucy and Paige outside to show Lucy the gardens, promising she could dig in a flower bed with him. After asking my permission, Evan headed downstairs with Ronan and Aiden. A few people went for a walk.

I sat with another cup of coffee and some of the women, enjoying their chatter. When the subject turned to books, they brought up the book club again, and I told them I was rereading *Her Virtuous Viscount* again. There was some sharing of favorite parts and lots of teasing about the steamy scenes. I was amazed at how open they were—all three generations. Sandy was as into the steamy scenes as Gracie, Addi, and Ava were. Their humor was evident and their love for one another clear as they laughed and teased. I wondered if my mom would have been as comfortable with the topic, then recalled her sense of humor and knew she would be. She would be thrilled that Evan and I had found a place in a family as wonderful as this one.

I wandered downstairs and found Evan with Ronan and his dad. Aiden was talking to Evan, who was listening intently. Ronan held out his hand, and I joined them, curious about what Aiden thought.

He held up Evan's file. "You've kept immaculate records, which have been a great help."

I waited.

"I'll lay this out as clear as I can."

I nodded. "Okay."

"I think Evan could benefit with more, consistent therapy. Some intense deep tissue work. Acupuncture."

I smiled sadly. None of that was new—the problem was affording it all.

Before I could say anything, Aiden smiled in understanding. "I know you have no benefits. The fact that Evan is walking is amazing given the extent of his injuries and the help you've been able to give him. The exercises he is doing are good, but they need to be great." He sat back with a grin. "And I can make sure they are." He clapped Evan on the shoulder. "With your permission, I'd like to work with Evan. See if I can't help build more strength. Between Ronan and me, I think we can help."

At my hesitation, he frowned. "I'm not guaranteeing anything, but I think there is room for improvement. I can develop a program and be there to help Evan." He waved his hand. "I have all the machines and the tools to do so."

"Please, Beth," Evan begged. "I want to try."

"I can't afford—"

Aiden interrupted me. "We look after family. That's what we do. And if you're part of Ronan's life, then you're part of mine. That makes you family."

"How will he get here?"

Aiden and Ronan laughed. "Someone comes and goes from here every day," Ronan said. "I can bring him out here to my dad, and we can hang out while you're at work. Come on the weekend. We'll figure it out."

Gratitude and relief tore through me. The thought of the chance of Evan being able to walk better, be in less pain. Without thinking, I flung my arms around Aiden's neck and hugged him. His returned embrace was firm, comforting, and warm. The perfect dad hug.

"I have to do something," I insisted, still hugging him.

Aiden pulled back with a grin. "I love cake."

I matched his smile. "Then you have a deal."

CHAPTER TWENTY-FOUR
BETH

"I had the best day ever, Beth." Evan grinned, fighting the exhaustion bearing down on him. He'd had a session with Aiden, swam in the pool, talked to every BAM man, and picked Paul's brain about the green project they were working on. He'd eaten more than I had ever seen him eat, laughed often, and had exhausted himself so much, he was struggling to stay awake. He'd fallen asleep in the car, and Ronan had carried him inside, laying him on his bed. He woke long enough to brush his teeth before crawling back on the mattress.

I brushed back the hair on his head and kissed his forehead. "I'm glad."

"They have a family," he mumbled. "I like them."

Ronan spoke behind me. "They liked you, bud. *Everyone* liked you."

Evan's eyes drifted shut. "I like you, Ronan. You're the best big brother I could ever dream of," he mumbled, his voice getting quieter as he slipped back into sleep.

I glanced over my shoulder, meeting the tear-bright gaze of Ronan. He held out his hand, and I took it, letting him lead me from the room. Lucy was asleep in her room already, not even stirring as Liam had carried her inside. Her day had been full, too, with all the attention and activities going on. She had rarely left Liam's side, although Ronan got a few of her snuggles and kisses she lavishly bestowed on people. I was pretty certain everyone received a few from her today.

We bypassed the living room since Liam and Paige were in there and headed downstairs. In my room, Ronan encircled me in his arms.

"I agree with Evan. Today was the best day."

"Your family is great."

"I know. They always are, but somehow you being there today made me feel closer to them." He ran his nose along mine affectionately. "As strange as that sounds, it's true."

"Your dad—all the guys—made Evan feel so special."

"He is." He slipped his fingers under my chin, looking down at me. His gaze was tender and soft. "You are as well." He bent his head and kissed me, his lips ghosting over mine. "So special to me, Beth." He groaned as I opened for him. "God, I love you."

There were no more words. With our lips melded together, we slowly discarded our clothing, worshiping the skin that was uncovered. Ronan was gentle as he laid me on my bed, his warm body covering mine. Endlessly, we kissed and touched, neither of us in a hurry. I gasped as he licked my nipples, sucking them to hard peaks under his tongue. He stroked me, teasing my clit until I was begging and ready for him. I ran my hands up and down his broad back, marveling at the strength of his muscles. I licked at his neck and bit down on the lobe of his ear, liking his response. The way his arms tightened, how his cock felt as I reached between us and stroked him, the heat and heaviness of him perfect in my hand. I guided him to my center, and he hovered over me with a frown.

"No condom?"

"I'm on birth control. It's been years for me." I knew he'd been tested and was clean. All I wanted was to feel him—just him—inside me. Moving. Bringing me pleasure. I wanted to give it to him. I wanted him to forget everything and everyone but him and me.

He slid inside slowly, groaning as I closed around him.

"Jesus, you are so perfect. I feel you, baby. So perfect," he uttered, his neck arched, the muscles taut and straining. "I never knew how good it could feel."

He began to move. Long, unhurried thrusts, hitting me exactly where I needed him. Waves of pleasure coursed through my body. He kissed me, his tongue mimicking his actions. He groaned and hissed. Made low sounds of satisfaction in his chest. Murmured my name. Whispered he loved me.

I shook and whimpered. I felt his possession, his love, through every inch of my body. The way he held himself in check, careful to not hurt me, but wringing every possible ounce of ecstasy from me as he could. He slipped his fingers between us, using his thumb to draw tight circles around my clit, and I was done. I arched my back as my orgasm hit, my muscles locking down and milking his cock. I rode out the waves of intense fulfillment, chanting his name like a prayer as I came apart under him. One orgasm bled into another, and tears slid down my cheeks at the intensity of our lovemaking.

He kept moving, burying his face into my neck as he came, wrapping me close, holding me tight as he rode out his orgasm. We stilled, wrapped around each other, our bodies slick with sweat, still joined. Neither of us moved, too sated to break our connection.

"I love you," I whispered into his ear. "I love you so much, Ronan."

His arms tightened.

"I am never letting you go," he vowed. "You are everything to me, Beth. I love you, little bird."

I snuggled closer.

That was all I needed.

I was still smiling as I stepped off the bus the next afternoon. I hadn't stopped smiling all day. Ronan had spent the night, and in the early morning, I had followed him up the stairs to let him out the side door. Outside, Liam had Paige wrapped in his arms, kissing her goodbye. They were as surprised to see us as we were to see them, but Liam gave Ronan a high five as he went by, and I disappeared back into the house, trying not to laugh.

When Paige came inside, she poured a cup of coffee and sat across from me, not saying a word. Then our eyes met across the table, and we both started giggling.

It was a great way to start the day.

My phone rang, and I answered. "Hello."

"Hey, little bird. Home yet?"

"Almost. What's up?"

"Nothing. Wanted to hear your voice, check on your day."

"It's been a good one."

"Yeah?" His voice dropped to an intimate growl. "Any particular reason?"

I began to answer when I saw Evan sitting on the front step, Paige beside him. Her arm was around his shoulders, and his head was down. I began to hurry, crossing the grass, the dried twigs from the tree breaking under my sneakers. Paige looked up, sad, and Evan lifted his face. His lip was cut and bloodied, his eyes swollen from crying.

I made a funny sound, and Ronan's voice became concerned. "What's wrong? Beth—what is it?"

"I have to call you back," I breathed. "Evan," was all I said, hanging up and kneeling in front of him.

"What happened?" I asked. "Did you have an accident? Why didn't the school call me?" I pushed back his hair, shocked to see a bruise by his temple as well.

He pushed away my hand and held the cloth back to his lip. "I fell," he said sullenly.

I met Paige's eyes and saw the subtle shake of her head.

"Evan," I said firmly. "What happened?"

"Can we just leave it?"

"No," I snapped. "We can't. Did you fall, or did something else happen?" I covered my mouth. "Did those kids who were picking on you do this? Did someone touch you?"

For a moment, he said nothing.

Then he nodded. "Yes."

RONAN

I made it to Beth's as fast as I could, cursing all the traffic around me. I drove like an asshole, not caring if I got a ticket, but I was grateful I didn't. I pulled up to her house, seeing her and Evan on the step. He was leaning against her shoulder, and her arm was wrapped around him. I shut off the engine and hurried over, dropping to my knees in front of them.

"What happened? Bud, are you hurt?"

He looked up, pain and embarrassment in his expression. His lip was cut, and a bruise was forming on the side of his mouth, plus one on his temple.

I had him follow my finger and asked him a bunch of questions. He seemed fine other than the cut and bruises.

"What happened?"

"I fell."

I looked at Beth, knowing there was more to the story.

"He fell," she acknowledged. "But he had help."

"Tell me," I demanded.

He sighed, shuffling his feet and looking down. "We were in class and talking about the BAM project. We were discussing different aspects, and Mr. Humphries said something I knew was wrong, so I spoke up. I told him why he was wrong. I said exactly what Paul had told me. Mr. Humphries asked how I knew such technical information, and I told him that I'd met Paul and all the BAM guys and talked to them. He was excited and asked some other questions, and it was good, you know? To be able to answer in class and know what I was saying was right."

I nodded, knowing how much that would mean to him.

"Anyway, after school, some of the kids called me names. Said I was lying about meeting the BAM men. I told them I wasn't. I told them my sister was dating someone in the new company. They pushed me around a little and called me a liar again." He huffed. "I got angry and pushed back."

"Did they hit you?" I asked.

"No. They're too smart for that. They picked on me and moved before they got noticed. But as I turned to walk away, someone yanked my crutches out from under me and I fell. I hit my face on the cement."

"Little fuckers," I growled.

"Ronan," Beth tsked.

"They are," I insisted. "The same kind that used to push my dad around because he couldn't fight back. I loathe little cowards like that."

"Your dad got picked on?" Evan asked, his eyes wide with shock.

"He was skinnier than you. Shorter, too."

"Wow."

"Ask him when you see him this week. He'll tell you all about it."

"Did you get picked on?"

"No, I was always big for my age. But my dad made sure my brothers and I always looked out for other kids. We never used our strength to hurt anyone or intimidate them. He knew what that did to a kid."

His lip trembled. "That's good," he mumbled.

"I'm going to talk to the principal tomorrow," Beth stated.

I nodded, knowing how little good that would do, even though she had to do it. Those little fuckers would taunt him even more when his big sister came to stick up for him. She could confirm what he said, but I wasn't sure that would help Evan's case much. They would assume she was lying as well. After seeing him fall, their bullying was going to pick up even more.

I stood, looking at them. I pulled my phone from my pocket. "I'm ordering dinner, then I have some work to do." I looked at Beth. "Can I have a little alone time with Evan?"

"Paige was looking after dinner."

"You go tell her I've got it covered. Evan and I will be in in a moment."

She hesitated, and I leaned close, kissing her forehead. "Please," I breathed out.

She stood and went inside, and I sat beside Evan. "You know what boys were there?"

"Yes."

"Where did it happen?"

"Around the corner where I wait for the bus. It was a little late today."

"Anyone else around who can verify it?"

He paused. "Jenny was there. She helped me up." He held up the wad of cotton in his fist. "She gave me this to stop the bleeding on my lip."

"This Jenny—she your girl?"

He muttered something I didn't catch. I bent closer. "What?"

"I'd like her to be. She's really nice. But she's quiet, and she gets picked on too. Her mom works, and she lives in an apartment. She goes home alone every day. She walks because it's right around the block." He sighed. "She has pretty red hair, and she talks to me. Sometimes she sits and has lunch with me." He peered up at me. "We share our lunch. She never has much, so I pretend to be full so she can eat more."

My heart almost burst with pride for this kid. His parents had done a tremendous job raising him and Beth. She had carried on instilling him with goodness, and he was awesome.

"You have any information on Mr. Humphries?" I asked casually. "An email or anything?"

He nodded. "We all have teacher contacts in case we need help. He is one of mine."

"Will you share it with me?"

He looked confused but agreed.

"I'm gonna help you, bud. You just have to trust me."

He slipped his little hand in mine and squeezed. "I do, Ronan. You—you're like a big brother and a dad all rolled into one."

I wrapped my arm around him with a hug. My dad always said things were better after a hug, and he was right.

"I got you, kid."

CHAPTER TWENTY-FIVE
BETH

I tried not to take out my sour mood on the customers on Wednesday. Ronan had been right. The principal offered little in the way of help, informing me that they had a zero tolerance for bullying, but Evan had never complained and no one had seen what occurred. I argued that my brother never lied and the principal needed to question the boys. He informed me they came from very good families, and he was certain there was a simple misunderstanding.

"It is slick on the grass. Perhaps Evan's crutches simply slipped," he said, his voice condescending. I disliked him immensely. Evan was just another kid. He'd given me little assistance with Evan's disability, never tried to help or make things easier for him, and always turned a blind eye to my complaints. I had no doubt it was because of who we were. Or, more importantly, were not. I wasn't rich, influential, or important. Therefore, neither was Evan. It angered me, but that was the only school in the district Evan could attend. Until I was done with school

and got a full-time job, living with Paige was the only place we could afford.

Sometimes, life sucked.

Ronan had come in from talking to Evan, carrying two bags of Chinese food. Liam showed up, and dinner was good. Evan even smiled and laughed. After dinner, the two men sat with him again, talking, and Paige and I stayed away, giving Evan the time he wanted with them. I assumed whatever they said encouraged him, and he'd gone to school the last couple of days without complaint, and nothing seemed to happen. Still, I worried.

Earlier that afternoon, I'd gotten a message from Mr. Humphries, asking if I could come to the school tomorrow morning at eleven and meet with him. I was glad it was a light day and I could do my schoolwork from home, so I replied and said yes.

The bell jingled, and I looked up, smiling when I saw it was Ronan. He was alone tonight, and he waited by his booth until I came over and accepted his kiss.

"How's Evan?"

"Fine. I'm not sure if it bothers me more that it happened or that he has just accepted it," I admitted. "But his teacher Mr. Humphries asked to see me tomorrow, so I'm hoping he can help in some fashion. He has always been good to Evan."

He nodded slowly. "Excellent."

"Hungry?" I inquired with a grin.

He flashed me a grin. "As if you had to ask. Hit me with the special."

"Coming right up."

Ronan drove me home but didn't come in. I knew he didn't want to make a habit of sleeping over with the kids around, although I was certain neither would be surprised nor object to finding him there. He kissed me long and hard at the front door, telling me he would see me tomorrow. He held me tight, pressing a lingering kiss to my head. "Everything is going to be fine, Beth."

"Doesn't feel like it," I admitted, upset I couldn't make this better for Evan.

He drew back, touching the end of my nose playfully. "You know, Nan always says it'll be fine in the end. If it's not, then it's not over yet."

Then he bounded down the stairs and waited until I went inside. I had a feeling he was up to something, but what, I had no idea.

I supposed I would find out soon.

But nothing prepared me for what he had up his sleeve.

I weaved my way through the busy halls of the school, heading for Mr. Humphries's room, where he'd asked me to meet him. I recognized many of the kids, who seemed to be headed in the opposite direction, and I was puzzled. They were in Evan's grade, most of them in his class. I paused at his door, making sure my dress was smooth. I caught sight of myself in the glass window and I wished my hair could be controlled, but I had long given up on that happening. I lifted my hand, knocked, and walked in, surprised to see Evan sitting there. And Ronan.

My breath caught as he stood. Dressed in a navy suit, a richly patterned tie, and his shoes glossy under the lights, he looked every inch the rich businessman he was. How I had thought him a trainer or construction worker seemed ludicrous now.

"Ronan?" I asked, confused.

Mr. Humphries stepped forward and shook my hand. "Thanks for meeting me here. I wanted to say hello before the presentation."

"Presentation," I repeated.

He nodded. "In the gym. We have a special guest meeting with us today."

It clicked. Ronan was the special guest. He was going to talk to the school, proving that Evan hadn't been lying.

"I thought we'd walk down together," Mr. Humphries added.

"Um, sure."

Ronan smiled at me with a wink, remaining uncharacteristically silent. He held open the door, waiting until Evan and his teacher walked through. He caught my elbow and bent close to my ear. "See, it wasn't finished yet."

I turned and pressed my lips to his. "I love you."

His smile was wide. "I know."

We were the last into the gym. Ronan squeezed my arm and followed Mr. Humphries to the stage. He spoke for a moment about the class he was teaching and how excited he had been when a member of the very company they were discussing reached out and offered to come in and talk to the school about their company and what it stood for. He introduced

Ronan, who stepped up to the microphone amid the applause in the room. He waved, confident and sure of himself.

"Thanks to Mr. Humphries for allowing me here today. More importantly, I'd like to bring a friend of mine up here with me. He inspires me every day to be a better man. He's smart, funny, and we have a blast building Lego together. Evan Jones, come on up here, bud."

All eyes were on Evan as he made his way to the front. I saw the kids turning to one another in disbelief, one small group seemingly especially animated, their heads bent together as they talked to one another. Paige suddenly appeared by my side.

"Did you know?" I asked, my eyes on Evan.

"Liam told me this morning. I hurried over—like I would miss this." She clasped my arm. "You have no idea," she breathed out.

Ronan high-fived Evan and turned back to the microphone. "Now, I'm just an architect. I draw the buildings for ABC, and I have a hand in a lot of the BAM work these days. But I think you should hear about the companies and the projects from the men who oversee it all. So, without further ado, kids, I give you—BAM and ABC."

From the side where I hadn't noticed, Bentley, Aiden, and Maddox walked to the center. Behind them were the members of ABC—all of them. I gaped at the show of solidarity. Ronan had done this for Evan. For me.

They were a formidable group. The men tall and confident. The women intelligent and well-spoken. It was an impressive sight, and Paige was correct. I had no idea.

I listened as they all talked, starting with Bentley. None talked long, but they spoke of the company, the buildings, their vision. Paul spoke about the green project he was in charge of and answered a few questions. Each company member had insight to offer and kept it entertaining and motivational. It moved to education, to friendship, and by the time Aiden came to the microphone, I knew how it was going to end.

He was tall and strong in front of the kids. He talked of his childhood, meeting the men he, to this day, called his best friends later in life. He spoke about his dyslexia and how it shaped him. How they accepted him and helped him.

"They never looked down on me," he said. "Life is too short to be a dick," he said, staring across the sea of upturned faces. "We need to help one another. *Be kind*. We run our business that way, and we live it too." He shook his head. "That shit is free, so you need to spread it around."

I saw Bentley drop his head to his chest with a sigh. Maddox's shoulders were shaking with unreleased mirth. All of Aiden's kids were trying not to laugh, but it was perfect. These kids understood that lingo.

Aiden lifted his shoulders, knowing he had crossed a line and not caring. "It's just as easy to lift a person up as to put them down. Easier, in fact. You'd be shocked how good it makes you feel inside. Remember—how you treat someone reflects on you, not them. Making someone else feel less is not going to help *you* feel better."

There was silence in the room.

"Bullying is not cool. Learning, helping, being a decent human being is. Trust me, I know."

He stepped back, stopping in front of Evan and giving him a high five then a fast hug. He stood next to him, a silent warrior. It occurred to me the entire family was circling around Evan. My heart was full seeing it, and I had to wipe my eyes more than once.

Bentley returned to the microphone and finished off the talk. He thanked the school and the principal for allowing them to break up a school day, then announced they would take questions. Hands went up, and for the next hour, they listened and answered every single one. Never impatient or rushed, they took their time, only cutting it off when signaled to do so, and even then, Aiden snuck in the last hands that were raised. Bentley made one last announcement.

"BAM and ABC Corp have sponsored a help line. If you need someone to talk to, if you're having problems at home, being bullied, or just need a friendly voice, you can call and talk to someone. It's open twenty-four hours a day and is completely confidential." He paused, casting his intense gaze around the room. "No one has to be alone. Pick up the phone and call." He smiled. "There are handouts on your way out, or ask one of your teachers. They all have the information. Remember what Aiden said." A smile tugged on his mouth. "Maybe without the cursing. Be kind."

The members of the company remained where they were as the school filed from the room, talking among themselves. They had applauded loudly at the end, a few whoops and cheers shouted.

I approached the group, unsure what to say, how to say it, or even if I could. The principal stepped in front of me, looking shell-shocked. His forehead glistened with sweat, and his voice was overly friendly.

"Miss Jones," he began. "I believe we need a private word."

Ronan appeared by my side. "Later."

"Of course," he muttered. "Whenever is convenient." He paused, obviously hoping for something else, but I remained silent, and he turned and walked away. Ronan led me to his family, and I looked at all of them with gratitude. "Thank you. For what you did for Evan, thank you."

Liam huffed. "We couldn't let them get away with calling him a liar."

"Or hurting him," Aiden added, his hand on Evan's shoulder. "Not happening again."

"The help line was very generous," Paige said.

Bentley smiled. "We sponsor a lot of help lines and programs. We do it for Aiden and kids like him. So they know they aren't as alone as it seems."

His words touched my soul. The stern businessman with a heart of gold. All of them.

"Do you think it will make a difference?" I asked quietly to Ronan.

He grinned. "All the firepower of BAM and ABC claiming Evan as one of ours? Absolutely. I think the little fuckers will think twice about bullying anyone."

"Ronan," Bentley hissed. "We're in a school, for heaven's sake. With kids. Watch the language."

"If my dad can do it, so can I," he protested. "Besides, there're no kids around."

"Evan is here," I pointed out dryly.

"Evan isn't a kid. He's family," Ronan stated firmly, erasing any lingering doubt I had left about our place in his life.

He was all in.

And so was I.

Ronan took Evan and me to lunch. Liam and Paige disappeared together, and I didn't ask where they were headed. She deserved a little alone time with him.

Evan sat with Ronan, talking to him, thanking him.

"How did you do this?" I asked.

Ronan smiled. "I contacted Mr. Humphries. Told him who I was and that we wanted to come in and talk to his class. He asked if we'd talk to everyone that he taught since they were all learning about green building and the future. I told him to open it to anyone at the school he wanted, but it had to be fast. He arranged it. I talked to my dad, and he got everyone on board." He shrugged. "Simple."

I laughed. "Yes, so simple."

He leaned forward, his hand on Evan's shoulder. "It's not going to solve everything. I know school is almost done for the year, but maybe they'll think about it over the summer. Come back as decent little humans instead of little shits that like to kick out the crutches of someone struggling. Maybe they'll think twice before they knock someone down."

"Maybe they'll help someone up," Evan added.

Ronan high-fived him. "That's the plan."

I smiled watching them. "What your family did was incredible."

Ronan met my eyes. "They did it for me. For you and Evan. Because they know how much you both mean to me."

My throat felt thick, and I could only nod.

Ronan turned to Evan. "I saw your girl. She's cute. I like the red hair."

I had spoken with Jenny too. She was a sweet girl, too thin and too serious, but I knew how much Evan liked her. I had a feeling the serious part was due to her life, not her personality.

"What does her mother do?" Ronan asked. "Do you know?"

"She works at a hotel. She works until six every day." Evan looked sad. "Jenny is alone until she gets home."

I frowned. "You never mentioned that before, Evan."

"You have enough to deal with," he said. "I can't go home with her because I can't walk home after. She can't come with me because she can't go on the bus." He shrugged. "Telling you wouldn't help because I know you'd only worry."

"What will she do all summer?" Ronan asked.

"Last summer, she stayed home most of the time. She walked to the park sometimes, but her mom was always worried. She went to a couple of free camps, but otherwise, she was on her own."

"Maybe we can do something this year," I told him. "We can help. I'll call her mom."

"That would be awesome." He looked at the clock. "I have to get back to school."

Ronan grabbed the bill. "Okay, bud. Gimme a minute."

Evan watched him walk away. "He is the best guy, Beth. We're so lucky."

"Yeah, we are."

———

After we dropped Evan back at school, Ronan glanced at his watch. "You have a couple of hours until you have to be at work. Are you wanting to go home, or can I keep you?"

"You can keep me if you want."

"Awesome."

He drove us to his condo, leaving me in the living room as he went to change. I looked outside at the people on the street below, rushing to get somewhere. To work, home, errands, appointments. The city always seemed busy. I sighed, suddenly tired as the day and the emotions hit me. What Ronan and his family had done for Evan. What a difference Ronan made in my life. Our lives. Evan adored him. He was right. We were incredibly lucky. He gave so much.

What did I have to offer him in return?

Ronan wrapped his arms around me, pulling me back to his chest.

"What are you thinking about? You look so serious."

"What you did today, Ronan... How can I ever repay you?"

He stiffened. "I don't expect payment, Beth. That's not how this works."

"I can't compete. I can't do what you do. You belong to this huge, wonderful family." I was horrified to feel tears filling my eyes. "Why do you love me? I'm a poor, struggling student with way too many responsibilities. I can barely keep up, and you just keep being more amazing." I sniffled. "I don't know where I belong," I added quietly.

He hugged me back, sitting on his chair and keeping me locked tight to his chest.

"I don't know where this is coming from, but let's address it, okay?" he murmured in my ear.

"I love you for many reasons. I don't give a shit if you're poor or how many responsibilities you have. You're strong, capable, talented, smart, and loving. You go to school, look after your brother. Help Paige raise Lucy. You work, study, bake, you look after everyone around you, and you never ask for anything in return." He shook his head. "You don't see yourself the way I see you. You have a beautiful soul that draws people to you."

"You might get tired of—"

He cut me off, turning me so I saw the intense, serious expression on his face. "Your life doesn't scare me, Beth. If anything, mine should scare you. My huge family, the company, the need I feel for you." He held my face. "That should scare you. *Fuck*, it scares me. I have never needed anyone the way I need you."

"Why?" I whispered. "I'm just me. Plain, chubby, overdone Beth."

He sat back in shock. "Surely to God you know that isn't true. You are none of those things."

I looked away, and he slipped his fingers under my chin. "Today was hard for you, wasn't it? Letting go of the reins.

Letting me and my family step in and take a little responsibility off your shoulders."

I blinked at his words. Was that why I was feeling so overwhelmed suddenly? So unsure of myself?

He smiled, his voice gentle. "It's okay to need help. It's okay to accept help. Especially from me. I want to help you in every way I can, because unlike what you think, you give it right back. You make me feel loved, Beth. Needed. Wanted. Just for me. When you show me this side of you, it shows me how much you trust me. But I need you to understand something."

I couldn't look away from his gaze. "What?"

He ran his finger down my cheek. "You are not plain. You are intoxicatingly lovely. Your hair, your face—everything about you pleases me." He smiled as he traced over the line of freckles on my nose. "Do you know you have a matching line of freckles, just like this, on the back of your neck?"

I shook my head. "No one ever told me that."

"I don't think you could see them unless you were looking. I love kissing both. Knowing I discovered it—like my own little secret about you." He ran his hand along my leg. "You aren't chubby. You have curves. I love every one of them. The way your waist indents above your hips. Your gorgeous breasts. And your ass." He dropped his voice. "It's spectacular."

He wrapped his hand around mine, pressing it to his erection. "I'm hard just thinking about you, little bird. I can't fake that."

"Oh," I breathed out, curling my hand around him.

He dropped his head for a moment, his breathing getting faster. He lifted his chin, meeting my eyes. "As for being overdone, you are anything but. You are easygoing and wonderful. Your heart is a gift. The fact that you love me is a treasure I will never take for granted."

He brushed a curl off my cheek. "Whatever brought up these worries, forget them, Beth. I'm yours. I adore everything about you. I want to mesh my life with yours not because I have to but because I want to. Maybe if we share our worlds, both of us will be happier." He smiled. "I will never get tired of looking after you, because I know you're doing the same right back to me." He studied me intently. "As for belonging, I'll say this. Yes, I have a big family I'm part of. Just like Evan is your brother, so he is part of you. But if you're wondering where you belong? You're looking at him. You belong to *me*. If you're ever lost and can't remember your place, look at me. You're mine." He cupped my neck, holding me close. "We belong to each other, and together with Evan, we'll make our own family. That's where you belong, Beth. With me. Never doubt it, and never forget it."

Something eased inside my chest. A loosening of doubt I hadn't known I was carrying broke away and vanished. "I love you," I whispered. "I can't imagine my life without you anymore."

"Good. Because you're stuck with me."

He stood, lifting me, and for once, I didn't worry about how I felt to him. I could sense his love in his touch, feel his strength. It was as if he had been made for me.

And as he laid me on his bed and gazed down at me, I knew.

I had been made for him, too.

CHAPTER TWENTY-SIX
RONAN

Beth stirred in my arms and slowly woke, confused in the early evening light. After I had made love to her, she'd fallen asleep, and I didn't move. I wanted her to rest, unencumbered by doubts or worries. I had a feeling she was rarely afforded that luxury.

She smiled up at me, her curls even wilder than usual, having been crushed in my fists as I drove into her over and again. She was sexy and sweet as she blinked, looking drowsy and content. Then she frowned, gasped, and sat up, looking around in panic.

"Ronan! I'm late—my shift started an hour ago." She started to scramble from my bed, and I grabbed her arm, laughing.

"Calm down, little bird. You, ah, you aren't working tonight."

She looked at me as if I had lost my mind. "Pardon me?"

"I called Mike this morning and asked him if he could get someone to cover. I told him I had something special planned.

He said no problem." I paused. "I also asked Evan for permission to keep you overnight."

She pursed her lips, and I waited for the explosion. She surprised me when, instead, she wrapped her arms around her knees calmly. "What did he say?"

"Little shit gave me a list of requirements and rules. Let's just say a new box of Lego is being delivered, pizza and ice cream are owed, and I have to treat you nicely. *Really* nicely."

She chuckled.

"I told him what I had in mind for you didn't fall under the nice category, and he shut up pretty fast. I think 'gross' was the word used."

She fell back laughing. Pleased, I lay down beside her. "You're not mad?"

"No. Thanks to the cake orders, I'm fine, and frankly, the thought of spending the evening and the night with you is too awesome to resist. Especially if you treat me *really nicely.*" She cupped my cheek. "I'll let it pass this time, but you can't do that without talking to me, Ronan."

"Okay," I agreed quickly, already knowing my plans for the future. I just had to talk to a few people about what I was thinking and see if we could move all the pieces into place. I was certain we could, but until then, I would stay quiet.

She narrowed her eyes. "What are you up to?"

I kissed her. "Nothing." Before she could question me more, I kissed her again. "Now, you have me all evening and all night. What would you like to do?"

She began to speak, then stopped.

"What?"

"It's going to sound lame."

"Tell me."

"I never get to do nothing, you know?"

I waggled my eyebrows. "So, you want to stay in bed all night? I can get with that plan."

She laughed. "No—well, yes—but no. Maybe early to bed."

I kissed the end of her nose, dropping a few fast kisses on the line of freckles that covered the bridge. "What do you want to do until then?"

"Could we just relax and watch a movie?"

"Popcorn?"

"Oh yes."

"How about I order some pizza?"

"Um, could we have some wings too?"

I pinned her under me, kissing her neck and growling. "I knew you were the perfect woman for me."

She pulled me to her mouth. "Yes, I am."

———

BETH

The door to the diner opened, the bell ringing out. I could tell it was Ronan from the loud, fast peal of the chime. He entered the diner quickly, as if he couldn't wait to get inside. I always knew when it was him these days. I picked up the order I was getting in the kitchen.

"Bert, can I have the usual, please?"

He chuckled. "Your man is in the house, is he?"

"Pretty darn certain."

"Coming up."

"Thanks."

I opened the door with my hip and carried the tray to the table, unloading it and checking on the customers. The place had been hopping all day but was finally quieting down. I turned and met Ronan's affectionate gaze, still amazed at how complete he made me feel just being in the same room together. I walked over to his booth and leaned down, accepting his kiss happily. I pulled back, smiling.

"Hello, Thor," I teased.

He grinned. I'd called him that one day while he was gripping me in the shower, holding me up and taking me again before I left his place. I still marveled at his strength, and it had slipped out before I could stop it. He liked it, so I used it.

"Hey, little bird. I'm hungry."

"I figured. Working out with the dynamic duo?"

He also liked my name for Paul and Jeremy. They made sure to spend time together every week, and they kept in close contact. I really liked Kim and Diane, and we went out together as a group, Ronan no longer feeling like a third wheel. He was open and happy when we were together, and I loved that funny, teasing side to him. I loved every side of him.

"Yeah. They were headed off in different directions, and I came straight to you."

"Good."

"Have time to sit with me?"

"Yep. Jane will take over. I already ordered your dinner."

"Awesome."

Ten minutes later, I slid the turkey club with extra mayo and tomatoes in front of him with a side salad and extra pickles. He picked up the massive sandwich, looking at it with appreciation. "Woman, you spoil me."

I smiled as I sipped my coffee.

"Evan excited over the last day of school tomorrow?"

"Yes, he is. He is even more excited about being in Port Albany for a week."

Aiden and Cami had insisted on him staying with them. Aiden had been working with him diligently, and I could see the improvement in Evan's leg over the past month. Aiden wanted to spend time with him daily, and Evan was so excited he was almost bursting.

Ronan looked thoughtful as he chewed. He cleared his throat. "Addi offered Anne a job today."

I blinked. "Anne—as in, Jenny's mom?"

We had gotten to know her over the past few weeks because of Evan telling us about Jenny. Anne wasn't much older than Ronan, pretty, with auburn hair and brown eyes. She was completely alone, with no family, very proud and independent, but struggling. They lived close to the school, and Jenny spent some days with Evan after school and we saw her a lot on the weekends. Anne took any hours she could at the hotel where she worked to make ends meet, even though she hated the time it took away from her and her daughter. With the help of Ronan's family, three days a week, Jenny was given a ride to our place. She and Evan studied together, watched TV with Lucy, and ate dinner with us. It took some persuading on my part, but Anne finally allowed it.

Ronan wiped his mouth. "Yes."

"Where?"

"She is going to be the liaison between the hotel in Port Albany we're opening and the winery. She's been taking business courses online on top of working. She does hours behind the concierge desk, as well as reservations and her work in the catering department. She has all the knowledge." He crumpled a napkin between his fingers. "And ABC is going to give her the chance for the experience."

"She'll be perfect," I enthused. Anne was warm and smart. Level-headed and responsible. Then it hit me.

"How is it going to work? She doesn't drive."

He inhaled. "She is moving to Port Albany. We bought a couple houses in town and have fixed them up. She can live there with reasonable rent, Jenny can go to a decent school, and Anne will have normal hours."

I smiled sadly. "That is awesome for her, sad for Evan. Jenny is his best friend."

Since the visit from BAM, there had been no more bullying. There had been a lot of fake interest in Evan, but he was too smart to fall for it. He stuck to the couple of people who had liked him before they knew of his association with BAM and ABC.

"He'll miss her."

"The position is perfect for Anne. Addi really likes her—so does everyone else. She'll be working with Theo, who is going to run both the winery and the hotel when it's complete. He thinks she is incredible and is very enthusiastic." He paused. "Very."

I widened my eyes. "Like, personally enthusiastic?"

"He's not saying, but it wouldn't shock me."

I laughed. "Reid and Becca would love an instant grandchild."

"We'll see what happens."

He entwined our fingers. "Addi has lots of plans for the winery. Big changes."

"Well, one thing that is certain in life is change, isn't it?"

He met my eyes, his gaze intense. "Yep. How open we are to that change depends on the outcome, I guess."

I stood. "Okay, Mr. Philosophical. Break's over. Finish your dinner, and I'll bring you a piece of cake."

He nodded, but I felt his gaze on me the rest of the night.

Sunday afternoon was one of my favorite days of the month. I spent it with the ladies of BAM and ABC, and we talked books. Our shared love of historical romance united us. I loved them all.

Cami, Emmy, and Dee were a tight unit, their friendship long-standing and wonderful. Becca, Fiona, and Liv were all enthusiastic participants. Sandy loved a "good read," as she called it, informing me once with a wink that "Jordan enjoyed the benefits as well."

The whole room burst out laughing when Addi grinned. "All the men do," she deadpanned.

Addi, Gracie, Ava, and Heather were always there. Chloe, Addi's sister, came when her busy schedule allowed it. Between school and her volunteer work at the animal shelter, she was always on the go. Shelby came and went as the mood struck her, still more interested in paint or clay than the written word. She was quieter than the other women of her generation, but I liked her and enjoyed talking to her. She often came into the diner when I was working, bringing other artists with her. She was eclectic and funny. I noticed how often one certain man appeared in her groups, always close, always watching her. He was an art gallery owner, and I had a feeling he was far more interested in her as a person than simply as an artist. I sensed his feelings and wondered if Shelby was as blind to them as she seemed.

Often, Katy would appear via Zoom. I had met her a couple of times while visiting, and I liked her a great deal. Gracie and Heather looked like her, and she was hilarious when she got going. I had been intimidated by her husband, Richard, the first time I met him, but he sat with Evan, talking to him about his back injury and what he had gone through, and I saw the gentle, loving man beneath the cool exterior and had grown as fond of him as I had his daughters. He loved to drop in during the Zoom meetings and say something outrageous to Katy, making us all laugh, then disappearing again. One time, in particular, she laughed and turned back to the camera.

"Always the star of the show," she muttered.

"I heard that!" he'd retorted in the background.

Everyone laughed with her, because it was true.

Not every "cousin" liked historical romances, which was fine, but anyone who did was welcome. It was a lively, fun group. There was wine, talking, sharing, and much laughter.

"What book is next?" asked Ava from the corner.

"I think we should start the Wicked Winters series," I offered. "The books are shorter, so we should be able to read two each month." I grinned. "They are very, ah, fast reads." I winked at Kim and Diane, who were joining us for the first time. "A good introduction for you two."

"Awesome," Diane enthused.

Shouts of laughter from downstairs made me grin. Evan and all the men were downstairs. A huge table had been constructed, and all the Lego was being built. They had competitions, teams, and the rules were easy—there was none. Stealing happened, towers were knocked down, and it was a general free-for-all. But they all loved it. Lucy was an honorary member, always perched on someone's shoulder—although Liam, Ronan, and Aiden were her favorites.

I loved being part of this group of amazing women. This wonderful, loud, loving family.

We finished our discussion and broke off into smaller groups as usual. I wandered to the library to have a cup of coffee and enjoy the view before I went downstairs to get Ronan and Evan. I was surprised when Addi joined me.

Addi looked tired, and I smiled as she put her feet up, sitting across from me.

"How are you feeling?"

"Grateful the first trimester is over." She grinned. "I missed food. And even though my caffeine intake is limited, I missed that too."

We were quiet for a moment, and I noticed she seemed to be waiting for something—or someone.

"What's up?" I asked.

Before she could respond, Ronan strolled in, dropping into the chair beside me. He leaned over and kissed my cheek. "Hey."

Now I knew for sure something was up. "Hi," I responded.

He took my hand. "I need you to listen with an open mind, okay?"

I frowned. "Sure."

He nodded at Addi. "You're up."

She shifted in her seat. "I have an offer for you. I'm going to make it, and you can think it over. Promise me you won't say no right off."

"You're making me very nervous."

She laughed. "Sorry, I didn't mean to." She paused. "I would like to offer you a job."

"A job," I repeated.

She nodded. "The winery is booked solid all summer and fall, and even winter now. We've always offered the best for catering and service, and we want to add another layer to that."

"I know nothing about catering."

"But you know about desserts."

I was more confused than ever. "You want me to make some cakes for the winery?"

She shook her head. "We want to offer your cakes exclusively. We want you to do all the cakes for the winery's functions." She rattled off a number, and I felt myself go pale.

"I can't possibly bake that number of cakes plus waitress."

She looked at Ronan, who turned to me. "You wouldn't have to waitress anymore, Beth. You would be under exclusive contract to ABC. You would have a kitchen here to work from. People to help you."

"But school and commuting," I sputtered. "Evan—how could I look after him when—"

He held up his hand. "Let me explain."

Addi stood. "I am going to leave you two to discuss this. But the offer is coming from ABC with full approval from every-one. In fact, it was Dad's idea. We discussed it thoroughly, and we all saw the value of it. Ronan knows all the details—I'll let him tell you because I know how it will affect the two of you."

She left, pulling the French doors shut behind her. I stared at Ronan. "I don't understand."

"It's simple, really. We have an excellent chef at the winery, but we contract out all the desserts. We've had a great place making cakes, but they sold, and we don't like the product the new ownership is producing. It's our reputation on the line."

"But Ronan, I only make cakes. I can't make pastries or anything else."

He nodded. "We know. But we checked our records. Ninety percent of the events request cake for dessert. Especially weddings. Your cakes would be a huge asset to the company."

"But school and commuting…"

He smiled. "School isn't an issue, nor is commuting. We can work around your schedule. The beauty of this is you would know months ahead of what is needed and when. It can all be structured."

My mind was reeling. The thought of not having to waitress. Be on my feet all the time. Deal with difficult customers. I hated all those parts of the job, but it was something I had to do. At least, until now. Still, it was a lot to wrap my head around.

I met his eyes. They were gentle and anxious all at the same time. "Evan," I began.

He shocked me when he slid to his knees in front of me. "Evan will be fine." He took in a deep breath. "Because I want you and Evan to move here to Port Albany." He paused. "With me."

I stared at him. *"What?"*

"I want you guys with me. I hate waking up without you. I hate wondering how Evan's day was and having to wait until I see him to ask. I worry about you all the time. I want you with me. Here."

I had no words, and he kept talking.

"Jenny is going to be in Port Albany. He can go to the same school as her. He'll still have his best friend. You'll be surrounded by family to help. Think how much easier it will be for Evan to get treatment. My dad is here every day. Evan will have access to the pool and the gym every day." He ran a finger down my cheek. "I'll get *you* every day." He smiled, his voice soft. "Nothing would make me happier than that."

"I don't drive," I objected.

He laughed. "Every day, little bird. There is someone in and out of Toronto every day. Multiple times. You would never be stuck. We'd figure it all out. And you'd have a more manageable schedule. No more working nights, no more Saturdays. Your life would be easier. Evan would be happier here away from that school. You would be happier."

"And you?" I asked.

"I would be ecstatic. I'd have you and Evan. We'd be together."

"Paige and Lucy," I whispered. "I can't leave them."

He leaned close. "You won't be. My brother is all in where they're concerned. He asked her yesterday to move here with him."

I blinked in shock. "He did *what* now?"

He laughed. "Last night."

"She didn't say anything!"

"Because, like you, she was concerned what would happen to you. She told Liam she couldn't leave you alone."

"So, if I say yes to you, then she'll say yes to Liam?"

His eyes twinkled. "Maybe?"

Suddenly, I began to laugh. "Incorrigible isn't the right word for you Callaghan boys."

He pressed closer, gathering my hands in his. "Say yes, Beth. Come live with me. We'll work it all out. Join me in this crazy place and make this our home. Together. Please."

This man.

This amazing, wonderful man had just offered me a new life. One with him but still including the people who were my family. We would all be close. I would have him with me every day. Evan would be happier. I would be happier. My life would be easier. Better. Brighter.

There was only one answer I could give.

"Yes."

I looked around the boxes, shocked at how little I actually had to move. Mostly books and clothes. The rest of the stuff was Evan's. A few pieces of furniture I had from my parents. That was it. Paige was staying behind, and Liam was planning on being here with her until the end of the month. The landlord had someone else wanting to move in and had let us out of our lease. It worked out well for both parties, so he hadn't objected much.

Liam was busy with the rest of the BAM crew creating a room for Lucy that he wanted ready before they moved in a few weeks. Evan had a fabulous time with Liv Morrison, Van's wife, who decorated his room in his favorite colors of blue and red. The rest of the house, Ronan and I decided we would work on gradually. Evan was excited to be moving—the thought of a new school, an instant big family, and Jenny still being around all making him happy. He adored Ronan, and I knew he was looking forward to the change.

I had sat and spoken with Addi and Brayden, then all the men of BAM. I looked over their numbers, satisfied this offer wasn't made up. The numbers Maddox had shown me were accurate and well-thought-out. The one stickler was that ABC had the exclusive rights to the cakes I made. Mike wasn't overly happy, although he'd known our arrangement wouldn't last forever. He hadn't been pleased that I was leaving the diner as a wait-ress either.

"You're one of the honest, hard-working ones," he said. "Dependable. Your cakes brought in a lot of business."

I agreed to fulfill all the orders that were waiting before I left, so I parted on good terms. Then I suggested he talk to Jane, who sometimes helped me bake.

"She's looking for extra money," I said. "Her banana cake is awesome. I bet she could fill in very well."

That tidbit of information helped smooth my way out.

I rearranged my upcoming school schedule. Some of my courses were online, and I was able to get the ones I needed to attend in person to Tuesdays and Wednesdays. Ronan made those his days to be in Toronto, and we would stay overnight in the condo. There were so many places for Evan to stay on a

Tuesday night—he was spoiled for choice. I was still getting used to having people around to help. I wasn't sure if I would ever get used to having that many.

Paige came in as I was sealing the last box. "Ready?" she asked.

I smiled. "Not sure I will ever be ready for this."

She laughed, nodding. "I'll miss seeing you every day."

"It's not for long. Soon, we'll both be at the compound. You can see Liam's house from Ronan's front door. We'll see each other all the time." I sat down beside her. "Life is going to be so different, Paige." I paused. "So much better, though." I nudged her with my elbow. "Who knew when you asked for a single brother this would happen?"

She laughed, but it sounded forced.

"What is it?"

"Liam wants to get married."

"Wow."

"And adopt Lucy."

I gaped at her. "Holy shit."

She plucked at the edge of her shirt. "And he wants to do it soon. Before I move in."

"And you don't? Too fast?" I guessed.

She sighed. "That's the scary part, Beth. I do. I want to marry him. I want to let Lucy call him Daddy. She's dying to do so." She laughed softly. "So is he, I think."

"But…"

"Shouldn't I be scared? After what happened before? Shouldn't all this scare the shit out of me? I mean, is there something wrong with me that all I can think of is how much I want that too?"

I took her hand in mine. "Some people would think so, but I don't. Liam is different. I've seen how he looks at you. The love he feels for you and Lucy. He's like Ronan. What you see is what you get. They're special. Wonderful. And you love him, don't you?"

She nodded. "I do. I know he's nothing like my ex. You would just think I would want to be more cautious."

"Or maybe your heart knows what is right. You said you had doubts last time. Do you feel those with Liam?"

"None. All I feel is an absolute rightness."

"Then say yes."

"Neither of us wants a big wedding. In fact, we only plan on getting married with our witnesses. Maybe a party after if anyone was interested?"

I laughed. "As if this family would let an occasion like that go without a party?"

She sniffled. "Our family," she said softly and flung her arms around my neck. "Now we get to be real sisters."

I hugged her back, my heart filled with happiness for her. "Yes, we do."

I woke up with a start, confused. Outside was dark, but the windows were open, a gentle breeze blowing in, stirring the curtains, and moonlight softened the blackness. Beside me, Ronan slept, his big body close to mine, his arm draped over my hip. When I jerked, he moved, lifting up on his elbow.

"Beth? Little bird? What is it?"

In the dark, I sought his embrace. His warmth wrapped around me, his strength real and needed.

"Tell me," he whispered.

"I-I was dreaming," I replied, swallowing the lump in my throat. "I dreamed *this* was all a dream. You weren't real, and I was still alone." A sob escaped my throat. "How silly, a dream about a dream."

He held me closer, kissing my head. "Not a dream, baby. I'm here, and I'm not going anywhere. We're just starting, and it's going to be great."

He slipped his fingers under my chin and kissed me, his lips soft and gentle on mine. I pushed closer, needing, wanting his touch. Wanting to feel him move with me. He groaned low in his chest, his arms tightening. We kissed until my body screamed with desire for him. I rolled on top of him, positioning myself and taking him inside.

"Holy merciful…" he cursed, gripping my hips.

I was glad Evan's new room was at the other end of the hall as I began to move. I rested my hands on Ronan's chest, rolling my hips, riding him.

The bed creaked, the headboard hitting the wall. Ronan reached up and grabbed it with one hand, anchoring it in place, the action causing his biceps to swell. He looked so sexy under me in the dim light, the look of pure pleasure on his face.

My muscles tightened and I moved faster. Ronan's pillow slipped, and he groaned as he orgasmed, his back arching off the bed, his grip tightening on my hip. I shut my eyes, color exploding behind the lids as I shook with my release.

Then I collapsed on his chest.

For a moment, there was only the sound of our heavy breathing. Then Ronan spoke. "Is this going to be a regular thing? Not the dreams, but attacking me in the middle of the night? Because I'm all for it."

I giggled.

"I need to anchor this headboard if it is. Oil the bedframe. I wonder if we could add extra insulation to the walls."

I began to laugh. "Maybe some headphones for Evan would be cheaper."

"Hmm." He ran his hand down my back. "I'll go on Amazon in the morning and get some." He lifted my chin. "Okay now, little bird?"

"Yeah. I think I was feeling overwhelmed and nervous. All the change," I explained. "First night in a new place and all."

"I understand. And if you need to work that shit out again later? I'm right here. Anytime. I'm your guy."

I smiled. "Yes, you are."

I fell asleep wrapped in his arms.

CHAPTER TWENTY-SEVEN
RONAN

I checked everything one more time, not leaving anything to chance. Evan shot me a grin. "Relax, it's all good. It's going to work perfectly."

I ruffled his hair. "Easy for you to say, kid."

He laughed. "I suppose."

I grew serious. "Thanks, though, for all this." I indicated the table. "She'll love it."

He beamed at me. "I know."

Upstairs, I heard the women moving around, and I huffed out a long breath. "Showtime."

"You got this," Evan assured me. "It's a slam dunk."

I grinned at him, still hard to believe this was the same kid I had met a few months ago. Since moving here six weeks ago, he had begun to fill out, and his walk was getting better. His leg was stronger and his gait more confident. My dad hoped that he might be able to walk with one crutch soon, and after that—none. Evan's posture had changed, and he had become surer of himself. A lot of that had to do with my family, but a huge part of it was his new home life. Beth was around more —she was relaxed. I was there. We were a family unit. I was part brother/part father, and I prized every aspect of both. It had taken Beth longer to settle than Evan. He was all too happy to embrace his new reality, Beth feared losing hers, but the past couple of weeks, she was better. I loved hearing her laugh. Sharing meals with her and Evan. Watching movies or taking walks on the beach. Lying in bed and having her tell me about the clouds we could see or listen about the approaching weather system.

Liam and Paige married quickly and quietly. Beth and I were their witnesses, and we went out to dinner afterward. We kept Lucy for the weekend, and on Sunday when they got home, they announced it to the family.

The following weekend, everyone celebrated. I swore no one could pull off a party the way my family could. Even short notice and low-key, it was epic.

And now, it was my turn.

I climbed the steps, hearing the chatter that always followed a book club meeting. Broken into smaller groups, they were having coffee or wine. Most of the men were back in the fold, always anxious to steal away their other half and find out what had been discussed. I personally liked it when Beth would read to me, and I would help her reenact my favorite parts of the book just so she fully grasped its contents. Scarlett Scott had become my favorite author, because her steamy scenes always made me smile.

Widely.

I found Beth in her favorite place in the Hub. Sitting in the library, quietly enjoying a few moments to herself. Those were still rare for her these days. But she welcomed me with a smile.

"Hey, Thor. What you been up to?"

"Evan and I made some cool stuff with our Lego."

"Oh yeah?" She laughed. "You two and your Lego."

I held out my hand. "Come see."

She let me pull her from her chair, and we headed downstairs. No one moved from their spot or followed us. They all knew better.

She shook my hand. "You're holding me too tight, Ronan. And why is your hand shaking?"

"Oh, sorry," I muttered.

Downstairs, I led her to the table, stopping in front of it. She frowned in confusion at the array of Lego bricks laid out in odd ways.

"Um, an abstract?"

I held out my hand. "It's better if you look at it from up high. Climb on the chair."

She chuckled. "You guys have gotten so complex." But she let me help her up, and I kept one hand on her to make sure she was steady. She rested her hand on my shoulder and looked down at the table, the abstract now clear.

Words, not objects.

Marry Me. Please.

She read the words once, twice. She covered her mouth with her hand, then turned to me, her eyes flying open wide when she saw me holding a ring.

"Ronan," she breathed.

"I love living with you. Having you with me every day. I want it—I want *you* forever. Marry me."

Tears formed in her eyes.

"Evan gave me permission to ask you. He gave me his blessing. Now I just need you to say yes."

"Are you sure?" she asked.

I lifted her from the chair and took her hands. "Beth. You make my life wonderful. Because of you, I found myself. I'm Ronan. *Your* Ronan. I found my heart the day I lost it to you. You hold it and keep it beating. Say yes, Beth. Give me your heart, and I'll keep it safe for you."

"Yes," she whispered.

I picked her up, holding her against my chest where my heart beat frantically. I kissed her cheeks, nose, and everywhere else I could find, before sealing my mouth over hers and kissing her with everything I had.

Then I slipped my ring onto her finger, marking her as taken.

Marking her as mine.

Evan's exaggerated whisper floated down the stairs. "What did she say?"

"She said yes!" I yelled.

Upstairs, my family exploded in celebration, the laughing and clapping loud.

"They all knew?" she asked.

"Yes. They had to keep you up there while we finished this," I explained. "I think the champagne is chilling."

"And Evan was okay with it?"

I grinned. "Once I bribed him with a retired Lego kit, he was all for it."

She laughed.

"Look at your ring, Beth," I said, loving the fact that she hadn't even glanced at it before saying yes.

She looked down at the three-diamond ring, gasping. "It's beautiful."

"It stands for past, present, and future, but I think of it as us. You, me, and Evan." I bent and kissed her again. "I'll get you a band and expand it when we start having kids. I think six would look nice."

"Six?" she squeaked.

I burst out laughing. "We'll discuss that later. Our family is waiting to celebrate."

She smiled. "Our family."

I followed her up the steps, where they waited to congratulate us. Evan was the first to throw himself into our arms. I held them both tight.

My Beth. My Evan.

My heart.

EPILOGUE

BETH

The Following Spring

I looked in the mirror, lifting my eyes to my about-to-be mother-in-law. "Cami," I breathed out. "It's so beautiful!"

She smiled as she smoothed her hand over the skirt of my dress. "*You* are beautiful," she corrected. "You make the dress that way." She beamed at me. "Ronan will love it."

It was unusual and perfect. The white lace top with long sleeves led to a graceful billow of tulle in shades of white and grays. I was a walking cloud. The dress was gorgeous, designed by Cami, who understood exactly what I was looking for and sketched out my dream dress right before my eyes. The first time I tried it on, I was speechless.

Today, I was enraptured. My hair had tiny pearls and glistening beads woven into the curls. My feet were encased in the lowest heels I could find.

Behind me, Paige smiled, her dress of muted blue suiting her coloring. Lucy wore a lacy dress in bright blue, which she loved, although her shoes with glittering bows were more fascinating to her than anything. Gracie and Ava wore pretty dresses in different shades of blue to complement them. I called my wedding party the colors of the sky. Weather was the whole theme.

Ronan chose a classic black tux to wear. Liam, Paul, Jeremy, and Evan were in gray. The flowers we chose were all my favorites, adding bright pops of color everywhere.

I met Cami's warm green gaze—so much like Ronan's, it made me smile. "Is he here yet?" I asked.

She touched my cheek in a maternal gesture. "Liam says he was ready to go at dawn. They kept him busy, but they arrived over an hour ago. He's as impatient as you are."

I felt tears threaten, as they had all day. I was happy—ecstatic—to be marrying Ronan. But the shadow of missing my parents on this day hung over me, and I couldn't shake it.

Cami took my hands. "I know you're missing your mother and father." She smiled in understanding. "I'm not sure you realize how many mothers and fathers adopted you when you fell in love with my son. We are all here for you. Aiden and I are proud to have you join our family. We know your parents would be so proud of you. Of how you have raised Evan. We think the world of you."

"Thank you," I whispered.

She pressed a small box into my hand. "We would like you to wear these today. Consider them a welcome to the family gift."

I gasped at the pretty earrings inside the box. The swirl of tiny emeralds and diamonds glittered in the light.

"We know you aren't much for jewelry, but we thought you could wear them on occasion. I know you love Ronan's eyes, so I thought the emeralds would suit."

"I'll wear them all the time."

She laughed. "I'm quite sure my son will gift you many pairs over the years, but these can be your first Callaghan gift."

I met her gaze. "Your son is the best gift."

She hugged me. "And you are his." Then she pulled back, dabbing at her eyes. "Oh dear, let's get you downstairs before I start blubbering all over you."

"Thank you, Cami," I said sincerely.

"You're welcome, Beth." She kissed my cheek. "Welcome to the family."

Ronan stood proud and tall at the end of the short aisle, the darkness of his tux making him more handsome than I thought possible. Liam, Paul, and Jeremy stood beside him, smiling. Gracie, Ava, and Paige walked up and took their places, and Lucy slowly meandered behind them, carrying a basket of flowers. She couldn't toss them since we didn't want Evan slipping, but she was happy to hold the basket of daisies. At the end of the aisle, she stopped, looking at her mother, then veering directly to Liam, who chuckled, bent, and lifted her into his arms. Everyone laughed, including me. There was no doubt she was a daddy's girl, and Liam loved it. The papers were official now, and he was legally hers, even though in his heart he had been right away.

Evan was beside me, his shoulders straight. We would walk slowly, him using a cane, but he was insistent it was his job to give me away. He was much stronger than he had been when we moved here, working diligently with Ronan and Aiden.

"Are you ready?" I asked quietly.

He glanced at me with a smile. His face had matured, and he was getting taller and beginning to fill out. He looked more like a young man now than a kid. "Are you?" he asked. "If you've changed your mind, we could run, but I suggest you ditch me if you want a shot. The big guy is fast." Then he winked. "And you'd miss a really good party."

We shared a chuckle, knowing how true that was. This massive, blended family knew how to throw an amazing event.

"No, I'm good."

"Whew," he breathed. "Ronan's got a line on a retired Lego Death Star set. I don't get it if I don't get you to the altar." He gave a thumbs-up to Ronan, who returned the gesture with a big grin.

"Well, heaven forbid, I stand in the way of a Death Star. I guess we'd better get going," I deadpanned. "The sacrifices I make for you…"

He grinned. "Love you, Beth."

I squeezed his arm. "Love you."

Then, slowly, we walked toward my future.

Two Years Later

I woke up leisurely, stretching. The breeze lifted the curtains, the scent of the water and the voices coming from the beach below making me happy. I sat up, looking around the room. The house had changed a lot in the past two years. Empty, plain walls now held memories, captured on film and hung on warm-colored palettes. Deep navy, brilliant greens, and warm taupes made the house cozy. Comfortable furniture filled the spaces, and the kitchen was stocked with every cooking implement I looked twice at.

I walked to the window, looking down at my favorite sight in the world. Evan and Ronan jogging together.

That was the biggest change of them all.

Through hard work and determination, Evan had overcome his injury. He walked slower than some, a slight hesitancy to his gait, but he did it without any walking aids. He had worked and pushed—Ronan, Aiden, and all the family encouraging him. Gradually, two crutches became one, then he used a cane, and finally, he walked unaided. He had grown as well—taller, filling out, his appetite rivaling that of any of the Callaghan boys. He smiled all the time, happy in life. Port Albany had been good for him. A fresh start—and he had blossomed.

Ronan had made sure we knew the three of us were in this together. He never left Evan out of anything. He was Evan's brother, his father, and his best friend, and I adored him all the more for being so. After we were married, Ronan sat Evan down and asked if he wanted to change his last name to Callaghan. Evan asked him why, and Ronan was honest.

"I don't want you ever to feel less than. You are a part of this family."

Evan had hugged Ronan. "I do feel part of it. My last name doesn't change it. I don't want to leave my parents' name in the past."

Ronan nodded, satisfied. I knew if Evan ever changed his mind, Ronan would be happy to help him.

More laughter drew my attention back to the window. Ronan was teasing Evan, calling after him as Evan moved away from him toward the girl sitting on the rocks.

Jenny's red hair gleamed in the sunlight, and she held out her hand for Evan to take. The two of them began to walk, their heads close together. She was still his best friend as well as something more. She now lived with her mom and Theo in a house on the property. Ronan had been right when he'd told me he was certain that Theo was interested in Anne on a personal level. It hadn't taken long for them to become a couple. Reid and Becca adored her and Jenny, and soon, Theo and Anne were married and there was another child for everyone to love. Evan was ecstatic that his best friend was around all the time, and as they'd grown the last couple of years, so had their feelings.

They sat and talked to us, as well as Theo and Anne, this past spring when they acknowledged how they felt. We set ground rules, reminding them how young they still were, and they had so far been very good about sticking to the rules.

At least for now. I had a feeling that might change.

Bentley and Maddox laughed all the time about Jenny and Evan, saying that history was repeating itself. I had a feeling they were right and Evan had already found his soul mate, the same way Addi and Brayden had years before. I supposed time would tell.

I got ready and headed downstairs. I brought coffee outside, finding Ronan on the deck, sitting at the table. I kissed him good morning and sat next to him.

"Deserted again?"

He chuckled. "I don't have red hair and a blossoming set of—"

I held up my hand. "Do not even finish that thought."

He laughed. "Whatever. He stares at them all the time."

"I'm sure you did at his age too."

He dragged my chair closer. "I still stare at yours." He leaned over and pressed a kiss to the top of my breast over my heart. "They are spectacular." He leered with a grin.

I had to laugh at him.

"Incorrigible."

"You love it."

"I do. I love you too."

His smile was tender. "I know."

For a moment, we sipped our coffee, watching Jenny and Evan on the beach. They were standing at the water's edge, talking, focused on each other. I sighed in happiness, and Ronan rubbed my shoulder.

"Okay there, little bird?"

I nodded. "Busy week at work."

"Lots of storms this week." He peeked up at the blue sky. "We're done for a bit, though, right?"

"Yep, clear skies for the next while."

He still loved it when I talked "clouds." I had taken a job at a small research center in Niagara, and he enjoyed hearing me talk about work. He also loved it when I played "weather girl" for him. Which was exactly what had gotten us into the situation I found myself in right now.

"I have a present for you."

His verdant green eyes lit up. "Oh yeah? I love presents."

I chuckled because that was true. He was like a kid on Christmas every time he got a gift—no matter how small. Especially from me since he knew they were just for him. I had a feeling he would really like this one.

I reached into my pocket and held out my hand. "Close your eyes."

He did as I asked, eager and anxious.

I dropped the fluffy ball into his hand. "Guess."

He touched it gingerly, frowning in confusion. "Yarn?"

"Nope."

"Lint?"

I took a deep breath. "Open your eyes."

He did, staring down at the puffy mound in his palm. He picked it up, studying the white and gray ball of fluff. "You made me a cloud?"

"You guessed it. I made you a cloud."

"Huh, it's a little cloud."

I waited, but he didn't say anything. I should have given him more coffee.

"Yes," I said. "It's a little baby cloud. I thought you'd like to have it until the other one shows up."

He looked up, confused. "You made two baby clouds?"

"Well, I'm hoping there's only one." I laid my hand on my stomach. "This time."

I saw the moment he caught up with me. His eyes grew round, and his expression became joyful.

He dropped to his knees in front of me.

RONAN

It took me a moment to realize what Beth was saying.

Baby cloud.

Baby.

My wife was pregnant.

I was out of my chair and on my knees in front of her quickly. I laid my hand over hers on her stomach, joy coursing through my body. I felt more alive in that moment than I had ever felt.

"A baby? You're—we're—pregnant?"

"Yes."

"Beth," I breathed out. I lifted my gaze to her tear-filled eyes. "Are you okay—is everything okay?"

"Yes. I saw the doctor yesterday, and he confirmed it. I'm about six weeks along." I lifted my eyebrow teasingly. "You got all excited over the cumulonimbus clouds I was describing that night on the deck. Your hands and mouth started a different kind of storm."

I grinned at the memory. "Obviously, my cock got in on the action. I think he was trying to hide from the storm." I leaned up and kissed her. "He does like cuddling inside you."

Her eyes softened. "Well, now your child is cuddling."

My child.

Was there a more beautiful set of words?

"Is there a chance there is more than one?" I asked, tracing my hand over her skin.

"He only heard one heartbeat. But I have an ultrasound booked. We'll find out." She cupped my face. "How would you feel about that?"

"I would love it."

"Then I guess we'll find out."

I gathered her in my arms. "Thank you. My parents are going to be ecstatic. There will be seven by the time our baby is born, including Evan and Lucy—they're beating Bentley and Maddox now."

Liam and Paige had had a daughter named Shannon less than a year after they got married. Then last month, Paige had given birth to another daughter, Erin. He had an entire houseful of women around him, and he loved them all deeply. Liam took a lot of ribbing about keeping Paige pregnant all the time, but he accepted it good-naturedly, claiming she never kept her hands to herself. She was unabashed in her passion for her husband, and I loved seeing my brother so happy.

Paul and Diane had gotten married not long after us and now had a son. Jeremy and Kim married last year, and she was expecting next month.

And Ava—well, that was a story. She had recently gotten married and was still in the honeymoon phase. Her husband was well liked by the family, and although it took a while, he had warmed up to them. It had been a roller coaster of a ride.

But that was her story to tell.

For now, Mom and Dad had lots of grandkids of all ages to keep them busy. Sandy and Jordan loved having them around, claiming they "kept them young."

I picked up Beth and sat her in my lap, gazing over the water. I kept her close, laying my hand on her stomach, knowing our child was growing, safe and sound and already loved, under my palm.

"Evan is going to be a big brother slash uncle," I murmured. "The age gap is bigger than yours, at least."

She chuckled. "There we go with the whole complicated, 'I married your sister, who is kinda like your mother, and I'm your big brother/daddy' thing. This family," she snorted. "Canadian rednecks are what you are."

I laughed. "You're one of us, woman."

She laughed again. "I guess I am."

Then she became serious. "He'll love it, though," Beth assured me.

"He'll be a great one. Brother, uncle—whatever it is. Bruncle. Our kid will be lucky to have him."

She grinned. "Here he comes."

"Can we tell him?" I asked.

"Just family. Immediate family," she amended. "I want to get past the first trimester. But I don't think we can keep it from him."

"Can I tell him?" I asked eagerly, holding up my baby cloud. "I want to use this."

"Sure, Daddy, you do it."

Daddy.

That, I decided, was the most beautiful word of them all.

And in that moment, I found the final part of my heart.

TEN YEARS LATER
EVAN

Sun beat down on my neck as my feet pounded on the compacted wet sand. Water lapped lazily along the shore as I maneuvered my way around the rocks of the cove, finally stopping by my favorite hiding spot.

I sat down on a flat boulder, pulling my water bottle from the clip at my waist and drinking deeply. I wiped away the sweat on my forehead, lifting my face to the breeze blowing off the water.

Aside from the waves hitting the sand, the gulls flying overhead, there was a stillness to the early morning hour. It was my favorite time of day. My favorite place in the compound. What better way to start what was going to be my favorite day of my life than here?

I opened my eyes, watching the mesmerizing, ever-changing water. With the sun breaking through the early morning fog, its rays cast a burnished glow on the water, throwing thousands of glittering shards of glass along the surface. I pulled up my leg, resting my elbow on my knee, the action causing my loose shorts to ride up on my thigh, the edge of my scar visible.

I traced the marred flesh, lost in memories. To this day, the sound of the out-of-control car, the screams of people as it tore into the crowd, throwing bodies, crushing others, echoed in my head. I supposed it always would. I lost my parents, the life I knew, and my ability to walk that day. When I woke up to a world of pain and grief, the only person, the only thing holding me to this earth, was my sister, Beth.

For a long time, life after the accident was numb and dark. We both struggled in different ways. As a child, I knew Beth was having a hard time, but now as an adult, I could understand how hard. She gave up her life, her plans, and became my caregiver, my parent, and the provider for us. Doing it all on her own, with little help, the weight of the world on her shoulders, yet she never faltered—at least as far as she let me see. She went to school, she worked, she created a home for us. Paige and Lucy became our new little family, and we struggled along until the day she met Ronan Callaghan.

I recalled the day I first saw him. Larger-than-life, he filled the doorway of the living room, looking like a giant to me. Strong, vibrant, confident. Yet his voice was gentle, his eyes kind, and he made me feel as if he saw me. Not the boy with the crutches who felt sad and tired all the time, but the boy I used to be. The one who loved to play and laugh. Build Lego structures and run in the backyard. He didn't pity me but asked me questions. Listened to my responses.

Became my best friend, big brother, and the father figure I so desperately wanted and needed.

Ronan Callaghan and his big, crazy, blended family changed our lives.

His love and dedication changed my world.

Because of him and his father, Aiden, I could now walk. Run. Jump over rocks. It took a long time, a great deal of patience, and months of tears, struggle, and pain, but the day I was able to walk without aids was one of the greatest days in my life. I hadn't stopped since then. I pushed and pushed until I could walk a mile. Then two. Slowly, I began to jog. Jogging became running. Marathons. I never wanted to lose the feeling of being able to use my legs again. It was a gift I was given that I would never take for granted.

When it was time to choose my career, there was one clear path.

I decided to become a physiotherapist. If I could help just one person the way Aiden and Ronan helped me, I would be satisfied. I immersed myself at school, the kinesiology courses absorbing and fulfilling. I already had a head start, having hung with Aiden so much, and I graduated with honors. We sat for hours talking about methods, approaches, other therapies aside from Western medicine. My favorite part of school was when I was able to have time in the clinic using the skills I was taught to treat patients. I loved the hands-on aspect and soaking up the wisdom of the more knowledgeable therapists as they shared their experiences and helped me to grow as one.

The sound of footsteps on the rocks made me look up. From around the bend, Jenny appeared, her red hair catching the bright sun that was now filling the sky. Tall and willowy, she was graceful as she picked her way carefully toward me, taking the hand I stretched out in welcome and letting me tug her to me.

She laughed as I pulled her onto my lap and kissed her.

"What are you doing here, Jenny? Isn't it bad luck for the groom to see his bride on their wedding day?"

She snorted, rolling her pretty eyes. "You know that's a bunch of BS. Seriously, when have we ever stuck with tradition?"

I laughed, tightening my grip on her. "Good point."

"Besides, I missed you last night. I can't start my day without Evan kisses."

I slipped my fingers under her chin, fanning them out along her cheek. "Well, heaven forbid, I not give you what you want." Then I covered her mouth with mine, kissing my future wife. She sighed the way she always did when I kissed her, opening for me, her cinnamon-scented breath filling my mouth. Our tongues slid together languidly, connecting us on an intimate level. I pulled her tighter, the emotion surging through me as it always did when she was close.

I eased back, holding her to my chest. "Excited?" I asked.

"Hmm."

"Nervous?"

"You plan on pulling a Forrest Gump on me and running?"

I chuckled and kissed her head. "Nope. I'm looking forward to our wedding. To being your husband." I tilted up her chin and kissed her mouth again. "Never having to be apart from you again."

Her eyes danced in the sunlight. "Me too. The apart thing. I'll play the wife."

"Hmm. My wife."

She sighed happily. "Your wife. My husband."

She snuggled into my arms. "I can't stay long. The women have a whole day of torture planned."

I chuckled. Jenny wasn't much for makeup, fussing, or dressing up. She wore her long red hair in a ponytail most of the time, preferred jeans and sneakers to dresses and heels, and her idea of getting "fancy" was a swipe of lip gloss, some mascara, and a clean shirt.

I loved that about her.

"Let them have their fun. Just wipe off the excess so I recognize you."

She laughed, playing with the edge of my sleeve. "My dress is pretty, though."

"Good. You'll be beautiful."

From above us on the bluff, I heard Beth's voice calling. "I know you two are down there, hiding. Jenny, it's time to get ready, and Evan, Ronan is looking for you."

"Do you think if we stay quiet, she'll go away?" Jenny asked, looking mischievous.

"I can hear you!" Beth laughed. "The acoustics are great right here."

Jenny looked at me, panicked, no doubt thinking of all the times we came here to make out and talk. I shook my head.

"She can't hear the words, just the sound," I assured her. "And you have to know we're here."

"We're coming!" I shouted.

"You better not be until later." Ronan's voice was amused.

"Oh shit, the big guy is there too," I breathed. "We better go."

We stood and made our way around to the beach where Ronan and Beth were waiting. He stood beside her, his arm around her protectively. He was never not touching her if they were close. He adored my sister and was a great husband to her and an awesome dad to their two kids. All these years, he'd shown me the same love and compassion he held for them, and I would forever be grateful. His friendship and guidance meant the world to me.

I looked down at Jenny. She was tall, although I was taller by five inches. I had filled out over the years, my shoulders widening, my waist thick, and my arms and legs heavily muscled thanks to the workouts with all the BAM men, especially Aiden, Ronan, and Van. I liked being taller and heavier—a protector for Jenny and, hopefully, for my family one day.

"I guess I'll see you at the altar?" I murmured, squeezing her hand.

"I'll be there."

We stopped before we reached Beth and Ronan, and I faced her.

"I can't wait, Jenny. Today, you'll be my wife, and I'll never have to leave you again."

She pressed a kiss to my mouth. "I know."

"Our life is going to be great."

She smiled. "It already is. It's only going to get better."

She and Beth left, but first, Beth kissed me and fussed a little the way she always did. She was my sister and my mother and had been my rock since I was a kid.

"I'll take care of her," she promised. "You only have a few hours until the service." Then she flung her arms around me. "I'm so proud of you, Evan. I love you."

I hugged her back. "Love you too." I pulled back and wiped at her cheeks. "I'm getting married, Beth, not dying. Stop with the crying."

I looked at Ronan, who shared a look with me before pulling her to his side and pressing a kiss to her head. "Wait until one of yours gets married."

I grinned. Ronan was a big softy when it came to their two kids, Zoey and Luke, who owned him totally. I had to admit, I was pretty much a pushover for them as well. Good thing Beth stood strong.

His words warmed my chest. "You are one of ours, Evan. Always will be."

That made Beth cry harder, and for some reason, my eyes began to water. I wiped at them, muttering about the sand being blown around by the wind.

Ronan dryly pointed out there was no wind.

I flipped him the bird, and Beth laughed at our antics.

Then she and Jenny walked away, leaving Ronan and me watching them. I adored my sister beyond reason. It was her strength, determination, and love that got me through the first rough months after the accident and losing our parents. I knew what she sacrificed for me, and in some small, crazy way, I thought Ronan was the gift she'd been given for her incredible work. I knew he was like a gift to me when he entered our life. It wasn't the money and the life we were able to have after he arrived. It was him. His heart, love, and devotion to us both. He never once made me feel as if I were a burden or something he had to put up with because of my sister. He genuinely loved me. His soul was a gift to us both.

He clapped me on the shoulder. "You ready?"

"Get me to the church, Ronan."

He grinned. "We have to observe the BAM custom first. Basketball and food at the Hub with the men. Then you get married."

I laughed. I was good with that.

———

Later that afternoon, we stood looking out over the water on the outside balcony of the winery. The game was done, the food eaten, and the trash talk complete. The hands on the clock slowly advanced to the moment I was waiting for. I knew Jenny was in the building, her mother and all her adopted aunts and cousins fussing over her. The room behind me contained the people we loved the most—our family and friends. I was ready to start this new chapter of my life. Husband, father, all of it. I had been waiting for this since the first time I'd kissed Jenny on the beach, our lips sloppy and messy, uncoordinated and inexperienced.

And perfect.

Together, we learned, grew, and fell in love. Together every step of the way, our future clear.

Ronan stood beside me, a silent support. Aiden was inside, making sure everything was in place. The two men I loved the most would stand beside me today. No friend could ever mean what these two did to me, and they were who I wanted with me. They had been at my side every moment since they'd come into my life.

"Ronan," I began, turning to him.

He was patient, waiting for me to speak. Still tall and strong, his shoulders were broad, his expression open and his eyes full of life.

"You, today, being with me. It means a lot."

"For me too," he said.

"I remember meeting you the first day when you came to pick up Beth."

He chuckled. "You were a kid. You looked at me like you'd never seen someone so big."

I laughed with him. "I hadn't. You were like a giant." I paused. "Your size reflected your heart."

He huffed out a surprised breath.

"I don't say it enough, but thank you. For being the husband you are to Beth. The dad you are to Zoey and Luke. The friend, brother, and father you've been to me." I had to clear my throat. "I wouldn't be standing here today getting ready to marry my Jenny if it weren't for you. Everything you've done for me. For her. For my sister." I paused, feeling like I was twelve again. I shuffled my feet, looking down. "You made my life better, Ronan. You made all our lives better. I wanted—I wanted you to know how much you mean to me. How special you are to me. I love you, and I'm glad you're with me today."

He was silent, and I looked up. His eyes were filled with tears he let overflow, not embarrassed to show his feelings. He rested his hands on my shoulders, the strength in his muscles belied by the gentleness of his touch. He smiled despite his tears.

"I'm proud of you, Evan. I've watched you grow from a boy to a man. I've seen how you've overcome. Pushed. Taken every obstacle in your way and kept going. You're an incredible young man." He shook me slightly. "I'm here for you—anything, anytime." He laughed and wiped his cheek. "But I think you're going to do fine on your own. You've got this."

Our eyes met. "I couldn't love you more if you were my own. You know that, right?" he added, his voice thick with emotion.

I nodded, unable to speak.

"Then let's get you inside and married. Today is a day of cele-bration."

He embraced me, his arms tight, his hold firm. He had always offered his affection freely. His hugs were legendary, and I'd often sought them as comfort when I was younger. Now, I used them to show my love, because my affection for this great man knew no bounds. He was the example I planned to follow in my life. I wanted to be the friend, the husband, and the father he had been to me.

Everything that was right and good in this world.

He pulled back.

"You ready?"

Thanks to him, I was.

"Yes."

And with him by my side, I headed toward my future.

Thank you so much for reading FINDING RONAN'S HEART. I appreciate all reviews. Make sure to drop me an email with a link or tag me on social media.

Would you like to read more about Liam and Paige? Subscribers get a first look at LOVED BY LIAM - Vested Interest: ABC Corp #3

If you have just started reading this series and would like to get to know the Ronan's parents, start with the prequel: BAM-The Beginning

LOVED BY LIAM
Vested Interest: ABC Corp #3

Liam Callaghan is happy with the way things are.

He has a successful business, a family he loves, and a life he thinks is fulfilling and complete.

Until a favor for his brother brings him to her.

She sparks something inside him. Something he had no idea he was missing.

One touch and he knows Paige Winters is the woman he wants.

She and her daughter become his focus. His world.

He only has to convince her to believe in them.

Liam entered Paige's life quietly, but from the moment he took her hand, her world exploded.

Larger-than-life, he stepped in, brightening her days and filling her with happiness.

But she has more than her own heart on the line.

Her daughter, Lucy, has to come first.

As much as her soul yearns for him, can she trust his words?

Can the seeds love plants take root and bloom, growing over the past?

If Liam has anything to do with it, they will.

AGE OF AVA
Vested Interest: ABC Corp #4

Ava Callaghan

A woman working in a male-dominated field.

Organized, strong, and tenacious.

That's how she has to be to succeed.

Hunter Owens

A loner.

He needs no one, has no ties, and his future is an unanswered question mark.

It's all he knows.

Until the day their lives intersect.

He sees the woman she hides from the world.

She nurtures the part of him he lost long ago.

But they both agree—their connection is temporary.

They are only for now.

Can their stubborn natures allow them to bend and accept that maybe, just maybe, there is more to life than they believed?

That love can heal.

That happiness can exist.

That *for now* can be forever.

ACKNOWLEDGMENTS

So many people to thank—so little space on the page.

Lisa—thank you for all your efforts and the smiles.

Your lessons are noted…just not often recalled. It's called job security.

Beth, Trina, Melissa, Peggy, and Deb—thank you for your valuable input, your keen eyes, and encouragement. Your comments make the story better—always.

Karen—there are never enough words. You are strong, fearless, and my rock.

Thank you will have to suffice. And I love you—tons.

Kim—thank you for all you do. I bow to your social media-ness.

My reader group, Melanie's Minions—love you all.

Melanie's Literary Mob—my promo team—you do me proud and I love our interactions.

Your support is amazing and I am lucky to have each of you in my corner.

To all the bloggers and readers. Thank you for everything you do. Shouting your love of books—of my work, posting, sharing—your recommendations keep my TBR list full, and the support you have shown me is deeply appreciated.

ABOUT THE AUTHOR

NYT/WSJ/USAT international bestselling author Melanie Moreland, lives a happy and content life in a quiet area of Ontario with her beloved husband of thirty-plus years and their rescue cat, Amber. Nothing means more to her than her friends and family, and she cherishes every moment spent with them.

While seriously addicted to coffee, and highly challenged with all things computer-related and technical, she relishes baking, cooking, and trying new recipes for people to sample. She loves to throw dinner parties, and enjoys traveling, here and abroad, but finds coming home is always the best part of any trip.

Melanie loves stories, especially paired with a good wine, and enjoys skydiving (free falling over a fleck of dust) extreme snowboarding (falling down stairs) and piloting her own helicopter (tripping over her own feet.) She's learned happily ever afters, even bumpy ones, are all in how you tell the story.

Melanie is represented by Flavia Viotti at Bookcase Literary Agency. For any questions regarding subsidiary or translation rights please contact her at flavia@bookcaseagency.com

Connect with Melanie

Like reader groups? Lots of fun and giveaways! Check it out Melanie Moreland's Minions

Join my newsletter for up-to-date news, sales, book announcements and excerpts (no spam). Click here to sign up Melanie Moreland's newsletter

or visit https://bit.ly/MMorelandNewsletter

Visit my website www.melaniemoreland.com

facebook.com/authormoreland

twitter.com/morelandmelanie

instagram.com/morelandmelanie